DAYS
OF POWER,
NIGHTS
OF FEAR

*A Novel of
Washington*

The Sound of Small Hammers
The Nazi Hunter
Divided We Stand: The Baptists in American Life

DAYS
OF POWER,
NIGHTS
OF FEAR
A Novel of Washington

Bynum Shaw

ST. MARTIN'S PRESS · New York

Manufactured in the United States of America

Design by Dennis J. Grastorf

Library of Congress Cataloging in Publication Data

Shaw, Bynum.
  Days of power, nights of fear.

  I. Title.
PZ4.H5336Day [PS3569.H375]   813'.54
ISBN 0-312-18483-2   80-14146

Author's Note

In this novel, the character of Sam Bradford was suggested by the career of Senator Joseph R. McCarthy. Bradford is not intended, however, to represent McCarthy, and all the other substantive characters and situations are products of the imagination. Any resemblance to actual persons, living or dead, or to actual events, is purely coincidental.

B. S.

For Brad and Molly Jacobs

DAYS
OF POWER,
NIGHTS
OF FEAR

*A Novel of
Washington*

☆ **I** ☆

WE SIT NOW ACROSS the breakfast table in the eight-by-ten nook between the kitchen and the dining room in the brick English Tudor dwelling in Chevy Chase, and wordlessly over the bacon and eggs and between the sips of coffee we exchange the ad-cluttered sections of the *Washington Post*. It is a familiar, comfortable ritual, and only occasionally do I look up over the top of the sports section, wondering at the composed face almost free of wrinkles and the absence of gray in the carefully-coached ash-blonde hair.

Why the *Post*? Because people of quality respect a newspaper which can bring a president to his knees. And besides, we have always read it, at least since we have been in Washington. And that is more than a quarter of a century now, and the days of glory—days when with nearly every edition we made the news or editorial columns of the *Post*—are long past. But after you have been in the thick of it in Washington, you do not go back to Boise, Idaho, or Yamasee, South Carolina. Not when you have really been one of the movers, the topplers, the ferrets, the creators, the powerful.

Not when just over there, moldering in Arlington under the rough granite slab—so typical—lies the body of the man who put it all together. For him there is no Eternal Flame, except what his life created. And the shotgun blast could not extinguish that.

The children—James and Luellen and John—are not here. James, the oldest, is on an extended pilgrimage to India in search of himself in the shadow of some leprous guru. Luellen is in her third commune, making birds' nests out of gourds and experimenting with the transcendental side effects of peyote. John, the youngest and the only one I understand, is a junior at College Park. He is pre-law, wears his hair short and chases girls. Normal in all respects.

Without the sounds of the children the house seems empty, ghostly, but there are times when I catch faint echoes of young voices, far off, fading. Of course, I know that my memory plays tricks, that these children whom I hear are not reality. A quarter of a century ago they had not even been conceived, and there was that one painful period when their conception was altogether in doubt, when, I guess, I had lost the faith, or for a moment had seen the cleft in the rock, the fissure in the wall, the clay in which all men's feet are inevitably grounded. And women, too, stray.

I drink the last of the coffee and excuse myself and go to the study for a letter that I must answer. From someone in political science at Auburn. "Dear Sir: Of all men, you were closest to him. After all these years, what is your assessment. . . ?" I am not in sympathy with political science, not as it is taught in colleges and universities, because it is not in touch with reality. But I will answer it as if I were a true believer, a stalwart of the academic disciplines, an ardent supporter of the quest for higher truth. I will answer it, just as I have answered hundreds of others, and my reply will be read to some bored class in Politics 271—the American Dream—as if it were purest gold. And no doubt some poor grabbling collegiate political theorist, battling for tenure in the publish-or-perish trenches, will write a worthless paper for some obscure journal of the higher intelligence and cite my handiwork in a footnote. That, at least, will classify me properly, for I am, indeed, a footnote to history. An asterisk.

I pick up the letter and turn, and there he is in the old portrait, the shadowed jowls a little fading, but with the bold penstroke of the inscription still bright and strong: "To Harry Dodge, my strong right arm—Senator Sam." He was called a lot of things then, "Savior," "Watchdog of the Public Trust," "True-Blue American," and less flattering epithets when the jackals got in after him, but that's what we on his staff called him, "Senator Sam." That's what he liked best, too, to be known as a duly exalted Senator of the United States, although to be sure he enjoyed the blind, lapdog affection that followed him to Arlington and still inspires the wreaths and flowers.

But to us he was Senator Sam. Senator Sam Bradford. Republican of Maryland.

Good old Senator Sam, my boss, my mentor, my closest friend.

It is hard to explain that relationship, because it was so complicated and we were so different. He used me, exploited me, reviled me and, in his mawkish way, loved me. There were times when in my heart of hearts, even in my intellect, I hated him as a thorough-going, twenty-eight-carat son of a bitch. But he had that magical charm about him, an ingratiating manner which could be overwhelming in its believability. He could turn it on as you run water through a tap, flooding you, floating you, possessing you. I do not pretend to understand the love-hate relationship. I know that a thin line divides them and that it is sometimes not distinguishable. How else could I have stayed with him after he had delivered to me the unkindest cut, and how else could I have flung myself between him and an assassin's bullet?

But that is a long story, perhaps too long.

Actually, it is not too long, and it should be told, and I am the only one who can tell it. I can remember how it began, or how the pieces thrown to the winds in a chaotic past suddenly resurrected and fell into place. It was just after World War II, and I had this little advertising and public relations agency in Richmond, Virginia. I was getting ready to leave the office on a cold March afternoon when the telephone rang. Selma, the office girl, had a sinus headache and had gone home early, and I snatched up the receiver and said something inane which to me at the time seemed funny, like "Dodge pick-ups." You do not know when the die is cast, when the dew rises upon the melon, when the stars are in their most malevolent configuration. A young lady with bright eyes, whom you have never seen before, stands next to you in the chow line, and you innocently admire the turn of the derierre, and you do not know that in six months, a year, five years, notwithstanding a brace of intervening involvements, she will be leading you to the altar. A car flashes over the crest of a hill in the darkness, its headlights beaming, and it crosses over the center line and crashes not into you but into the tractor-trailer rig tailgating; and in the small hours of the night you ponder over those ten extra feet, that fraction of a second that saved your life when three others died. But that day the timing was exact. There on the other end of the line was a voice that bridged thousands of miles and hundreds of days, a living echo from the Pacific Theater of Operations, rasping over an intercom on a Vultee dive bomber thrusting at Bougainville.

"Harry," the voice said after the opening amenities, "I need you."

"Nah, you don't," I said. "Not unless you've got a bag of money." I needed anybody with money. It takes a lot of years and a lot of well-heeled clients to make a public relations agency work. I had been at it only since the end of the war, and there hadn't been enough time or opportunity to build much. The bankroll, most of it saved from the occasionally serious war-time crap games, was getting pretty thin.

"I've got money, and I've got connections," Sam said. "And I'm going to the United States Senate. I want you to go with me."

"The Senate? I thought you were a judge."

"I am a judge. Hell, yes. And a damn good one. But the bench isn't where the action's at. Washington, old buddy. That's where all the marbles are."

"Why do you want me?"

Sam's voice changed a little. It came across much more warmly. "I never told you this," he said, "but I think you're one of the savviest guys I ever met. You've got brains. I need a brain trust, and I want you to be part of it."

I knew from experience that Sam was capable of throwing out compliments as if they were dishwater, but I have to admit that I was flattered. Just why I don't know. At that time I remembered Sam as something of an ass, and who can be flattered by braying? But I had had some hard days, I wanted to hear nice things, and there was also the faint memory that Sam always got what he wanted. No matter how. And so I played along with him. "Who you gonna run against, Sam?"

"In the primary? I've filed against Blair."

"How the hell do you think you can beat E. Northrop Blair? He's one of the heavyweights in national politics."

"Yeah, but he's vulnerable, and I'm gonna grab the old fart by the balls."

"What would you want of me?"

"Just the usual stuff in the primary and the general. Speech writing. Gung-ho propaganda. Press releases. You P.R. boys know all about that. And when we get to Washington I'll make you my administrative assistant. Fair enough?"

"Fair, maybe, but not enough. Not precisely enough. It's not something I could go into on speculation. I'd have to have a salary. From the start. No other way I could do it."

"No problem. There're plenty of people want Blair out.

And not just in Maryland. I've got a good war chest. How much do you need?"

I did some quick figuring. "A thousand a month."

Sam came back without a quibble. "It's yours. Until we get to Washington. And I think the staff rate there is, oh, eighteen to twenty. Whatever is tops is what you'll get."

"I've got to think about this some, Sam. It would mean closing my agency and arranging a temporary transfer of my accounts. Temporary in case Blair whips your ass. And I've got this girl here—"

"Romance?" Sam had a leering way of saying it, imparting lust to the word.

"That, too. But I'm thinking about the girl who works for me. I don't want to leave her out in the cold."

"Hell, bring her along. We can use typists. What's her name?"

"Selma Gadowski."

"Selma *what?*"

"Gadowski. A good Polish Catholic."

"Well, all right. There's a strong Polish vote in Baltimore. What is it with the other girl? The love bit? Is it serious?"

"If I can persuade her. These First Families of Virginia types don't like to marry below their class."

"Well, good luck on that. It would help for one of us to be married."

"You're not?"

"Nah," Sam said nonchalantly. "I just haven't had time for that kind of fluff. Are you coming with me?"

"Give me a few days to think about it."

"A week. I'll call you back in a week." He made incoherent noises, belches and rumblings, and I knew he was groping for the final pitch. When it came it was about what I expected. "Just remember, Harry, we fought the war together."

As I hung up and swiveled back in my chair, I knew I would never forget. A strange thing about war: you don't remember the heroes. I had seen live heroes and dead heroes, dead seven ways, and I couldn't remember their faces. In combat, heroism is commonplace, and except for the winners of the Congressional Medal of Honor, who do manage to catch your eye, you don't attach names to it. The ones you remember are the cowards, the nonentities, the goldbricks, because they are out of place in a company of men. Sam I remembered not because he was any of those things but because he was different. The war was not using him, as it was the rest of us; he was using it. He made it work for him, like no one else I ever saw, and he did it without risking his hide.

He arrived at Munda, a rear-echelon Marine airbase in the Pacific, in July of 1943, a newly ordained Captain with an exaggerated limp. He was so green he even knocked on my door to tell me that we were billeted together. In appearance he was not particularly impressive, stocky, with a heavy foot, short, dark hair already slightly receding, looking, as he would forever look, as if he were in constant need of a shave. He came in and threw his flight bag on the empty bunk—vacated by a jaundiced gunnery officer—tossed his jacket carelessly alongside the bed and turned to me, hand outstretched. "Lieutenant," he said, "I'm Sam Bradford. Out of Maryland."

I took his hand. It was soft but big and strong. "Dodge. Harry Dodge. Norfolk, Virginia. I guess that makes us neighbors." He turned back toward his bunk, dragging the wounded leg, and I took the cue. "Got a charley horse there?"

He slapped the leg and laughed. "Not quite. My baptism of fire. The seaplane tender that ferried us over took some strafing, and I got knocked around a little bit." He pulled up his trouser leg to expose a healing yellow bruise. The flesh had not been torn.

"Tough," I said. I had seen men blown apart; I had seen men whose flesh was spaghetti; a bruise didn't impress me.

Sam let his trouser leg fall, not at all unruffled by my lack of concern. "You guys get much action here?" he asked.

I leaned back on the bunk, my hands clasped behind my

head, elbows out. "Who briefed you?" I asked. "Don't you know about this outfit?"

"Not very much. Just that it's operational. A lot of time in the air."

I laughed grimly. "Oh, we get air time. Flight pay. But this is an ex-combat unit. We've all had more than eighteen months out here, and we're freaked out. Combat fatigued. Do you know what that means? Instead of sending us to some stateside looney bin, they regrouped us here. You'll see guys who cry a lot, and some who just sit and stare. They're the worst. In an emergency they could send us back, but mostly we patrol. And see nothing."

"You mean you're not fit?" There was disapproval in his voice.

"Fit in the sense that we can still fly and navigate and drop bombs if necessary, but we don't intercept Zeroes or go looking for flak."

"You look all right. What are you?"

"What do you mean?"

"A crier, or one of the silent ones?"

"Oh, me? I laugh a lot. Without reason. Everything's funny. Dead men, a battleship to be bombed out of the water. I go crazy."

"Everybody here's been in it?"

"Up to their asses. And it's not likely we'll go back."

"Shee-it!" Sam exploded. "I wanted combat. That's where the ribbons are."

"I got a chestful. Four Air Medals. The DFC. You can rent 'em for two bits. Wear 'em to the Saturday night USO dances."

"Are you kidding?"

"About the medals?"

"Nah, I believe that. About the dances."

I sat up and laughed. "There isn't a broad within 500 miles of this island. No nurses. No native girls. There's a canteen. We drink a lot. An awful lot. And dream about Betty Grable."

He stood and paced the room, the limp momentarily forgotten. "Just what in hell," he finally asked, "does an intelligence officer do here?"

"That what you are? It's easy duty. When we come in from patrol, you ask us if we saw anything worth reporting. We say no. You file a negative. No prisoners to interrogate, no enemy troop movements to anticipate. Mostly, at this point, you sit out the war. How the hell did you get assigned to this unit?"

"I didn't ask for it. In fact, I enlisted. As a buck private. And they gave me a commission."

"You must've had some clout."

"Back in Maryland, I'm a judge. Elected by the voters. I guess it makes a difference." He sat back down thoughtfully.

I didn't understand, even though as a patriotic kid just out of college I myself had volunteered for Marine flight training. Without clout. "If you were a judge," I asked, "what're you doing here? Public officials are exempt from service."

Sam looked at me shrewdly, with a slight, hard smile that I would come to recognize as his trademark when he was serious. "I know that," he said. "But in the business I'm in, especially if you're able-bodied, you need a war record. I don't want any voter ever to be able to say that Sam Bradford hid out from the war behind his judicial robes. Tell me, is it possible that I'll get any air time?"

"If you want it. These planes have a place for a gunner. Two, in fact. We usually don't carry one, because we don't expect any opposition and run from it if we encounter it. But many of the ground officers and enlisted men often go along for the ride, just to break the routine."

"Can I fly with you?" His appeal was that of a small boy.

I laughed. "Any time."

He laughed back. "You *can* fly the damn thing, can't you?"

"Upside down. In my sleep. Dead drunk."

That was my rather unpretentious introduction to Samuel Raynor Bradford, a bulldog of a man then thirty-five, at that age older even than Col. Alfred Slater, our skipper, but with more raw energy than half the squadron put together. Along with that tremendous drive there was a strange curiosity about small things and a total disregard for large ones, a bluntness that was not meant to be, but generally was insulting, a sometimes God-fearingly pious pose that could be double-clutched instantly into the grotesquely obscene. As a captain he had rank and authority, but he knew how to handle neither well. In serious conversation he never made a point once, whether it was about politics, war or women. "The Japs," he would say, "are barbarians. Total barbarians." "Roosevelt is an impotent old man, and always has been. An impotent old man." "Jane Russell has too much tit for any one woman. Too much tit." Very quickly the squadron divided into three distinct camps in its attitude toward Sam Bradford. A hard core hated him roundly, largely because on that easy-going base he insisted on the proprietary salute due him as a senior officer. Until he came no one saluted, except when an overload of scotch regenerated and over-emphasized the basic instincts. The vast majority ignored him as a self-inflated but innocuous blowhard. A few of us genuinely liked him, despite his faults. I was one of those, because in the year and a half that I shared a billet with him I learned that on a one-to-one basis he could be considerate, generous, even sensitive. It was only in crowds or when he was on stage that he became a boor.

Sam lost no time in alienating Al Slater. I was in the officers' canteen one night about a week after Bradford had arrived when the colonel approached me, drink in hand. "Hey, Harry," he asked, "what's with this captain of yours? The judge?"

It passed through my mind that news travels fast, but I didn't comment on it. "What do you mean?" I asked.

"He requested an appointment with me the other day." On Munda nobody ever made an appointment with the skipper. They just barged in.

"What'd he want? Or is it a military secret? He's intelligence."

"He's dumb-ass," Al said. "You won't believe it, I don't think. Came in with some cock-and-bull story about an injury on the boat that brought him over. Wanted me to put him in for the Purple Heart. I talked to the commander of that tender when they put in here. Beach, I think his name was. He didn't say anything about any action. And he sure as hell didn't recommend any bastard for a medal." Slater took a long drink of scotch.

"So what'd you tell Sam?"

"What you would. That the ship was gone, that there was no corroborating evidence or witnesses. In other words, to go fuck himself."

I nodded and thought no more about it. Not then. But if in that first week Sam made himself odious to the skipper, he also picked up a disciple. He was Navy, a Filipino steward assigned to the Officers' Mess, efficient and courteous to the point of servility. I had never paid much attention to him until he started showing up daily in our hut, making up Sam's bunk, polishing his shoes and looking after his clothes. It puzzled me when I first came in and caught him at it. "Numeriano, isn't it?" I asked.

He made a slight bow. "Numeriano Lopez." His pronunciation was stiff but eloquent.

"What are you doing here?"

"Tidying up for Captain Sam." He went about his business.

"You don't have to do that. We don't have servants in the Marine Corps. Not captains, anyway. Maybe generals."

"I know," Numeriano said. "I am not a servant. I do this because I want to. Captain Sam is a very nice man."

"Did he tell you that?"

"No. I can tell. I can feel it. You very nice man, too."

"Well, you don't have to do my stuff. I'm not that nice a man. And make Sam pay you."

"Oh, no pay. No pay. We have other arrangement."

Numeriano finished his work and left. For eighteen months he came almost every day, turning Sam out as the most resplendent officer on the base, and I wondered all that time what "the arrangement" was. But I didn't find out. Not then.

Sam had been on the base about three weeks when he again broached the subject of flying. We had turned in, killed the lights and opened the blackout curtains to let in some of the night air. In the other bunk Sam was smoking, and I could see the red glow of the cigarette slightly brighten the room as he inhaled. "Harry," he asked "you awake?"

"Yeah."

"Where you guys flying in the morning?"

"Won't know until the briefing, but it'll probably be the usual. Patrol out a couple hundred miles, make a wide turn, return to base. Boring as hell. Sometimes I think I ought to send my pajamas to do it."

"I think I'd like to take a look."

"Sure. You ever flown?"

"Oh, commercial a lot. Couple short indoctrination flights in the trainers. But nothing serious."

"I'll wake you up."

There was no need to. He was up, had eaten and was waiting in the ready room, already flight-jacketed, when I checked in. Slater was late, which meant that nothing special was on tap, and as he glanced around checking the pilots his gaze stopped at Sam.

"I'm flying observation with Lieutenant Dodge," Sam explained.

Al merely nodded and went into the monotone that passed for our daily instruction. As we walked out to the flight line, Sam asked, "Was there anything unusual in that?"

"Nah," I said. "Al's more animated when there's a change of routine or anything that we have to be warned about. Here. You have to step up. Take either of the gunners' seats. There's the headphone. Do you know how to fire that damn gun? For Chrissake don't take off the back of my head. And don't shoot any of the squadron down."

"I know, I know," Sam said.

"Okay. We'll be fifth in line, and you won't even know it when we're airborne." I scrambled past him, perfunctorily ran the checklist, revved up the single engine and taxied slowly toward the runway. He said nothing, but there was a slight gasp on the intercom when I turned her loose and roared down the Seabee concrete. I could hear his held breath exhale as we waggled into formation and began a long, slow climb.

When his voice came it was slow and grating. "How high're we gonna fly?" he asked.

"We'll level off at about ten thousand."

"Is that the top for this craft?"

"Oh, hell, no. We can fly at twenty-five. But we don't do it unless we're going in for a strike. And striking is not this squadron's business."

"How fast?"

"Cruising at two fifty. We can kick it up to about two eighty if we have to. At three hundred the wings fall off."

"What's our range?"

"We won't push it. If we have to, we can go out about a thousand, with plenty of reserve for return. But this is a piece of cake. See anything?"

"Lots and lots of water."

"Check over there at three o'clock. A carrier, converted job. A wagon. Supporting craft. And I count about six freighters. They're ours."

"How can you tell?"

"They haven't put anything up. If it were a Jap convoy we'd be running our asses off by now."

"What's the procedure?"

"We'll roll over them, just to say 'hello.' And then we return to base." Our conversation was cut off by Hank Bostwick, the patrol commander. Back this far we didn't maintain radio silence, and Hank came in weakly. "One pass," he said.

We screamed in, rocking slightly. "I can see the men on the deck of the wagon," Sam said. "Are they tracking us?"

"Sure. It's a drill for them, too. If we were unfriendlies the sky would be black by now."

"I hope nobody pulls the trigger."

"Nah. They got precautions. We're going to climb now and make a steep turn. It's a little breathtaking. Hang on."

I heard from him at the apex but nothing else for the rest of the flight, and when we climbed out of the plane at Munda, I asked him, "How'd you like it?"

"No sweat. Just like training."

"Sam, be honest. Would combat scare you?"

"I'd wet my pants."

He didn't fly with me again for several months, until one night I told him we were going to fly a raid on Bougainville.

"Why Bougainville?" he asked.

"There are some old airstrips over there. Deserted. We bomb them occasionally to make sure the Japs don't come back. Lot of fun. We go in at about twenty, dive like crazy, level off and drop the eggs. No resistance. No risk at all. Want to go?"

"No flak?"

"Nothing there. Not a living thing."

"I'll be right behind you."

His enthusiasm for attacking a helpless objective should have told me something, but it was a long time before I put all the associations together.

Right behind me he was. We decided, for kicks, to make it a record strike, and I flew three missions, delivering 15,000 pounds of explosives on a helpless, inert foe. Sam seemed to enjoy the idea of nesting all that energy on a defenseless target, and he got into the act with the machine guns—which was not part of the briefing. Every time we made a run into the target, he blasted away at the coconut trees, and by the time the day was finished he had expended all the ammunition in both the tail and waist gunners' slots. I calculated that he had fired more than 5,000 rounds, as excited as a small boy with a new toy, and when Joe Frawley, the squadron Public Information Officer, was writing up a news release for the record day of bombing, I happened to mention that Sam surely must have set an all-time record on the 50-caliber machine gun.

"Hell, we'll get some mileage out of that, too," Joe said. He was an old flak, without conscience, and with tongue in cheek he ground out a news release from "an advance Marine base" saying that Captain Sam Bradford had fired 6,000 rounds, thought to be a record, in a hectic day of forays against the enemy. The Associated Press picked it up, of course, identifying Sam as an on-leave judge from Maryland, and about two weeks later Sam came around with a handful of clippings from Maryland and D.C. papers cataloging his record. The newspaper reader could be forgiven, of course, for imagining that Sam had indeed been gripped in mortal combat with the enemy, but that piece of deceit never bothered Sam. He waved the clippings gleefully and said, "These are worth at least 50,000 votes."

I drank with Sam to his success—he was already addicted to scotch—and I was in fact a little pleased to have been a part of his exploit, to have invented it, to have become the shirttail of a legend. I felt so good about it, in fact, that I conspired with five other junior officers to get Sam the Purple Heart. One dark night Sam stumbled over an errant shovel on his way to the latrine and sprained his ankle. We all gave depositions that Sam had triggered a land mine and had been thrown off his feet by the blast. Although Munda had never been occupied, much less mined, Al Slater expansively signed the recommendation, and Sam got his first medal. He was to get more, but they were on his own initiative. For us, on that lonely, forsaken, wearisome atoll, it was enough that we had put one over on the brass.

I talked casually to Al after Sam had been decorated. "You knew we were lying," I said. "Why'd you sign it?"

He looked at me soberly, which was not his accustomed mien. "I always trust the word of my men," he said. "And besides, we need heroes. It's good for the morale back home. But don't put him in for the Silver Star. I have to draw the line somewhere."

"You're gooder'n ary angel, Al," I said.

"Don't give me that *Snuffy Smith* routine," he replied. "But you can buy me a drink."

Sam didn't fly much after that. There was nothing to be gained from it that he had not already won. And besides, a plane might at any moment become disabled and fall out of the sky. Mostly, he contented himself with playing poker. For a war, in which anybody could go at any time, he was a strange player. Most of us traded markers, for mind-boggling sums, but not Sam. He played for keeps, paid in cash and collected in cash, always with a lame explanation: "I always pay my debts." "I always collect my debts." Through paying and collecting, he endeared himself to no one. To the rest of us it was make-believe, a game; Al Slater owed me $213,000. It was a meaningless sum. But not to Sam.

Sometimes we talked, and on one moonlit night in the South Pacific he told me about his background. "I come from a big family," he said. "Farm folks in Southern Maryland. We were white trash, recent immigrants from Ireland, and my own brothers and sisters made fun of me. I was clumsy, like a bear, and they were unmerciful. But I was my mother Abigail's favorite. Abigail Bradford. With her little savings— I don't know how she did it—and a small scholarship I got to the University of Maryland. And washing dishes and carrying out garbage put me through law school. Except for my mother, I don't owe my family anything. The old man was a son of a bitch, and what with childbearing—she was a little woman—and the farm drudgery he sent my sainted mother to an early grave. Someday I'll show my brothers and sisters that they picked on the wrong pigeon."

"All kids fight," I said. "It's part of being a family."

"Not mine," he said with bitterness. "They actually conspired against me. I can't forgive them for that."

"Forget it, Sam," I said. "Go to sleep."

He didn't go to sleep, and there were many hours on Munda when he lay awake, brooding, planning his future. I didn't brood; I didn't plan. I only wanted the war to be over.

For Sam it was over earlier than for most of us. He was on leave as a Maryland judge. He was up for reelection. Legally he couldn't stand for public office while in uniform. But he wangled a month's leave and went back to Maryland and ran a shadow campaign, telling the voters what he would have said had he not been muzzled by the military. He got his name on the ballot, which itself was a piece of skullduggery, and by exploiting his war record he won enough votes for reelection. He didn't come back to Munda. With his influence as a judge he applied to be decommissioned from the Marine Corps, and I didn't see him again, or hear from him, until that postwar day in my Richmond office, when I was the guy with the kind of "savvy" that could help him in his campaign against Senator E. Northrop Blair.

I had to talk it over with Patricia. Patricia Mason, my love. Patricia Mason of the Virginia Masons. She had made her debut in Richmond in 1945, accompanied by three VMI cadets and sponsored by her father, Stanwick Byrd Mason, president of Commonwealth Federal Savings and Loan. I was not there for her formal presentation to society, and I would never have known her except that she was a careless driver and allowed her MG to crash into the side of my parked pre-war Chevy. I didn't see the accident and would only have cursed over the damage had she not had the honesty to leave a note under my windshield wiper. It was in a round, feminine hand, quite neat, and it said, "I am sorry I struck your car. If you will call my father, Stanwick B. Mason, at Commonwealth Federal, he will arrange to take care of the bill."

So I called Stanwick B., and he invited me to his office, where the old biddy who was his receptionist informed me that I was to ask for *Colonel* Mason, and by God, he was a colonel of infantry in World War I. He liked the cut of my jib or some damn fancy a C. Aubrey Smith would take, and invited me out to Mason's Bluff, the family mansion overlooking the James River near Hopewell, to talk about what he referred to as "the incident." I did not really want to talk about "the incident," as it seemed to imply that I was to blame for not parking my car in the Fiji Islands, where his daughter would be less apt to get at it. But I had a warm feeling for the Colonel and was compliant. I supped on Smithfield ham stuffed with Virginia oysters on a bed of wild rice, smoked a Havana cigar over a large snifter of Napoleon brandy, and after I had visited for a few hours with Colonel Mason and his darling blonde daughter Patricia who would lose her driver's license unless I cooperated, I was persuaded by her Dresden doll face, small voice and meticulously sculpted lines that my parked car had indeed leapt out at her MG, and I didn't file an insurance claim. Commonwealth Federal paid the repair bill, $215, and I inherited Patricia.

I say inherited, but that isn't the right word. It started with small things, on weekends when she drove home from her junior studies at Mary Baldwin. There were lunches at modest restaurants, Sunday afternoon strolls along the banks of the James, tennis matches on the Mason court, mornings of the Henrico hunt. Inevitably, too, there were fumbling encounters in the back seat of the repaired Chevy, which would not have been ample for the purpose had she been a larger woman. Gradually it dawned on me that Patricia Mason had sacrificed marriage within the tight Virginia aristocracy to think of me as her consort. In a very short time we had worked out an unspoken understanding, an arrangement. When the agency had made it and could support me and a bride, Patricia would be waiting. There was no exchange of promises or stones or formal announcements, but the Mason household, right down to Peyton, the oldest black retainer, accepted the projected union as inevitable. Even though I was not of Virginia Society, or First Family association, I came from sturdy Tidewater stock, had graduated with honors from the College of William and Mary and had a respectable war record.

From the first, Commonwealth Federal chipped in, steering several small accounts in my direction, although Stanwick B., to his credit, never offered me a place in banking. He simply tried to assure that my agency, within a reasonable time, would develop a reliable cash flow. It mattered little that Patricia had from her long-deceased mother, who had been a Taliaferro, money of her own.

So it was with some trepidation that I went out to Mason's Bluff the Saturday after the call from Sam. Patricia had already driven down from Staunton, and she met me at the door. "Harry," she said, "you're early. You must have brought me a surprise."

"Well, I guess I did," I mumbled. In lieu of surprise I was fitting her diminutive frame to mine and kissing her quite hungrily when her father walked into the drawing room.

He cleared his throat with great exaggeration and Patricia turned to him without embarrassment. They had a good relationship. "Father," Patricia said, "Harry has brought a surprise. I want to see it."

We situated ourselves on a velvet sofa and Stanwick B. took his favorite chair near the massive fireplace. "It isn't something I can show you," I said. "I have to tell you."

"Well, let's hear it," Patricia said impatiently. I think she was disappointed that I had brought only talk.

"I don't know exactly how to begin," I said. "But it's—well, I'm thinking about closing the agency."

"Isn't that a rather serious step?" Colonel Mason asked. He chewed over some of the words, but there was not a hint of approval or disapproval.

"But what would you do?" Patricia asked. "I thought you loved the agency. You are extremely good at what you do. Your clients are happy. I just supposed that you love your work."

"I do," I said. "It's fun, and I can come back to it if I have to."

"After what?" She was doubtful, her psych major causing her to be quite logical.

"Let me lay it out for you," I said, spreading my fingers. "I got a telephone call from an old Marine buddy in Maryland. He's a judge now and he's going to run for the United States Senate."

"Against whom?" her father asked. This was his ground.

"Against E. Northrop Blair. In the Republican primary."

Colonel Mason snorted. "Against Blair? Nobody can beat Blair in Maryland. Why he's—well, Blair House was in his family."

"I know that," I said. "But I don't think the Maryland voters are influenced much by Pennsylvania Avenue real estate. Blair's old, almost senile. My friend thinks he can win. And he'll pay me to help. Quite well."

"What is your friend's name?" Patricia asked.

"Sam Bradford."

"I've never heard you mention him. Why?"

"I just lost touch with him. And then, out of the blue . . ."

"Bradford, Bradford," Colonel Mason mused aloud. "If he has the right connections, he might bring it off. Maryland had a Governor named Bradford during the Civil War. A Yankee, but a damn good man. From up around Bel Air. What was his name? Bradford. Augustus Williamson Bradford. Would your friend be from that family? Quality counts, you know."

"I'm not sure," I lied.

"Is this something you *want* to do?" Patricia asked.

"I guess so. If I didn't, I wouldn't be bothering you with it. Would you mind? Living in Washington?"

"Of course, she wouldn't mind," her father broke in. "Her people—my people—have been in politics since before the Republic was established. It's honorable work. If not, why would the Byrds and the Masons and the Llewellyns and the Taliaferros have been in it? To say nothing of Thomas Jefferson. And Jeff Davis dined in this house. We'll help you wind things up here and you can have a go at it."

It wasn't her father's permission I wanted. I needed hers. "Okay?" I asked.

She frowned, shook the long blond mane, wrinkled her nose and then nodded resolutely. "Oh, hell, why not?" she said.

"Patricia!" her father scolded. "In this house the 'hells' and 'damns' belong to me." Discreetly, he charged out, and we were left to much more intimate concerns.

I FLEW INTO Harbor Field, the sinking old landfill in Baltimore, on a cold day in March of 1946, and as I crossed from the old DC-3 to the small terminal a few flurries of snow were whirling in the air. Sam had said that he would send a car to meet me, and as I started toward the flight desk to ask for a page a familiar voice rang out. "Lieutenant Dodge," it called with some urgency. And there I got the answer to an old question, because waiting for me with a flash of white teeth was Numeriano Lopez, the Filipino whom Sam had impressed into wartime service on a barren Pacific isle.

I shook hands with him warmly and said, "You can forget the 'Lieutenant' now, Numeriano. The war is over. I'm just plain Harry."

"Sure, Lieutenant." Numeriano took my light bag, and as we walked to the parking lot, he explained. "The Judge—the Captain—sent for me right after the war."

"Didn't you want to go back to the Philippines?"

"Oh, I did. But everything was all changed. Most of my people were dead. From the Japanese, from hunger, fever. There was nothing to stay for. So I wrote to the Judge and in about a month I was here. He arranged everything."

"And you're a citizen?"

"Oh, damn right." He opened the door on the passenger side of the Packard, which was as solid as a Sherman tank, closed it behind me, went around to the driver's side and crawled in.

As we headed toward the exit road I asked, "What do you do for Sam?"

"Everything. Chauffeur, cook, housekeeper. I do it all."

"But not for free anymore?"

"Oh, no. Very good salary." He was on a rutted route that wound through East Baltimore, and he poured on the coal. It was evident that he and the Packard got along well, the one anticipating the moves of the other.

"You could have been career Navy, with a good pension."

"I didn't want that. And, besides, the Judge needed me."

"I guess he did, at that," I said.

"He needs you, too."

"Not very much. There are plenty of people who do my kind of work. And some of them are better than I am."

"But it is not the same. It is not done with love. Do you understand me? The Judge told me once you were his best friend." We pulled into the downtown traffic, made a few turns and slid to a stop in front of the Emerson Hotel. "You go on in," Numeriano said. "His office is on the mezzanine. I'll put the car up and bring your bag." He revved up the engine and squealed off in front of a cruising taxi.

I stood on the broad sidewalk, momentarily bracing myself against a stiff wind blowing up Calvert Street from the Baltimore Harbor. Over my head, on the protruding hotel marquee, were three signs, in bold black letters against a gold background, advertising "Bradford for Senator." The lobby of the Emerson was festooned with red, white and blue bunting, and another banner hanging from the mezzanine called attention to the "Bradford for Senate Headquarters." I climbed the stairs, found the headquarters suite and entered a workroom dotted with typewriters placed on long tables. A lone woman, wearing a "Volunteer for Bradford" tag, looked up at me questioningly, and I said, "Where's the Judge?"

"Is he expecting you?"

"You could say that," I said.

She thumbed me toward an inner office, but before I could enter, the door burst open and Sam dashed out, hand outstretched. He was a little heavier, a little fuller of face, the hairline had receded slightly, but otherwise he hadn't changed. He slapped me on the back and pushed me toward the inner office, made up of two rooms. "I recognized your voice," Sam said. "Come on. I want you to meet my political consultant." We went into the second room, which had an exit to a mezzanine corridor so Sam could come and go without detection, and a tall, older man stood up. "Harry Dodge," Sam said, "I want you to meet Jack Symington. Jack, this is the brain I've been telling you about."

"We've been waiting for you," Symington said, giving me a nice grip. The name registered with me, and I looked at him with some care. He was well turned out in a navy blue suit with a contrasting vest and a maroon tie. I was slightly mesmerized, because Symington to me was spelled m-o-n-e-y, and I wished later, for very particular reasons, that I could remember him as I first saw him. He was a presence, exerting itself. Old, I don't know how old. Old for fiddling around with political neophytes. Sixties, surely. He was sincere, earnest, kind, thoughtful—all the Boy Scout virtues. Money, character, ambition, inscrutability. But I do remember his first words to me. "There's a lot of work to be done here." He seemed to be in perfect control, perhaps even with a sense of dedication.

Sam broke in, ending my assessment of Symington. "Don't make it sound so hard," he said. "If a young Marine like me can't beat a seventy-two-year-old—"

"He's sixty-six," I said. "I've been checking."

"A few years don't make any difference to the voters," Sam

said. "The point is, he's senile. This is an age of youth, and the old guys have just got to step aside."

I shot a glance at Symington. He was taking it very well. Blair was his generation, but he seemed perfectly willing to sacrifice and to ignore the barbs. "Blair is very popular in Washington," I said. "Here, too, I'd imagine." I was still looking at Symington, and there was a slight ghost of a smile on his face. I think he could have backed Blair, had there been any personal gratification in it. But, obviously, he had made his choice.

"Blair is popular," Sam replied. "We're changing that. We haven't turned it all the way around yet, but we're going to. The old bastard is helping us, in a way. He doesn't even concede that he has any opposition. And I been doin' my homework. Runnin' all over the state meeting lawyers, legislators, newspapermen. And I've been very discreet in my judicial decisions."

"Playing politics from the bench?"

Sam grinned. " 'Politics' is a dirty word in jurisprudence. Let's just say I haven't forgotten where the votes are."

"That's another thing that bothers me," I said. "Under Maryland law, isn't a sitting judge prohibited from running for any other office?"

Sam's face was blank. "I hadn't heard anything about that," he said. "Jack, is that true?"

Symington was equally unmoved. "State Elections Board accepted the filing fee," he said. "They wouldn't have done that if it was illegal."

"Okay," I said. "Where do I sit?"

"Out there," Sam said. He pointed to the adjoining office. "There's a place there for that Polack you're bringing up, and yours is the desk with all the papers piled on it. I have to hold court in Marlboro the next couple days, and while I'm gone I want you to go through the *Congressional Record*, *Congressional Quarterly*, all those news clippings. Dig up anything we can use against Blair. Dirt. Speech ideas. Anything for promotion. And you've gotta find an apartment. Do you need money?"

"No. Not yet."

"Well, if you do, speak up. There's plenty."

"Where's it all coming from?"

"From little people. All over the country."

"The hell you say," I said. "To run a senatorial campaign you have to have some fat cats."

"Fat cats, eh?" Sam cut his eyes toward Symington and then back to me. "We got fat cats. But you shouldn't get into that. It's not for news releases." Numeriano came in quietly, and Sam turned to him. "Take Harry out and find him an apartment. Something convenient. And Harry. We're glad to have you aboard. Aren't we, Jack?"

"More than glad," Symington said, looking me over carefully. I tried, later on, at a particular period, to remember exactly how he looked when he said that, but I could never recapture it. Of course, at the time I was distracted.

I took a $75-a-month furnished flat on the second floor of an old row house in Govans, and every morning at 8:30 I caught the No. 8 Towson-Catonsville streetcar. In precisely twenty-five minutes, barring unusual traffic jams, it delivered me within thirty yards of the Emerson Hotel entrance. Daily, I pored over the *Congressional Record,* picking up the spirit of the senatorial debates. From *CQ* and a collection of old Blair newsletters, sent out under his frank, I compiled his voting record. When I was honest, I found myself envying it. E. Northrop Blair was a thoughtful, conscientious public servant, not flamboyant or golden-tongued, but quietly going about the business of government. He was the ranking Republican on two important senate committees, would chair Foreign Relations if his party ever won a majority. But more and more he was becoming a Senator of the United States rather than a Senator from Maryland. He had been a Washington fixture for twenty-three years. For his reelection he had come to depend more on his national stature than on his local appeal. It is a credit, no doubt, to be a Senator of the United States, but the people of the United States vote for senators by state, not as a nation, and Blair, in short, had neglected to keep his fences mended back in his home state, even though it was nearby. His residence was in the prestigious Columbia Towers on New Hampshire Avenue, and he no longer bothered to introduce small private bills benefiting his constituents. He left that to junior members of the House and co-sponsored them only as a courtesy when senate action was required. He was big on the budget, big on economy, big on business interests—and it was all there in the *Record*. If he consistently voted for "Big Oil" or "Big Steel," his reasoning was public and judicious. But my job was not to applaud him; it was to dissect him.

To be sure, he was vulnerable. In the "bring-the-boys-home" debates that began just after VJ day he had delivered a major speech opposing full-scale occupation of Germany and Japan. The public, he declared, deserved "to be relieved of the unnecessary tax burden of supporting a large military establishment." I batted out a memorandum to Sam: "Blair wants to cut the armed forces to a level that would be highly dangerous if this country were challenged once again on the field of battle. You can't oppose demobilization but you have to argue for a peace-through-strength posture." At about the same time Blair had made a courageous but ill-timed attack on the Soviet Union, citing its swallowing up of Estonia, Latvia and Lithuania and its dominance in Poland and Eastern Europe as "a pattern for world conquest." He apparently saw no incongruity in his appeal for reduced defense spending and his warning of the Soviet threat, but it was not my business to repair his mistakes. I turned out a memorandum to Sam reminding him that Russia was an ally and that in his speech Blair had echoed the charges of Fascist sympathizers.

I gave some of the reading to Selma Gadowski, who had

arrived by bus in the middle of my first week. We got her a
small apartment on Mount Vernon Place, within walking distance of the office, and she plunged into her work with a
vengeance. She marked every page of the *Record* that might
give me an idea, because she knew how my mind worked, and
she arranged the news clips in an order of priority. In another
way she surprised me. While she thought of me as her employer and respected me, she worshipped Sam. She was Jell-O
around him, collapsing into little jiggly mounds. "He is like a
little boy," she confided to me, and he rendered her helpless.

"He's no little boy," I told her. "He's a barracuda."

Selma was not pretty. She was lumpy and did not curve in
the right places, but she had an engaging smile and a disarm-
ing naiveté. "You have never known little boys," she said. "I
have brothers."

"Before I became a man, I was a little boy myself," I said.

"No, you were born old. Some men do not go through
boyhood."

I'm not sure how I got Selma. I think as a gift of the gods.
She arrived in my Richmond office the day I opened it, asking for a job. "I can't afford a secretary," I told her bluntly.

"You can afford me."

"How much will you work for?"

"Almost nothing, at first. And when you start making
money, whatever I'm worth."

"How much is almost nothing?"

"Twenty-five dollars a week."

"Can you type? Take dictation?"

She waved a secretarial school diploma on which the ink
was barely dry. I was never sorry I hired her. She could work
so cheaply because she still lived with her parents, immigrant
Poles, and they were frugal people. Her father worked in a
paint factory, a big slab of a man whose English was poor but
who had shortened some polyglot Polish name to Justin; her
mother sewed, doing very careful handwork in which she took

great pride. Even the high-school-age sons—Selma was the oldest and the only girl—had part-time jobs. Several times I was there in the modest, frame Gadowski house, on the Midlothian road, nursing a generous shot of 100-proof Zubrowka, the Polish vodka. It was a warm, loving place, and I was treated as some visitor from the mansions above.

Baltimore was Selma's first foray into the world, and she made the adjustment nicely. She was subservient to Jack Symington, friendly with Numeriano, firm with the volunteers who came to address letters and lick stamps. But she lost all her poise around Sam; she simply melted. When I saw those attacks coming on, I sent her out for coffee.

"But we have a coffee urn," she would protest.

"I want a sandwich, too. Polish sausage."

"Is that the sandwich, or are you calling me names?" Happily, a first-rate delicatessen was only a half block away. Selma wore out a lot of leather on those errands, and I glutted on corned beef, pastrami and Polish sausage.

I mentioned the volunteers. I must mention one in particular. On a rainy day, when volunteers don't show, I went into the workroom and was staggered by one of the loveliest brunettes I have ever encountered. She was something out of a dream, a fantasy, but she was stuffing envelopes and putting a red tonguetip to the mucilage. When she was aware that I was watching her she turned, and her radiant smile lit up the room. "You're Harry Dodge, aren't you?" she told me.

"At the moment, I'm not sure," I said.

"Take my word for it. That's who you are."

"And who might you be?"

"Meg Symington," she said, extending a hand that was angelic. "Jack's wife."

"Nice of you to come down," I blubbered.

The smile had faded, and there was an iciness, an aloofness about her. She trod paths most mortals do not know. "I want to help," she said, and turned back to her work. I went back to mine, but I could still see her face, that jet-black hair, the perfection of skin, the lushness, the ripeness, and it struck me that she was half Jack's age. Barely half.

I wrote the speech, to be delivered before a women's club at Havre-de-Grace, for the first "peace-through-strength" blast. We didn't expect to get much mileage out of the appearance itself, but Selma oiled up the mimeograph machine and I got out a news release to every paper in the state and the District of Columbia, capsuling the point. "Sam Bradford charged last night that Senator E. Northrop Blair, his Maryland Republican primary opponent, would denude this country of its striking power if he is returned to Washington. Bradford based his charge on a claim by Blair that the people of the United States are 'tired' of paying for a first-rate defense force. . . ."

About 200 women with their husbands, including several minor-league, local politicians, showed up for the dinner, and although Sam had read through the speech several times and had the salient points in mind, he didn't follow the script. And I soon learned that he never would. When he was introduced, with notes we had supplied identifying him as a respected judge and a hero of World War II Marine combat, he stood up with that slight smile, acknowledged the introduction with what he thought was graciousness, and launched immediately into a dissertation on the horrors of war. "Ladies and gentlemen, I have seen it firsthand," he said. "Firsthand. Many was the night that I sat up writing letters to the mothers of men I had seen die cruel deaths. Cruel deaths. And I never want to see anything like that come to our shores. Or to see our sons sent off again to perish on foreign soil. The only way to avoid that—the only way—is to maintain a fighting force so powerful that no alien ruler will ever again attempt another Pearl Harbor. And that is what my opponent stands for. Pearl Harbor. Oh, not in those words. Not in those exact words." And he fumbled through the text until he found the passage, which he paraphrased. " 'An adequate defense,' " Sam quoted Blair as saying, " 'is an unnecessary tax burden.' I don't think you believe that. These are the thoughtless mutterings of a senile old man. Now I respect age, but I don't believe that a seventy-two-year-old man should be entrusted with six more years in the United States Senate."

In Northeast Maryland, disregarding Blair's stated opposition to Soviet expansionism, we attacked him as a Red sympathizer for favoring reductions in the defense budget. In Southern Maryland, at the La Plata Rotary Club, we characterized him as a "fascist" favoring a return to power of Hitler's Germany and Mussolini's Italy. "Our brave Russian allies helped stamp out the Hitler menace," Bradford intoned. "And yet Blair prefers the Nazis to our wartime allies. He prefers the Nazis." And he cited yet another line I had dug up from an obscure Blair speech. "He does not even favor world cooperation. Gentlemen, in this postwar world we cannot go it alone. We cannot."

And at Ocean City, we made Blair a Jekyll-and-Hyde whose true position, unknown, was therefore sinister. The Ocean City speech was before the Maryland VFW, and when Bradford got going on his "peace-through-strength" pitch, the audience, mostly young World War II veterans, rose in a body and gave Bradford, one of their own, a unanimous endorsement.

The most unexpected support came from the Maryland-D.C. Labor Council, for most part representing steel, dock and shipyard workers. They reacted to Blair's denunciation of the Soviet Union with a vigorous editorial in *Labor Watch*, the state union paper, followed two days later by a statement of support for Sam Bradford. It did not matter to us then that the *Watch* editorial staff was dominated by Communists and that nearly every union local in Maryland had an organized Communist cell. We took support where we could get it.

Along with the speeches and press releases, we flooded

Maryland with postcards soliciting support for a "Marine hero" and a "true-blue American," all signed personally by Sam Bradford. Sam did, indeed, spend a half hour every day signing the cards, but most of the signatures were crude forgeries handwritten by volunteers. The recipients were none the wiser; they wouldn't have known a genuine holograph if they had seen one.

Radio was also an outlet. We got as much free time as we could through press releases, but we volunteered for talk shows, bought time to encourage the interviewers and provided Bradford tapes of his most effective stabs at the incumbent. We knew that Blair, if he wished to take advantage of it, could have the facilities of the Congressional tape room free, and we tried to dull that edge.

Blair realized too late what was happening. On the age issue he protested that Bradford had overstated his birthdate by several years, but no one paid any attention. Bradford had successfully portrayed him as senile, and that senility seemed to be magnified by Blair's feeble attempts to clarify his stand on military spending and his antipathy toward the defeated Germans and Italians. We responded to his press conferences by citing chapter and verse in the *Congressional Record,* and if we didn't have appropriate quotes we made them up. No one ever bothered to check. The attacks came from so many different levels and directions that poor Blair, accustomed to gentlemanly encounter, could never successfully counterattack.

Blair was, of course, the anointed of the Republican organization, but that blessing did not bind the Young Republicans of Maryland or the Women's Auxiliary. These electors were of Sam's generation, and they gave him a healthy if unofficial boost. The League of Women Voters scheduled both Blair and Bradford on the same program and because Blair was ill he sent his regrets. Sam portrayed Blair's bronchitis as a malady of convenience and swore that he himself would have entertained the ladies even if it had been necessary to hire a stretcher. Sam was, in his own words, "the only one who cares about you." The League offered no endorsement, but it gave Sam a lot of sympathy, and the brash young judge, hardly known statewide, became the hottest number on the campaign trail.

He was, to give him due credit, absolutely inexhaustible. The energy that I had seen trapped on Munda, he expended in a whirlwind of speechmaking, interviews, handshaking, supermarket visitations and press conferences. No group was too small for him to meet, not even a coffee klatch, and on some evenings he visited organizations separated by as much as a hundred miles. He was shooting at coconut trees again, delighted with the sound of the machine gun, this time his own voice. He went to bed late on those out-of-town excursions, rose early, ate and drank sparingly. Although Numeriano always accompanied him as driver, I did not; sometimes Jack Symington was with him, his jet-maned wife alongside, particularly if there were men to dazzle; sometimes Selma made the trips, especially to women's organizations. We all made notes on audience reaction, which of his lines went over best, how he could improve his image.

And I made a few private notes. One morning at a small hotel in Western Maryland I got up early and surprised a woman ghosting out of his room. She glanced at me and hurried away in some confusion, and I recognized her as one of the organizers from the event of the night before. At breakfast—juice, toast and coffee for Sam—I braced him about it.

"Did a little wenching last night, didn't you?"

"Who said?"

"That wasn't the chambermaid popping out of your room an hour or so ago."

He laughed. "No, I guess not."

"An old friend?"

"I never saw her before last night. Don't even know her last name. Ethel somebody. Or Esther."

"How'd you hook up with her?"

"She came calling to see if there were anything I needed."

"And it just happened there was."

Sam carefully spread butter and marmalade on his toast. Between bites he said, "Women in politics are the easiest lays in the world. Didn't you know that?"

"No."

"That's because you haven't been paying attention. You're thinking too much about the broad in Virginia. Get with the bird in hand. All those babes on the fringes of politics are fascinated with men in the center of it. They all have a case of the hots, the way some women go for quarterbacks or tennis bums or movie types. This is a breed apart. I could have a different woman every night. But don't put that in a press release. Sam Bradford is not at stud."

"Aren't you afraid it might get out? Even without the press release."

"Wouldn't hurt a damn bit. Pussy is international currency, as neutral as money. There isn't a congressman in Washington that hasn't got a woman stashed away somewhere. Generally on the payroll."

"That doesn't make it right."

"Harry, you're not goin' to turn the fuckin' world around, so don't try. I didn't get much sleep, so don't preach to me. Not now. Not ever."

"Whatever you say."

He wiped his mouth with his napkin and changed the subject. "We're goin' to win. I have a gut feeling."

"I hope so." I really did. I had invested some of my best talent in Sam Bradford, even though he sometimes spurned it. A loss I would have taken personally, as if I had been rejected by the voters.

Suffice it to say that we won, not overwhelmingly, but with a respectable margin. It was not a presidential election year, party cross-overs were not allowed in the Maryland primary and fewer than 100,000 Republicans turned out. We built up a good margin in Baltimore, where the votes were counted first, and we never fell behind. Sam, Jack and I and a few others sat in the inner office at hotel headquarters and listened to the radio and caught telephoned reports from observers at the Elections Board. Selma kept a running total on a small blackboard set up where we were and on a larger one installed in the lobby. The volunteers drank coffee. We drank scotch, some very smooth stuff that Jack had had sent in. Sam never worried at all. He simply did not believe he could be beaten.

When the majority was clear, Blair called to concede, and Sam listened to the "We want Bradford" chants from below and beamed. "This is one you don't have to write me a speech for, Harry," he said. We all went out to the balcony of the mezzanine and the rest of us flanked Sam. With that little half smile he gazed down at the cheering crowd, his eyes blinking from the pop of the flashbulbs. He held up his hands for silence and roared, "A great night. A great night for us, for the Free State of Maryland, for America. We have pulled down the temple. And I thank you. I thank you. All who licked stamps and envelopes, all who practiced my signature, all who provided cars today and all who, if only in their hearts, wished us well. This has been the big one, and in November we're going to roll over the Democrats." He stopped, and a note of puzzlement crept into the smile playing across his dark features. "Funny thing, I don't even know who I'm running against." He turned to me. "Who's winning the Democratic primary?"

"St. Clair."

He returned to the crowd and shouted, "We're going to beat the pants off John the Divine St. Clair. Beat the pants offa' him. We're going to put him right back in the classroom where he belongs. Can't do any harm there."

The crowd exulted, and Sam got the first taste of what blind adulation was really like. It created in him a hunger that was never to die, and that appetite was ultimately to lead to his undoing. I could not see it written there then, on the lusty winds of the Emerson Hotel lobby, and with him I enjoyed the evening. In the reflected limelight I basked, for I felt a strong sense of personal achievement. I couldn't wait to tell Patricia about it, to tell and to show.

So between the primary and the gearing up for the general, I brought her up to Baltimore. I didn't really bring her up. She tooled herself up 301 in the MG and coolly rejected the room I had reserved for her at the Emerson. "Darling," she said, "don't be so *conventional*." So we weren't conventional. I took her out to Govans and introduced her to my landlady as my fiancée, and Mrs. Fisher, long widowed, liked us both and posed no objection to Patricia's sharing my flat. We were, after all, adults, and Patricia was clearly a lady of quality. It wasn't even awkward. On the first night Patricia came to my bed, and after a few minutes she said, "Darling, I do hope you *have* something," and I had something I had been saving for just such an exigency, and we were one flesh. She had a healthy enthusiasm for sex, without weeping or self-reproach afterward, and after the third night I felt that we were old married hands, even though the matings always had a quality of newness and discovery.

Just before she went back to Virginia we had dinner with Sam, who had been holding court at La Plata, and it didn't go at all well. They were natural-born adversaries. At one point, I think it was over dessert, Patricia said, "Sam, what do you honestly think you have to offer the people as a United States Senator?"

"Leadership," Sam said.

"On what basis?" she came back. "What have you done that suggests you have that quality?"

"I have adjudicated. I have been an officer in the Marines. I beat Blair. Give me a chance, will you?" He was getting slightly peeved.

Patricia was blunt, in a fashion which seemed unlike her. "You'll make a lousy Senator," she said.

Sam looked at me. "What do you feed this girl?"

"He beds me," Patricia said, "but he doesn't tell me what to think. Or say."

I yawned. "We better go," I said to Sam. "She has to leave tomorrow. And I assure you, she's a lot better in bed than she is at dinner." Patricia stood up and I said gently, "Say something nice."

She nodded. "The baked Alaska was good."

We retrieved the MG, and I drove out Calvert Street and cut through Guilford to York Road. We were waiting for a streetcar to pass, and Patricia said, "Did I make you angry with me?"

"Not at all," I said, making the left turn, "but you were a little rough on him. One could get the distinct impression that you didn't like Sam."

"Like him? He's the biggest ass I've met in ten years."

"Ah, come on. Be generous."

"I'm being generous. He is dumb, boorish, maybe even dangerous."

"Dangerous! Sam?"

"I think so. He has a bad look."

"Plato was ugly."

"Ugliness I can stand, but not meanness."

"Patricia, you've spent a little more than an hour with the man, and you've already figured him out completely. He's— why are we doing this?"

"What?"

"Fighting?"

She was instantly chastened and leaned over to kiss me. "We won't fight. I'm sorry."

But later, much later, when we were spent and lying very close, she murmured, apropos of nothing, "You shouldn't be working for him. You should be working against him." In the dark I stroked her fine blonde hair, sought out the sweet places, turned her thoughts to more immediate needs. And Sam was forgotten.

Yet but briefly. After she had gone I had to get back to work, and the work was the one Sam liked to call "the Divine." John St. Clair. A sociology professor at Johns Hopkins University.

Maryland has some fine universities, even if it did once allow its state university to fall into the hands of a football coach. But Johns Hopkins, world-renowned because of its Hospital and associated Medical School; St. John's; the Naval Academy; Goucher—all fine institutions of learning. Which cut little ice with the rank-and-file Free Stater. In mass, Marylanders are suspicious of education, and professors on a printed ballot are regarded as typographical errors. There is a lot of old money in Maryland, and its owners move in a tight little circle and get immense enjoyment from the good life. By and large they have no traffic with the common people, and by and large, despite their cash balances, they have little influence on how the state mandates its politicians. For years the biggest political boss in Baltimore was a bricklayer who quit school in the fourth grade and learned how to vote dead people. He never set foot in the Maryland Club on Charles Street, but he had more practical power than most of the old millionaires. Occasionally, as in the cases of Blair and Symington, a member of the aristocracy dabbled in politics, but for the most part the governing of the state, of Baltimore, of the counties—and the division of the oft-times malodorous spoils—is left to rising young lawyers, ambitious Italian-Americans or Greeks, a representative Jew out of the Northwest Baltimore precincts. The state's government, at all levels, has sometimes been very good, and there have been instances when it was incredibly bad. But it is no place for educators. The system does not adapt to them.

And so John St. Clair, Ph.D., had no business in the race

for the senate, even though he was a Democrat and Democrats outnumber Republicans on the Maryland registration
books. St. Clair's doctorate was from Harvard, he was not
native, he labored in a discipline beyond the comprehension
of the average voter, and he had a known record of vocal
support for even the most radical proposals of the Roosevelt
Administration. He had been an inveterate author of letters
to the editor of the Hearst and Abell newspapers, and as I
culled through these writings I prepared a memorandum for
Sam saying that at the very least, John the Divine St. Clair
was "leftist-oriented."

Sam didn't care for such ambiguous phrases. In his first
major speech of the general election campaign he attacked St.
Clair as being "Communistically inclined," thereby tacitly
disavowing the Communist support that had helped him win
the primary. If in that maneuver he lost some slight support,
he picked up additional backing from right-wing organizations which had just begun to surface nationally. The Maryland director of the Committee for Conservative Action,
Leonard Meecham, issued a statement attacking St. Clair as a
"dangerous revolutionary" who would "sell out the basic
principles of the Founding Fathers," and a scattering of
America First splinter groups coalesced into an "Indepen-
dents for Bradford" campaign committee. The Abell newspapers, aligned financially with Valley and banking interests,
took a brave plunge with a tippy-toe endorsement of the
Hopkins intellectual, but their Hearstling counterpart was
fulsome in its praise of Sam Bradford, "by word and deed the
epitome of a one hundred percent American."

If Bradford toppled Blair by a sheer onslaught of words, he
skewered St. Clair on a dirty lance and cooked him to ashes.
The Hopkins professor, Bradford declared, had sat out the
war "sharpening pencils." Actually, St. Clair had a heart flut-
ter as a result of childhood rheumatic fever and had been
classified 4-F. On the contrary, Bradford, who could have

been exempt from service, had volunteered "for some of the heaviest fighting in the South Pacific." St. Clair's senatorial program was a "pipe dream, probably from an opium pipe," while Bradford had presented "a concrete program for the supremacy of American defense, the American economy, full employment, and an end to governmental interference in private business."

Sam's program was worded thus vaguely for good reason: he had never bothered to sit down with his advisers to work anything out. He insisted that "programs are not elected, people are," and if pressed for his stand on any particular issue he became evasive and contradictory. We had not written him any formal position papers, and he flew by the seat of his pants. If St. Clair had bothered to assign a leg man to monitor Bradford's speeches, interviews, ads and off-the-cuff remarks he could have painted his antagonist as one of the greatest chameleons of all time. But St. Clair lacked that political necessity, the instinct for the jugular, and he allowed himself to be browbeaten, slandered, misrepresented and crucified. His major pitch was that the voters can tell a good man from a bad one, and he placed his fate and faith in the ballot box.

He was, indeed, a misguided idealist. Anyone who stakes his future on the wisdom of the electorate is building his house on quicksand, because the voters respond to their emotions, not to their intellect. American politics also requires one all-important ingredient—money. St. Clair had modest backing, paid mostly in words. But during the months I spent in the Emerson Hotel headquarters, I saw the big checks roll in for Sam. From Texas oil. From the manufacturing associations. From the banking interests. From the medical monopoly. From munitions makers. From the aviation lobby. And some of the checks came in with foreign stamps from strange banks in obscure little countries. Sam Bradford got the cream, and he used it to butter up nearly every communications medium in the state. With ads he could buy endorsements, and with judiciously placed envelopes of cash he could line up ward heelers in every strategic district in the constituency.

The tide of words and dollars swept us to victory on election night, about three-to-one, and Sam grieved that it was not six-to-nothing. To those same faces in November that had gapped with frantic cheers in May, assembled once more in the Emerson lobby, he said, "Friends, we made it. We are going to Washington like a fresh wind. We are going to air out all the dark corners and hidden places, all the rotten handiwork of the do-gooders. It is a new day in American politics. A new day. I want you to share it with me, and to all of you, my door will always be open. Come to me with your problems. Will you do that?" He waited until the swelling applause died down, and then he said, "I am going back into my office now, to relax a little and to wait for the call from St. John the Divine. Go home now and get some rest. We all deserve it."

St. Clair lacked the grace of E. Northrop Blair. He never conceded. But concession or not, Sam Bradford, judge, Marine hero, despoiler of coconuts, he of the facile tongue, was on his way to the seat of power.

☆3☆

UNLESS THEY ARE UNNATURALLY PRESTIGIOUS, freshman senators make very little splash in Washington, and Sam Bradford was no exception. In January, 1947, we moved into the least impressive of the ninety-six suites in the old Senate Office Building, signed the government payroll forms and studied the black-lined maps of the Capitol Hill premises. Sam had a private office with a bar, and in the larger working quarters, we were a staff of five. Selma, bulky even at a large desk, sat nearest the door, greeting visitors as receptionist, handing out the impressive gallery passes with the rubber-stamped signature, handling the routine correspondence over which she sometimes had to confer with me. My nook was toward the back of the room, with a large window overlooking a courtyard, and we had taken on two of Senator Blair's unemployed secretaries, professional Hill types who had no political allegiance whatsoever but who from years of experience knew how things were done. At a very small, unadorned desk in a corner, almost hidden by filing cabinets, sat Numeriano, who was listed euphemistically on the organizational chart, and the pay forms, as "clerk."

Numeriano did not spin and he did not sew, much less tinker with the office equipment. He was Sam's shadow, and the familiar navy-blue suit, his lifelong habit except that the hash marks were gone, now bulged slightly at the chest. The protuberance, thought by casual observers to be a pocket full of documents, was a .32-caliber, blue-steel, automatic pistol lodged in a black leather shoulder holster. Until he met Sam, Numeriano had never carried or fired a gun in his life. It was not a necessity for a Navy steward or a judge's chauffeur, but a week after his election as senator, Sam had taken Numeriano down to a pawn shop on East Baltimore Street and picked out the weapon for him. Even after ten days of constant practice, Numeriano couldn't hit an elephant at twenty paces, but he could make one helluva racket. I had personally given him instruction because Sam was a hunting type and didn't care much for handguns. After extensive battle with tin cans and beer bottles, I despaired of Numeriano's ability. "Look," I said, "if we are ever together and you have to pull that cannon, let me shoot it. And if I'm not there to help, be sure you get the gun out of the holster before you pull the trigger. You could wind up with a new belly button. And that would smart." Gradually, Numeriano got accustomed to the weight, and he was as at home with the holster as he was with the flashy cuff links he fancied.

When I say that freshman legislators make no splash, I don't mean to imply that they are ignored. There are ten thousand lobbyists in Washington. They are all eager to get on familiar terms with members of congress, and daily, at the beginning of every session, they throw breakfasts, brunches, luncheons, morning and afternoon coffee hours, cocktail parties early and late, receptions, dinners, formal and informal, and midnight stag parties. By "stag" I mean, in addition to the vacuous nudes, the real, hard-core stuff. At that time the biggest national dealer in pornographic films operated out of a basement two blocks from the Capitol, just behind the Supreme Court. For a premium he could provide 16 millimeter films of some of the biggest names in Hollywood practicing fellatio, cunnilingus or homosexual shenanigans. In all the years that I was on the Hill, he was never bothered by the police or the postal authorities. There were certain perquisites that were just generally accepted, legal or not.

Sam was flattered by the attention of the lobbyists, sometimes to the neglect of his Senate duties. He was at some association's breakfast nearly every morning. He took a morning coffee break, with bloody marys instead of caffeine; he dallied at expense-account luncheons and enjoyed martinis at the afternoon breaks; and he was always at someone's dinner. Senators are, of course, a prize catch at these functions, lending them more prestige than house members, lower-level bureaucrats, newsmen and minor ambassadors, and only slightly less than cabinet members, Supreme Court justices or the envoys from the great powers.

Bradford didn't apologize for his attention to these gatherings. "I've got to sort things out," he explained to me. "Learn the ropes. Find out who's who. If you think all the power is over there under the dome, you're nuts. Money changes hands around here. I want to know who's giving it and who's getting it. I want to sit in on the sessions where the votes are traded. And at some of these cocktail parties you can find out more about what a committee is up to than you can at its public hearings." But he never brought out the new broom to clean up the dark corners of the seat of government, even though one of his gullible Maryland supporters had had one sent special delivery as a symbolic gesture. I don't mean that Sam was idle or that he loafed. All that energy inside him had to find a way out. But little of it was expended in the passage of legislation or on its consideration in committee.

Oh, he sponsored a few bills. One to provide price supports for chicken (there are a lot of chicken ranchers on the Eastern Shore of Maryland). It was never reported out by the Agriculture Committee, even though we flooded Maryland with flyers on its prospects. He went along with all the legislation extending veterans' benefits; he was a veteran himself. One curious anomaly was his opposition to a federally funded public housing program whose principal beneficiaries would have been GI's. In a minor senate speech he insisted that the private sector was "fully capable of providing all the housing the country needed, at prices more favorable than a government bureaucracy can assure." All he wanted congress to do was to guarantee the builders of cheap prefabs that they wouldn't lose money on their investment—"a gesture which would cost far less than the Treasury raid we are considering." He was beaten soundly, but he didn't care; his speech had been delivered to please a construction lobby whose association he had addressed earlier for twelve minutes—and a $2,000 fee. Sam easily rationalized his position. "One way or the other," he told me, "the veterans are going to get housing. That's for sure. It doesn't make much difference who provides it."

The thing he had us working hardest at during the first year was sugar, which was still rationed. A Baltimore brewery wanted to expand its production, Jack Symington held a lot of stock in the company, and Sam went on the floor of the Senate to plead for an end to rationing. We had supplied him with production and usage figures which he rattled off, and at the end he ad-libbed that he had been in constant touch with the appropriate officials in the Agriculture Department "and they assure me that there is no need for the further rationing of sugar. It could end tomorrow." A North Carolina senator, close to the canning industry, got up to second Sam's case. The proposition was derailed, however, when cagey old Senator Burroughs, of Illinois, returned to the floor after a short visit to the lobby. He said he had talked with the Secretary of Agriculture himself not three minutes before "and the Secretary has authorized me to say that sugar is in short supply, that increased production cannot be expected within the foreseeable future and that it is essential that rationing be continued." Naturally, Sam had not been "in constant touch" with anybody at the Agriculture Department, nor had those of us on his staff. We had asked for some statistical material and it had been routinely supplied. We had fashioned it to suit Sam's case. Breweries are important to Baltimore, and the rationing of sugar after the war's end was generally unpopular. In this case Sam did not lose altogether, because he and the sugar lobby got to enough senators to advance the date of the ending of sugar restrictions, originally scheduled for March, 1948, to October, 1947. This meant a lot of extra bottles of beer. Before the vote, Sam quietly instructed his broker to invest heavily for him in sugar futures. The price, he knew, was bound to rise. He was generous enough to offer me a piece of the action, but I declined.

One thing I never fully understood was Sam's opposition to the Marshall Plan, which was framed as legislation after Gen. George C. Marshall, then Secretary of State, made his famous address at Harvard in June 1947. "I'm going to vote against it," Sam told me over and over as the $12 billion measure shaped up in the following months.

"But why?" I asked. "Wasn't it you who said in the Blair campaign, 'international cooperation'? Isn't that what the Marshall Plan is all about?"

"It isn't Marshall's plan."

I could get no more than that out of him at first, but a few days later he called me into his office. "You still worried about my vote on the Marshall Plan?"

"Not worried. I don't represent anybody. But it seems a humane, generous thing for the United States to do."

"I have evidence," he said, "that it's a Communist-inspired giveaway. Communist-inspired."

"Are you saying that General Marshall is a Communist?"

"I wouldn't go that far," Sam said conspiratorially. "But people around him are. Do you know who thought up this scheme?"

"Marshall proposed it. I suppose he had help."

"Who do you think helped him?"

"I haven't any idea. Who helps Sam Bradford? Nobody ever heard of Harry Dodge."

"You're getting off the point. It's Acheson's plan." He pulled a clipping out of a folder and handed it to me. It was an account of an Acheson speech in Columbia, Missouri, some months before Marshall's Harvard address. Essentially, Dean Acheson, Marshall's Under Secretary, was giving voice to what Marshall had proposed later.

I handed it back to Sam. "So maybe it should be called the Acheson Plan."

Sam's voice became confidential. "That's just it," he said. "Everybody knows that Acheson is hand in glove with the Communists."

"I didn't know that."

I didn't realize it at the time, but to Sam, "Communist" was a scare word, and anything tainted with communism, however remotely, was automatically suspect. I never found out where he picked up the slur on Acheson, but it was enough to decide his vote against the Marshall Plan.

Actually, for the first four years in Washington, we marked time. It is not surprising that Sam commanded little respect from his colleagues or from the press corps. He had done nothing to earn it.

As for me, the period was of great consequence, highlighted by an incident which in my memory occurred at my small carriage apartment house in Georgetown. The telephone rang, and it was Patricia. She had visited Washington a few times, I had been down to Richmond, we had exchanged letters and calls. I had not detected impatience, but I got the full blast of it that night. "Harry," she began, "it's about time you made an honest woman of me."

"Are you serious?" I said. "You haven't been drinking anything?"

"I have never been more serious in my life. I've been sitting here. Thinking."

"About what?"

"About how much time we've wasted."

"Wasted? Hell, you've been getting educated."

"I will have that proof shortly. In a scroll of lambskin. But it says nothing. Do I have to goose you?"

"About what?" This was very serious business, and I couldn't afford a miscue.

"Harry, I want to get married." In her voice there was a note of desperation.

"Do you have to?"

"Damn you, Harry. No, I don't have to."

"You're sure about this?"

"Positive."

"Well, I've been thinking about it. All the pros and cons. And if you insist . . ."

"Oh, you heel, you heel."

"Suppose I come down this weekend, and we'll talk about it."

"Will you let anything keep you from coming? No Saturday sessions for that Sam."

I broke down and turned honest. "Patricia, nothing will stop me. Nothing. You mean more to me than the whole United States Senate. And for that matter, the future of the Republic."

"Just hurry."

By that time I had acquired one of the new-generation Studebakers, a coupe, the old Chevy having expired, and early Saturday morning I drove down through the maze of motor homes and places of illicit liaison on U. S. 1 to Richmond and through the heart of that city to the James River Road off Hopewell. When I reached the entrance to Mason's Bluff, with the broad sweep up to the portico, I proceeded slowly up the graveled lane. Once slaves had tilled these fields and carriages with liveried footmen had rolled this path. A faint voice somewhere in the back of my mind asked, "Is this what you really want, Harry Dodge?" and it was an impudent question and I dismissed it and stomped down on the accelerator and made the small stones fly. I slid to the front of the house and Peyton, the man of all work, came out and got my bags. "Miz 'Tricia, she in the garden," Peyton said, and I walked around the wing of the house and found my love on a cast-iron chair. She advanced with both hands outstretched, this perfect blonde miniature, and I took them and squeezed them and laid a kiss on her.

She motioned toward a matching chair, painted white like the rest of the outdoor ensemble, and she paced in front of me, rather singlemindedly, I thought.

"Did you have a nice trip?" she asked.

"Okay."

"Was the traffic heavy?"

"Fierce."

"What about June?"

"June? June is all right."

"Six weeks. June 20."

"June 20. I'll try to make it."

"Put it on your calendar. Under 'Things to Do Today. Marry Patricia.'" She came and sat on my lap and put her arms around me. "Harry, this is what you want, isn't it?"

I hesitated long enough to embarrass her. "Yes."

"Why?"

"I don't know," I said. "Because you're a good lay."

"No, be serious. I know that isn't it. Why do you want to marry me?"

"Do I really have to tell you, Trish?"

"Yes. For my pride."

"All right, Miss Mason. Miss Mason of the Virginia Masons, of the First Families. I'll tell you. Because without you, my life isn't complete. When I first met you, after you had beat up my car, there was a voice inside me that said, 'Harry, this little blonde is the girl you are going to marry.' It was inevitable, ordained, predestined."

"Do you really believe that?"

"Of course."

"And you don't think I'm—rushing things? I feel shameless, wanton."

"We've waited too long already."

"You won't be sorry? Giving up your freedom? Bachelorhood?"

"It's not as much fun as you are."

"I don't come to you a virgin."

"I know. We'll just have to live with it."

"But you were the only one."

"Then where did you learn all that . . . ?"

She put her finger on my lips. "The Masons are hot-blooded women." She lapsed into silence, and when her voice came again it was smaller, with a note of pleading in it. "You know what?"

"What?"

"I think you should give me a ring."

I turned away as if she had made me uncomfortable. "I hadn't thought about making that much of an investment."

"Not a big stone," she said quickly. "Nothing expensive. A token."

"Diamonds are pretty serious."

"Not even a diamond. A zircon."

"Well, a zircon. That's different." I reached in my pocket and took out a small box wrapped in white. "Will this do?"

She tore at the ribbon. "Harry, you haven't had time. How could you . . . ?"

"It was my grandmother's. Eight-tenths of a carat. And I had the silversmith add the baguettes. It represents the entire Dodge fortune. I hope you like platinum."

"Oh, I do. But the size? It fits perfectly."

"I borrowed a piece of your old junk jewelry. Peyton conspired with me."

"I love it, I love it," she said, dancing around and flinging her lithe body against me.

Colonel Mason had joined us on the terrace. "What is going on here?" he asked gruffly.

"Harry has given me a ring," Patricia said.

"Why would he do that?"

"As part of the plans for our wedding."

"It's about time," snorted Stanwick, in his best C. Aubrey Smith imitation. "Congratulations, Harry," he said, shaking my hand firmly. "And God help you. This woman is incorrigible."

"I know that. I'm going to beat the hell out of her about twice a week."

"It's the only way," the Colonel said. "When is this ill-fated union to be legalized?"

"June 20," Patricia said.

"Your mother was married on June 20," her father said. "Come to think of it, so was I."

"I wondered if you would remember."

"Where will you live?"

"In Chevy Chase," I began.

"In Harry's carriage house in Georgetown," Patricia said firmly.

It was a big wedding, at St. Ann's Episcopal Church in Richmond, with third cousins and maiden aunts, striped pants and an antique satin gown made over from a previous June 20, a reception at the James River Country Club with lots of champagne, caviar, truffled goose liver and jumbo shrimp. There was one little nicety that I hadn't seen at a wedding before and haven't seen since. At a table in one corner of the huge hall a wiry little black man deftly shucked oysters and set them out on the half shell as fast as they could be gobbled up. Colonel Mason explained it to me. "Old family tradition," he said with some embarrassment. "Goes back to the early days of the Bluff. One of those old geezers had the idea that every bridegroom ought to eat at least a dozen raw oysters in preparation for his wedding night. You know, they—don't know if there's any truth in it. But we've kept it up. Kind of a joke."

"Damn good joke," I said, dousing one of the bluepoints in the fiery sauce. "Damn good tradition. Is there a limit on the bridegroom? I've already had eighteen."

"I like a man with that kind of ambition," the Colonel said, patting me on the back. He seemed really fond of me, and I felt tremendous warmth toward him.

In the arrangements for the nuptials, Patricia had disputed me on only one point. I wanted Sam Bradford to be my best man. She was too caught up in coordinating the colors of the gowns for her attendants to protest too much, and Senator Sam did indeed stand up for me, and it was he who sent us off to Bermuda for a week as his wedding present.

When we headed back to Washington, it was with joy unbounding. In the Georgetown carriage house Patricia busied herself with the drapes, filled the walls with bright prints, recovered the sofas and chairs, made me French toast for breakfast, pleasured me in the nights—oh, how she pleasured me—and I wondered why it had taken us so long to set up housekeeping.

In the intimacy of one late night I asked her, "Do you like this?"

"Being married? Sleeping with you? *This?* What a foolish question."

"No, I mean Washington. Georgetown. The cocktail parties and political dinners. This life."

"Yes. Why?"

"I don't think it'll last."

"Does anything ever? What's wrong?" She sat up in the darkness and hugged her knees.

"Bradford isn't going to be reelected," I said. "He's a lousy Senator."

"Is that news to me? I told you, back there in Baltimore, that he's a jerk."

"Oh, jerks get reelected. He just hasn't *done* anything. There's no way to make him look good."

"So. Have you made any plans?"

"The obvious. Go back to Richmond. Reopen the agency. Would that be too bad?"

"No. I'm ready to go back when you are. All right?"

"Yes. I wanted to be sure."

"Okay. You have my word. Going back to Richmond will be no great disappointment." She settled back under the sheet, her mind on more pressing matters. "Now could we try that again?"

The muggy August came, and recess, and we forsook Washington for Rehoboth, taking long walks on the strand. We made love behind the sand dunes, and on some nights, when there was little traffic, we shamelessly went skinny-dipping. There is something about the ebb and flow of the tide that is aphrodisiac, and we allowed ourselves to be swept up by it. I think it was not so much that we were in love with each other, although that was certainly there. But we were in love with youth and its extravagance, with the blessed years wasted, with the knowledge that time, inexorably, moves onward, passing you by. It does not wait, and although on Rehoboth, Washington and Sam Bradford seemed far away, and we made desperate love, we had, inevitably, to go back in the fall—away from the creeping tide, away from those surges which seem to suggest absolute abandon, away from that enveloping warmth that diverts one into strange and wondrous experiments.

And, politically, the fall brought no changes. Sam continued to play the cocktail circuit. He missed more roll calls than any other senator except Perry, of Maine, who was in

Walter Reed with incurable cancer. He slighted committee meetings. He drank. Oh, how he drank.

Faithfully Numeriano practiced with the .32. Faithfully Selma Gadowski clipped, marked, filed. Faithfully I got out the newsletters to the Maryland papers, chronicling in imagined detail the daily battles of the junior Senator from Maryland. We covered, we stalled, we protected him from his constituents. When he had a hangover, we were ready with an excuse. "The Senator is on an investigatory trip." Not "junket," you will notice. "Junketing" was in bad aroma. The office ran smoothly. It was a gem of coordination and precision. But it was a hollow operation, because it lacked a moving force, a center, a man who cared enough to do his job. We talked about that necessity, quietly among ourselves, evading the central issue. Selma, who loved Washington, put her lines out in the Capitol Hill Club, hedging her obvious future unemployment. The two professionals, attuned to the winds of the Hill, already had their applications out. They would be available, and they would be hired. In Washington, on the Hill, the political eunuchs thrive. I myself could not reach the man, the senator around whom all this action vortexed. He was leading the gay life in the capital, courted, complimented, pandered to. He was still a vote, and therefore he was still worth a drink, a luncheon tab.

The day of reckoning, I thought, must surely come.

☆4☆

THE DAY OF RECKONING CAME, to be sure, but not as I thought it would. On a January day in 1950, Sam called me into his office and said quite astonishingly, "Harry, I'm in trouble."

I was so taken aback that I said, "What do you mean?"

He looked at me in disgust. "Shit!" he said. "You know fuckin' well what I mean."

"If you put it that way, I guess I do."

"What can I do about it?"

"Let me think. Will you let me think?"

"Okay, think. But come up with some answers. That's what you get paid for, isn't it? Answers? I'll be at the Congress Hotel."

I went back to my desk and thought, which was what I got paid for. My mind was utterly blank. I paced. Selma sensed that I was earning my pay, and she brought me coffee. I drank it and walked. I was so deep in thought that I almost didn't hear Selma say, "Can you talk to this man? Colonel Skinner?"

"I had hoped to see the Senator," Colonel Skinner said. He was a small, nervous man with a fat briefcase. Short for a colonel. Unkempt. Apologetic.

"Sit down," I said. "Senator Bradford is tied up in commit-tee. I'm his administrative assistant, very close to him. Can I help?"

Colonel Skinner was nervous. "I think I can only talk to the senator."

"Talk to me. Trust me. Tell me what you want. The sena-tor will get back to you. I promise."

Skinner looked around him, ill at ease. He patted his brief-case. "This is very confidential material. I can't show it to just anyone."

"Would you feel better if we went into his office?"

"I think so."

We got up, and he followed me into Sam's inner sanctum. "Would you like a drink?" I asked.

"No."

"What do you want to talk about?"

"It's what I have here." He began to drag out photostated sheets of paper. "Someone has to do something."

"About what?"

"Look at this." He handed me document after document.

"What are you trying to tell me? For God's sake, come out with it."

His lip trembled. "The Communists are taking over the Pentagon."

"The hell you say. That's very serious."

"Serious? It's traitorous. The Defense Department is full of spies. Do you know what that means? Do you have any inkling?"

"No inkling. I'm not clued in. What does it mean?"

"All our defense secrets are being handed over to the Rus-sians. That's what it means."

I nodded reassuringly. In Washington I had seen nuts of every stripe. I tried to cajole this one. "You leave this stuff with me," I said. "The senator will study it, and he'll get back to you."

"I have an unlisted number."

"Of course you do. Will you give it to me? I won't spread it around. In harm's way."

Skinner jotted the number on a scratch pad and handed it to me. "Will you tell the senator that this is of the utmost urgency? Our country is being sold out. I think that's very serious."

"Damn right, it is," I said. "I'll tell him. And thank you for coming to us. You won't be sorry."

Skinner bowed out, and I resumed my pacing, little caring about what he had brought. I picked up a magazine from my desk. *Aviation Age.* And it struck me. I called Jack Symington in Baltimore, because I thought Sam would want him close by. "Can you be over here about five this afternoon?" I asked. "It seems to be a matter of life and death."

"Sure," Jack said, "and I'll bring a priest."

"For God's sake," I said, "we don't need the last rites. Not yet."

"Nah, this isn't a sin-eater. It's a guy who's been dying to talk to Sam. Chewed my arm off up to the elbow. We'll see you at five."

Sam came in from the Congress Hotel bar about 3:30, rocking slightly, and I went in to set him up. "Jack Symington's coming over at five. With some power in the church."

"The church, for Chrissake!"

"Well, we need all the help we can get."

"You had an idea yet?"

"Yeah."

"It better be good."

"It's damn good. A brainstorm. One of those fevers of the cerebrum. Or the cerebellum."

"What the hell are you talking about?"

"My idea."

"Do you want to tell me now?"

"Let's wait until Jack gets here."

"Set up something somewhere. A dinner. Make reservations at The Last Resort on Mass. Ave."

I went back to the outer office and told Selma, "Call The Last Resort on Mass. Ave. and make reservations for Senator Bradford. Table for four. Something after six." I went over to my desk and picked up the papers Skinner had left me. Classified documents. Depositions. A chronology of how the atom bomb was stolen for the Russians. A chart alleging a network of deceit at the Pentagon. Conspiracy on conspiracy. A lot of it was stuff I had heard rumored. I crammed it in my own briefcase for a going-over; I'd do a *précis* for Sam and let him handle it. Skinner was a kooky zealot, perhaps mad. Let one kook do for another. I forgot Skinner.

Jack Symington, fresh from his bath and anointed with oil and precious spices, arrived shortly after five in tow of a Jesuit priest. Father Baugh, of the Society of Jesus. We all went into Sam's office and poured scotch, and Father Baugh gulped it as if he were afraid the miracle at Cana might be suddenly reversed. We were all quite companionable by the time Sam called Numeriano. When the white Olds drew up to the curb, we tumbled into it loudly, I with Numeriano in front, Sam and Jack in the back sandwiching the good Jesuit. The Olds moved smoothly along Constitution to New Jersey, bore left at the Government Printing Office on Massachusetts and carefully negotiated Mount Vernon Square. Just beyond Thomas Circle, Numeriano deposited us at The Last Resort, and we went in and raucously claimed our table.

"This is on me, Sam," Jack said.

"Why should it be?" Sam asked. "I called this cabinet meeting. Through the good offices of my trusted associate."

"I owe you," Jack said. "The brewery owes you."

"Let the brewers, the dispensers of malt, feed us, then," Sam said. "They have good shellfish here. And the steaks are sensational."

I eyed the menu. "The prices are sensational, too. Now I

know why they call this The Last Resort. It's the last place you ever will be able to afford."

"Think beer, boy," Sam said.

"Think beer," said Jack. "And we need more scotch."

When we had settled into the dinner, Sam began, punctuating his pitch with gulps of filet and chunks of buttered French bread. "I don't have to fool any of you," he said. "You've all been around, and you know that I haven't compiled the kind of record that inspires voters. Two more years like this, and it's back to the farm. I ask you; what can I do?"

"Your record's not so bad, Sam," Jack began. "At least you haven't made any mistakes."

"That's not the fuckin' point," Sam said. " 'Scuse me, Father. I just haven't been effective."

"What you need, Senator," Father Baugh said quite soberly, "is a cause. A fresh one. Something striking, that hasn't made the rounds before."

"That, Father, is why the fuck—excuse me—we're here. To put something together. My genius here has been cogitating. What did you have in mind, Harry?"

Jack had ordered burgundy, and I took a sip to clear my adenoids. "Two things," I said.

"Name one."

"Space. Missiles. For the next twenty years, that's going to be the big thing."

"Just how?" Sam asked.

"Any future war is going to be fought with missiles. Long-range rockets."

"They didn't do much for the Germans," Jack said. "They weren't much more than toys. Nuisances at most."

"But suppose you could marry an atomic warhead to a missile?" I said, not at all put off. "Suppose you could develop a missile that would cross oceans? Or continents? Hit Moscow? Tokyo? Suppose you could deploy them not only from land bases but from planes and subs?"

"Cost a lot of money," Sam said. "And the public mood isn't for spending. You're talking about, I dunno. Billions. And suppose you have this huge arsenal and have spent all this money and there's no war. What good is it?"

"Listen, Sam," I said earnestly, and I was really trying to sell him. "Space is the last frontier, and all this technology could be put to peacetime uses." I made my final overture. "We could explore the universe."

"Just why the hell would anybody wanta do that, Harry?" Jack said. "Even if they could. Who gives a damn what's out there? It's comic page stuff. Buck Rogers. Leave it for the funny paper."

"Nah, Jack," Sam said. "Harry's got something. Why did Columbus cross the ocean? In his time that was Buck Rogers stuff. And gunpowder. For a long time all it was used for was firecrackers. But I ain't Queen Isabella. And I ain't Genghis Khan—whoever the bastard was that put the first cannonball in front of a glob of that gunpowder. I don't think pushing an expensive program of any kind would necessarily endear me to the voters. But I'll ponder on it. You got anything else, Harry?"

I finished my steak and nodded. "One other thing. If you could be a voice warning against the production of shoddy goods, you'd be a public hero. There are any number of abuses we could look into. Automobiles. Housing. Five and dime items. We could come up with a new revelation every week. 'Sam Bradford, friend of the little man.' "

"Yeah," Sam said, "and cut my throat with the moneybags. They'd stomp me into the ground. You can't go fuckin' around with people like General Motors. They're too powerful. In many ways the large corporations run the goddamn country. And the profit comes from shaving a little here and shaving a little there. They're too powerful, and they sure as hell know how to play politics. Any other ideas? Anybody?"

"All I could think of was the St. Lawrence Seaway," Symington said. "If it goes through it's going to play hell with Maryland shipping."

Sam shook his head. "As an issue it's too narrow," he said. "I can't go around making a St. Lawrence Seaway speech every day. And, incidentally, it's going through, and Maryland will have to suffer the consequences. I'll vote right on it, but I can't stop it. And besides, what we need is a national forum, something to stir people up all over the country. At the crossroads grocery stores, around the pot-bellied stoves, those old bastards don't give a damn about no hole in the ground."

Father Baugh had been sitting quietly, listening, grunting occasionally, but holding his peace while he cleaned up his victuals. Finally, he pushed his plate away and said, "Senator, may I make a suggestion?"

"I'd hoped you would," Sam said. "But I warn you, I don't want to fight the Protestants. Let the Pope do that."

"Not Protestants," the priest said. "Communists. Fight communism. I've been in Russia, and I teach a foreign policy course at Loyola. Has it occurred to you that this country has no secret that hasn't been—or couldn't be—stolen by the Russians? Take the atom bomb. The Russians didn't devise their own. They stole ours. With the help of native-born American Communists, or Communist sympathizers. That's the biggest threat to this country today. Internal subversion." He looked at me. "Why develop your rockets, young man, if Moscow is going to have a complete set of plans as soon as we draw them up? Senator, this country is being sold down the river. In the government agencies, in the schools, the civic organizations. Millions of our people are being brainwashed by cold, calculating schemers. I know what I'm talking about. I've seen it in action. At every level. Somebody has to wake the American people up. You go in after the Communists, the fellow travelers, I mean really let them have it, and your name will make headlines in every newspaper in this country."

I could see the change come over Sam, the massive shifting

of weight, the coordinating of the fibers, the intensity of every muscle. This was a kind of language he could understand. Rich in conspiratorial overtones. His mouth tightened in that little smirk, his eyes came aglow, the muscles in his jaw became knots. And he began to nod in appreciation, slowly at first and then vigorously. "I think that's it," he said. "I think you have the answer. St. George and the dragon. St. Patrick and the snakes. Or was that someone else? I have the feeling the country is ripe for just this sort of thing. Flailing out the little dragons, the little snakes, at almost no cost to the taxpayers. Hasn't Cardinal Spellman been sounding off about this occasionally?"

"He's very concerned," Father Baugh said, "but he isn't as effective as you could be. Anti-Communism is the official posture of the Roman Catholic Church. Since Pius XI. But a priest, even a Cardinal—who listens? Outside the Church? But I'm sure Cardinal Spellman would place all his records at your disposal, and the Vatican must have volumes. Rome might even help you with money, if you need it."

"Are you speculating?" Sam asked slowly.

Father Baugh was very deliberate. "No. It's not speculation."

"You were primed when you came here?"

"Certain suggestions had been made. And assurances."

"Because it was known that you were going to have the ear of a United States Senator."

The priest shriveled slightly. "That is true."

"Well," Sam said, "I don't give a damn whose idea it was. It could come straight out of the Sistine Chapel. I don't care. Now, money is no problem. That'll be easy to come by. But anything documentary would be good. Will you tell them that? On the threat to America, I mean. I don't give a damn about Italy or France. Or Pago Pago. Nobody there votes in our elections, if you get my drift." He was excited, and he turned to me. "What do you think, Harry? Can we handle this?"

"I had in mind a coincidence," I said. "There was a guy from the Pentagon in the office today. A Colonel Skinner. He left me a stack of raw information. I haven't had time to look through it, and I don't know what it's worth. What it indicates is concern. We could pirate all the old House Un-American Activities Committee material. Sift through the Attorney General's list of subversives. The Hiss trial transcript. Sam, it's a goddamn gold mine and there are lodes—I know there are—that haven't even been mined yet. We can churn out enough sensations to keep you in business for years. When would you want to get going?"

"We've got to time this right," Sam said. "Something national. Off the floor. Wait. The Lincoln's Day dinners are coming up. I can get scheduled for a tour. Everybody goes out on these things. That'd give us about a month. Get cracking on it, Harry, will you?"

"First thing," I said.

"Drop everything else. Highest priority."

I nodded. "Triple A."

We went outside to where Numeriano was double-parked, untouchable with that Senate plate, and I packed them into the Olds and caught a cab to Georgetown. I was fumbling with the key when Patricia flung open the door. "You dog," she said, putting her arms around me.

"What have I done?" I said, kissing her rather imprecisely.

"You were out living it up. Filet mignon and fancy girls. I had a dry crust of bread. Moldy. Do you want a drink?"

"This time, I pass. Keeping up with Sam is ruining my liver."

"Don't louse up your liver, lover."

"Why do you alliterate at me? Without any provocation."

She laughed. "Was it anything special?"

"Very special. High strategy. Symington himself. The Church of Rome."

"You mean drunk strategy."

"There was that element. Your robe is distracting me. It

gaps. No, this was the real thing. Sterling. Sam's future. He finally admitted today that he doesn't sparkle, that he might not be a United States Senator much longer if he doesn't get off his duff."

"So what do the high priests propose to do?"

I looked around me carefully and held a finger to my lips. "Sh-h."

"Yes?" she whispered.

"Fight Communists."

"Fight Communists!" she shouted, and I tried to quiet her, but she would not be calmed. "You have to be kidding!" she upbraided me.

I looked around conspiratorially and said, "No. Very serious. Papal blessing. Major campaign. Turn over every rock."

"In Washington?"

And then I raised my voice. "In—the—whole—damn—country? Can you grasp that?"

She nodded soberly, thoughtfully. "Harry, will it work?"

"It just might."

"Do you have to run it?"

"At first. And then you get help. People deluge you with leads. Sick, scared people. There was a funny little man from the Pentagon in the office today. Weird. Pathetically weird. But he has the goods on a gigantic conspiracy. It's all in there." With my toe I nudged the briefcase I had dropped on the floor.

"I don't think I like it," she said slowly. "Wasn't there any other way?"

"I tried to sell him on missiles. Men walking on the moon. Intercontinental rockets. He wouldn't buy it."

"I like the moon better."

"That's because you're a hopeless romantic. Did you eat?"

"A peanut butter sandwich."

"Do we have a bed somewhere?"

"What's left of it. We have to get a new one. The neighbors are complaining. The springs squeak."

"Does a new wife come with the new bed? A new bed sleeps clean."

She punched me with a balled fist. "Oh, you are going to suffer, Mister Dodge."

"Suffer me. Suffer the little children. I read that somewhere." She had gone into the bedroom ahead of me, and it occurred to me some time later that we really *did* need a new bed. The springs were raucous, tattletales.

That evening was the beginning of something too large for me to grasp, too gigantic for me to envision. For three weeks I lived in an unreal world of phantoms, traitors, ingrates, spookiness beyond credibility. First I went through what Skinner had brought. It was fearful stuff. According to the papers, largely photostats of raw counter-intelligence reports, the entire defense establishment was riddled with deceit. By piecing together little bits and oddments, a case could be made to show that from the beginning of the mathematical computations leading to the development of the atom bomb, the Soviet Union had had a network of informers in high places who passed along each step-by-step advance to Russian agents. Moscow had sources at every level, some paid, some collaborating out of leftist idealism, some betrayed by tawdry romance. The network was not exclusively defense. It included scholars working under grants on the Manhattan Project, and it had close ties with Communist-sympathizing liberals in the State Department. In the course of my search I turned up a copy of a letter from Secretary of State Bryan to a member of Congress, in which Bryan stated that 284 State Department employees had been the subjects of loyalty investigations at the end of World War II. Of that number, 79 had been discharged, and 205 were still the subjects of inquiry. That was old hat, not sufficient for a live challenge, but I put it into one of the memos I prepared for Sam. Another old report, this of the House Appropriations Committee, showed that 108 employees and applicants for jobs at the State Department were under suspicion. A later survey placed 57 of those 108 on the State Department payroll, although by that time 35 of the 57 had been cleared in FBI security checks. Selma typed up a memorandum to Sam on that, too. We wanted him to have all the information available, and the confusion on the number of security risks in the State Department was tailor-made for obfuscation and inexactitude.

His application to the Republican National Committee for Lincoln Day appearances paid off, and he was scheduled for a barn-storming tour that began in Ohio and ended in Duluth, Minnesota. We laid him out a careful series of texts, each building on the other and the whole bundle hammering away at the Communist-betrayal theme. He read through them, digested them, committed the main points to memory. I was scheduled to go with him on the junket, and I urged him to follow the scripts as closely as possible because they were interlocking.

"Don't worry about me," Sam said.

"I'm not worried. I just don't want you to foul up."

He looked at me with complete self-assurance. "I never foul up," he said.

He never fouled up, but his sense for the dramatic was unbearable.

The first stop on the tour was Athens, Ohio, and we had very painstakingly prepared the text. It was before the Ohio Women's Republican Club, and some 300 had turned out with their husbands. There was one of those interminable dinners, at which I was consigned to a back table, followed by the introduction of local dignitaries.

And then it was Sam's turn.

He had thought about this performance, had thought about it a lot. It was the kickoff, the opening gun. But more than about content he had thought about his own impression, the live, breathing Senator Sam. And he was a caged lion. He paraded, he pranced, he preened. He got so far from the podium that his text was lost. Never mind. The theme was uppermost, and he ad-libbed. As nearly as I can reconstruct the speech, from the notes I made at Athens, he said, after the opening acknowledgments, "I have to tell you tonight that our country is in grave danger. Grave danger. We are a free people, an open society, and yet our freedom and our openness will be our downfall. Because there are traitors in our midst. Foul traitors. This surprises you? It shouldn't. You know and I know that since 1945 our country has been sold out. All of our national secrets, strategic and tactical, have been traded to the Russians. To the Russians." He paused dramatically and reached in an inner pocket, withdrawing a sheet of folded paper. "I hold in my hand," he said, waving the paper, "I hold in my hand—a list of two hundred and five employees of the State Department—who are card-carrying Communists."

I swore under my breath. We had not intended for him to use that figure, or any precise figure. It had been our plan to make the charge but to veil it in ambiguity so Sam would never have to produce names or substantiating evidence.

But he was not concerned about such trivialities. He plunged the paper back into his pocket and asked, "Do you realize what this means? Can you comprehend it? Two hundred and five Americans that we can identify, and God only knows how many more that we haven't unearthed, in this and other departments. Two hundred and five traitors, privy to our highest secrets, are turning everything over to Moscow. Methodically, systematically. We are a nation betrayed, sold out, undercut, weakened by the most gigantic conspiracy in history. I want you to think about it, to ponder it carefully. I say two hundred five, but I am only one senator, chipping away at this monstrous conspiracy alone. A voice crying in the wilderness. How deeply does this conspiracy run? How many other departments have their web of informers? How far do these tentacles reach out into the heartland, the state governments, the towns and villages, the schools, the universities? Even—and I hesitate to say it—the churches. The churches. Have you thought about your neighbor, your employee, your subordinate? I call for vigilance. Vigilance! We must weed from our midst these fellow travelers, these ingrates, these charlatans. It is not enough to expose the pinkos in Washington. They must be rooted out here, too, in Athens, Ohio, and this search and exposure must be our first priority as a nation. It is the only way that we shall remain free."

There was a newspaper reporter at the Athens meeting who just happened to be a stringer for the Associated Press. Within an hour after Sam concluded his speech AP tickers were chattering his name all over the country, and Sam became an overnight celebrity. After breakfast we stopped at the newsstand in the lobby of the Athena Hotel and picked up an armload of out-of-town papers. Sam had made the front pages of every one, and whether the headline was a banner at the top or a more modest two-column dingbat below the fold, the message was essentially the same: a United States Senator had charged that the nation was in the grip of a mammoth Communist conspiracy. Back in the hotel room the phone was ringing off the hook. The wire services and radio networks were pleading for more information—names, places, specific examples of skullduggery. Sam fended them off, saying that he would make more revelations in the course of his tour but that he was not yet ready to lay the whole plot bare—that would come. He was careful to exude cordiality and warm friendship. It was the first time he had been courted by the national press, and he wanted the association to continue. His whole strategy depended upon that. When Numeriano came to pick up Sam's bags for the trip to the airport, the telephone was still ringing. As we closed the door and walked toward the elevator, Sam said to me, "We really got things stirred up, didn't we?"

"Isn't that what you wanted?"

He slapped me on the back effusively. "Hell, yes. We're on our way."

I couldn't resist the obvious question. "Sam, what was that paper you pulled out of your pocket last night?"

He looked at me with mock sternness. "You doubt that it was what I said it was? You don't think you're the only leg man I've had at work?"

"Come off it."

The elevator door creaked open, and we stepped in, just the three of us. "It was an old laundry list," he said, laughing. "Just something I happened to have on me."

From Athens our tour took us to Fort Wayne, Indiana, Elgin, Illinois, Waterloo, Iowa, and Duluth. The houses were packed to the rafters every night, and special press tables appeared magically to accommodate the roving newsmen who had suddenly descended on us from as far away as Washington, New York and Chicago. At Sam's specific orders we did not supply advance texts, and the junketing scribes, fretting over it, were reduced to taking notes in longhand. Sam's explanation was ingenious: "I want this whole thing to be as spontaneous as possible. Sure, I've got notes [he had four carefully prepared texts], but I like to sense the mood of a crowd. Sense the mood. I play them like the strings of a harp." That was the first time I had heard that line. But I understood about not giving the reporters copies of the speeches. Months earlier, I had told Sam that no two reporters ever take the same notes and very few reporters get quotes accurately. Thus, from paper to paper, there can be considerable variance in what was alleged to have been said. We needed that kind of confusion.

Waiting for us in Elgin was a telegram from the Secretary

of State. Icily, as was his custom, the secretary demanded to know the names of the two hundred five "card-carrying Communists" whom Sam had unearthed in the State Department. Sam had fun with that. Before the Elgin crowd, panting for his revelations, he waved the Secretary's wire. "I have here," he said, "I have here, on this paper, an order from the Secretary of State in Washington, that delineator of our non-policy toward the Russians—an order to me to turn over to him the names of the two hundred five Communists I have discovered in the State Department. Mind you, I never said that there were *only* two hundred five. I said that two hundred five were verifiable. How many more there are, God only knows. And God knows they are betraying our country." He waved the telegram again. "I tell you what I am going to do with this directive from the Secretary." He could make the title sound profane. "I am going to tear it up." And here he actually did rip it to shreds and cast away the tiny pieces. "Why would I do that? Because, I tell you, if I, as a lone United States Senator, have been able to come up with two hundred five names, the Secretary, if he is interested in doing so—if he is truly interested in ridding our country of this cancer—can come up with twice that many. And I challenge him to do so. Here in Elgin, Illinois, before all you good people, I challenge the Secretary of State to clean out the stables, to exterminate this spreading rot before it destroys us all. I ask you, what should we do with traitors? I don't know how you feel about it, but I think they should be lined up and shot!"

And sure enough, the next day the headlines proclaimed, "Bradford Says Communists in Government Should Be Executed," "Bradford Challenges Acheson to Root Out the Reds." Sam had ventured nothing. He had dropped a random number which generated a velocity of its own. He had put the State Department on the defensive. He had named no name, except his own. Yet in the conservative bastions of the

Midwest, the fundamentalist strongholds of the South, given bloom by the reactionary press, Sam Bradford was the man of the hour, the name on the lips of every doubting Thomas, every exorcist of un-Americanism, however interpreted, every priest involved in the worldwide Roman confrontation with the Soviet anti-Christ.

In Waterloo and Duluth the tour was a triumph. The burghers of the heartland turned out by the thousands, decorating the parade routes, hailing the "Savior Sam," strewing flowers in his path. That last is figurative, of course, except that in Duluth an eight-year-old girl actually was delegated to present him a bouquet of pure white carnations. He kissed her, waved, shook hands. He was no longer the nonentity of the Senate Office Building. He was a force, a presence, a dynamic power clothed in the legislative toga. He gave articulation to the most dread fear of the grass roots—the conviction, not clearly coalesced but there just the same, that Red agents would insidiously take over the nation and destroy democracy, free speech, free press, free worship and the freedom to assemble. In a flash, Senator Sam embodied the hopes, ambitions, frustrations and ignorance of millions of small people, and he returned to Washington a conquering hero.

Washington, of course, is not persuaded by the grass roots, their hopes or frustrations. Washington is guided by pragmatism, by the easy compromise, by the fast buck, by evasion and triple talk. Back there Sam was not going to make headlines with meaningless figures. And so his first resort on his return to the capital was a grand indictment, dealing in case histories of known unreliables in the State Department. No names, please. Just damaging dossiers, with enough detail to seem to sound authentic. May the Lord help me, I provided the entries in those portfolios. From scabrous right-wing books, from old committee files, from the paranoid papers of the Pentagon colonel, from discredited FBI droppings, I put together the most bizarre collection of questionable materials ever carried into the Senate chamber.

In fact, I carried them. Sam had informed the Senate and the press galleries that he was prepared to make a major presentation based on his study of subversion in the State Department, and we stuffed an old blue denim duffel bag with the drawstring—it was rapidly becoming his trademark—full of "incriminating material." It bulged, and how Sam ever could lay his hands on exactly what he wanted was always a mystery to me. What we had assembled, without theme or order, was Case Number One, Case Number Three, Case Number Eighteen, Case Number Twenty-seven—instances of suspected homosexuality, wife-beating, forgery, theft, drunkenness, security risks all. There was not an actual provable instance of Communist connection in the whole lot, but Sam presented the material with such masterful and dogged conviction, faltering in the right places as he dug into the bag, hesitating over the innuendo and the guilt-by-association, regretfully giving voice to scurrilous matter, that the Senate was mesmerized by Sam's sheer effrontery. It was, of course, the old shell game, and not all were mesmerized. Some rose up to challenge, to question, to chide, but Sam brooked the interruptions with a tolerant, cynical little smile, as if he were dealing with morons, and brushed the questions and objections aside as irrelevant. And when he himself did not do it, the objectors were shouted down by his Republican colleagues. That the colleagues did not believe in Sam—not for one minute—did not matter. Sam had put the rusty bugle to his lips and sounded the tocsin. He had given his party a cause, a viable issue, and anything that advanced Republican chances in the forthcoming elections was an elixir of marvelous restorative powers. So Sam droned on into the night, fumbling in his pouch for case after case, grabbing the freshest headlines in the morning papers. The Democrats retreated, because it is far easier to make charges than it is to defend against them. Sam Bradford had about him an air of absolute confidence, and the Democrats had no answer.

After his breath and his clutch of "documents" gave out, I went home to Georgetown. Patricia was already in bed, but she sat up and had a nightcap with me. "How did it go?" she asked, sipping at her scotch.

I changed slowly into my pajamas. "You wouldn't believe how it went."

"Victory? The Gauls sacking Rome? Christ once more risen?"

"Verily. The second coming."

"And the gentlemen of the brotherhood? The Senators? How did they take it?"

"Like hungry seals catching fish. On the Senate floor you can get away with any outrage."

Patricia sighed and shook her head. "What he is doing is an outrage."

"He's just trying to get reelected. Under the circumstances, one is allowed certain excesses."

She swirled the ice in her glass and said thoughtfully, "No, there's more to it than that. A lot more. This is a bad, bad man. A demagogue."

"Sam?" I shrugged. "I think you give him too much credit."

"I'm sorry you're involved."

"You want me to quit?"

"No. No. You're trapped. I think the fever has gripped you, too."

"Fever! I'm not trapped. I could pull out tomorrow."

"But you won't."

I lifted the sheet and crawled in the bed beside her. "No, I guess not. I'm on this roller coaster, and I've got to see where it goes. Can't you understand that?"

"No!" she cried out. And then in a smaller voice, "Good

night. Sleep well, if you can." She turned her back on me. Even in her sleep, she shrank from my touch, balled up within herself there, a tiny, precious thing, tightly held, in a dream world I could not fathom, could not enter, could not share. For the first time in our married life, lying there in the darkness, I felt deserted, really alone. If it would have done any good I would have pounded on her back, in tears, crying, "Let me in, let me in. Do not forsake me, not now. Please?"

But I went to sleep.

☆ 5 ☆

BEFORE FEBRUARY 20, 1950, the mail to Senator Sam Bradford's office was delivered twice daily in a neat package tied with fuzzy brown string. On February 21, a Tuesday, the morning round was supplemented by a white burlap basket half full of telegrams. The afternoon mail brought a stuffed postal pouch, with letters carrying the official markings of nearly every government office in Washington. By the end of the week a truck was dispatched from the Central Post Office with a noon delivery of at least a dozen dirty gray bags.

Almost without exception, the wires were congratulatory. At last somebody was doing something about the "Communist menace." Many of the interdepartmental memoranda were unsigned and contained very explicit suggestions that Bradford and his team of skilled investigators ought to look into so-and-so in such-and-such an office handling sensitive government material.

There was a lot of crackpot stuff in the general flow from out of town, notes in crude block letters, cutouts from newspaper headlines, crayoned drawings. But a lot of good people were writing in their fervent thanks that one senator of the United States had the guts to warn that this country was being sold down the drain to the Red tide, and a lot of good people, who were quite willing to sign their names, were wary of skullduggery at their own crossroads and wanted it looked into. We got whole dossiers, with names, dates, places and even pictures.

A North Carolina shrimper was sure that Soviet submarines were poisoning the fishing grounds along the entire Atlantic seaboard and probably off the Newfoundland banks.

A retired schoolteacher in Texas had had a "vision" of an advanced Muscovite plot to blow up the New York subway system and the Empire State Building. She had had "visions" all her life and she had never been wrong.

A housewife in Rapid City, Iowa, had been surreptitiously wired by Russian agents and was being subjected to Cossack renditions of the "Volga Boatman" all day and all night.

That was some of the nuttier stuff, but absolutely sane people were writing in too, and from a sampling of their fervid letters it appeared that overnight a monstrous web of conspiracy had been discovered enmeshing the whole broad land.

On Wednesday Sam, not in one of his more perceptive moods, walked in through the outer office, took one look at the accumulating *incunabula,* kicked at a bag and said, "What is all this shit?"

As I looked up from a Communist-front whorehouse in Columbus, Georgia, Selma, who was going through some of the same stuff, winced. She didn't like to hear Sam swear. "All this shit," I said, tapping the letter I was holding, "is gold dust. Your future."

"My future," Sam said, yanking unsteadily at the door to his office, "my ass."

"Wait a minute, Sam," I said, following him, "this mail is dynamite. There are at least twenty senate speeches in all that mess, and there are enough leads to keep you going for years. Don't you see what's happened? You've suddenly got your own private network of informants all over the country. Preachers, schoolteachers, little old ladies, laborites, fringe politicians. We're really in business."

Sam had opened the fake bookcase to get at the bar. He poured himself a slug of rye, put the bottle down and held up the Jack Daniels. I nodded and took the drink he handed me. He thought for a moment, savoring the alcohol, and his whole attitude changed. "Really that good?" he asked thoughtfully.

"I think so. This stuff doesn't have to be phonied up. We gotta be careful with names and selective with what we use, but my God, with what's already come in we can scare the bejesus out of the whole country. I mean really shake things up."

I heard the telephone ring in the outer office and I picked up the line on Sam's desk. He waggled a warning finger at me. "Senator Bradford's office," I said.

The male voice on the other end was crisp, efficient, authoritative, accustomed to command. "Mr. Hoover calling Senator Bradford."

"I'm sorry," I said. "Mr. Bradford is on the Senate floor. This is Harry Dodge, his administrative assistant. Can I take a message?"

"Would you ask him to call Mr. Hoover?"

"Which Mr. Hoover might that be?"

There was a pause as if I had asked an idiot question. And then patiently, "The FBI. I'll give you a private number."

I took down the number and hung up and handed the scratch sheet to Sam. "Jehovah is calling," I said. "J. Edgar Almighty. From streets paved with shit."

Sam shoved the paper in his pocket. "I'll get back to him," he said. "Oh, say. Jack Symington wants us all over Saturday night. To celebrate the good press." He lumbered over to his desk, the glass refreshed, and picked up a fat sheaf sent over by the clipping service. "I thought we'd get some sour reports, but it's all there, just like I said it. More or less. Look at the headlines: 'Bradford, Bradford, Bradford.' And some of those sonabitches can be mean as snakes."

"You made good copy," I said. "And you gotta understand

how the gallery operates. When a Senator says something on the floor, it gets reported like he said it. As gospel, within the bounds of human error. But no digging under the surface. That's a cardinal rule of the game. There are one or two bastards up there who'll crucify you just for the hell of it, but most of those guys live on handouts. Or ride the UP pony. With most of them there's one guiding principle: don't alienate a source. There're a couple you'll have to steer clear of. Martin of the *Post*. That cadaverous Parker from the Baltimore *Sun*. Mullenhaupt. Those guys wouldn't believe their own grandmother. But the rest are just pounding typewriters."

"Give me a press memo some time, and make sure to point out the ingrates. But about Jack's thing. Six-thirtyish. You'll be there? And your bride?"

"Oh, sure, we'll come."

"You know the way?"

"We've been there a couple times, Sam. With you. Remember?" I backed out of his office, stumbling over a mailbag. "Don't forget to check in with God. And I don't think he holds with drinking. Or fornication."

The rest of the week we sorted and filed, sorted and filed. Selma rarely complained, but as the stack of mailbags grew, getting rapidly ahead of us, she said, "We've got to have more help."

"I can't take the eunuchs off the routine," I said. "The day-to-day stuff has to be handled. They've got all they can do with that. And we can't bring in anybody."

"Why not?" There was an edge to her voice.

I looked at her and could see that she was desperately tired, this ox of a woman. She had never been caught in an avalanche before, and I relented. "All right," I said. "Call the steno pool for Monday. We'll draft a form letter. 'The Senator regrets that he cannot give you a personal reply, but he would like to express his deep appreciation for your interest.

We can assure you that your information will be evaluated, and your name will be held in strictest confidence.' Something like that. But just give the gals the addresses and let them stuff the envelopes."

She stared at me incredulously. "We're going to answer all this?" she asked.

"Oh, not the psychos. See, I got a big nut pile over there. Ignore that. But something else. In the form letter put in a line like, 'Any further information you may develop should be sent to this office to the personal attention of Senator Bradford.' "

"Haven't we got enough mail already?"

"All right, Selma. If any of the temps look good, we'll give them a permanent appointment. We've got a couple slots open. But nobody with big eyes and a loose mouth. Nobody lookin' to get laid."

"Are we guarding the U.S. Mint?"

"Selma, the mint is for money. What we've got is dynamite. And nobody but us has access to this material."

"How can I tell if they want to get laid?" The line was uncharacteristic of her and bespoke some of her weariness.

"Use your instincts, Selma. That's what I always did."

Under the circumstances I even went in on Saturday to winnow some of the stuff. Just after mid-afternoon I took a cab back to Georgetown, collected Patricia and headed out through Silver Spring over old 40 toward Baltimore. It was chilly, and we took the Studebaker because her second-generation MG didn't heat very well. "Do you mind this?" I asked.

"Only the ride. I get a charge out of parties at the Symingtons'. They're so different from the Washington cocktail routine. The protocol isn't the same."

"Protocol bother you? The D.C. pecking order?"

"It's so dumb."

"The wife of an administrative assistant to a junior senator sits pretty far below the salt."

"We all eat too much salt. And we're changing all that, aren't we?"

"Salt?"

"Oh, you know what I mean. It matters what senator you are administrative assistant to, and we are about to become famous."

"You've been reading the papers."

She put her hand on my leg. She liked to travel that way. I think the slight play of the muscles along the femur in accelerating and braking excited her. "That's what this shindig is all about, isn't it? The Great Bradford Breakthrough? Onward, upward."

"Don't do that. Not when I'm driving. We could wind up in the ditch. There'll be a strange mix here tonight."

"That's what I like about the Symingtons. Not like the rest of the Maryland Valley set. They do acknowledge that other people exist. How old is he?"

I checked for patrolmen and put the Studebaker on seventy. "Jack? I don't know. In his sixties."

"And Meg is what, thirty-two? I wonder how that came about? It's not a—natural—alliance."

"Sam told me. Meg is—was—the daughter of old Senator Black. Served one term, I think. Way back. He made some poor guesses on the market and lost everything, all of his money, all of his wife's. Meg's mother married her off to Jack to get back in the chips."

"I know Jack's loaded. How much?"

"I don't know, but heavy. Maryland money is hard to figure. There are rich people, who count for very little, and then there are very rich people."

"How rich is very rich?"

"Starts at about fifty million. They don't know how much they've got. It floats by, and every once in a while they reach out and pick up a piece."

"Is Jack in that league?"

"Somewhere up there."

"I wonder if he got his money's worth?"

"With Meg? I don't know. Two kids, I think. But in the times I've seen her, flitting around campaign headquarters or checking in at the office in Washington, she's struck me as a pretty cold fish."

"That pure skin. The raven-black hair. She reminds me of Hedy Lamarr in *Ecstasy.*"

"Trish, you never saw *Ecstasy.*"

"Yes, I did. On a back street in Richmond. An 'art' theater. With a lot of dirty old men. One tried to feel me up. I was only sixteen. Scared hell out of me."

"I never saw *Ecstasy.*"

"You didn't have to. You've seen me. Hedy was flatter."

"I've never seen you skinny-dipping."

"Oh, you saw that, too. We can do that. Watch out for that Buick. He wants the whole road."

I swerved for the centering car, and in gathering darkness we drove into Baltimore and out Park Heights Avenue toward the Worthington Valley. The Symington manse naturally was secluded, naturally had a broad, sweeping drive and naturally provided abundant parking space, which was well-filled. "Christ," I said, "a mob."

"Not for this cottage."

We walked to the entrance, glowing with light and vibrating with noise, and the doorway was thrown open at our ring by a massive black man in a short, white coat. He had barely taken our wraps when Meg materialized, demure in a high-necked black cocktail dress so obviously unaccented that it couldn't have come off a rack. She greeted us with genuine warmth. "Finally, human forms," she said. "But you're so far behind you'll never catch up. Let me take you to one of the watering troughs. They're all over the place. Jack really knows how to 'likker' people. And I hope you don't mind if it's buffet." She slipped the hand with the glass through the crook of my arm, at the same time catching Patricia by the wrist.

"I didn't know it was going to be informal," Patricia said. "I'd have worn my painting smock."

"You don't fool me, Trish," Meg said. "You'd look smashing in a gunny sack. I didn't know you painted."

"Just the walls. I'll have something with gin."

"And you take bourbon, don't you, Harry?" Meg said. "With branch." She nodded to a black bartender. He was perfectly trained. He had overheard the right words, and nothing else. We took the drinks and Meg said, "Harry, I guess you'll want to check in with the authorities. I think the senator and Jack are holding court in the drawing room. I'll take your wife and introduce her to some perfectly dreadful people. Come on, Trish."

I held up my glass as a momentary adieu to Patricia and she wrinkled her nose at me in acknowledgment. I crossed the broad center hall, shouldering through the gaggle, to what seemed to be the center of the madness. Sam and Jack had their backs to one of the two huge fireplaces in the room, but before I could elbow my way to them I was intercepted by Father Baugh, whom I had not seen since the strategy session at The Last Resort.

"Mr. Dodge," he hailed me, "we meet under more auspicious circumstances."

"Somewhat," I conceded.

"What do you think of my little suggestion now? I got the feeling you weren't too enthusiastic about it at first."

I crunched a piece of ice. "Father, you were right on target."

"He's a different man, isn't he, the senator?"

"No, not really."

The priest persisted. "But his fortunes have changed, haven't they?"

"Oh, vastly. He's not a dead duck any more. Or a lame one."

"To the contrary," Baugh said. "He's found a national platform."

"Have you personally had any reaction?" I was interested in the position of the church hierarchy, and the good father instantly chose his words more carefully. He was deliberate, thoughtful, and his words came in small doses.

"The response has been noted," he said. He covered his face with his glass, and his features were distorted behind it.

"I mean, beyond the diocese."

"I grasp the thrust of your question. I think it's safe to say that delight has been expressed in high places. There is just one large concern, and I have been . . ."

"Instructed?"

"No. Asked. I have been asked to convey it to you personally."

"Not to Sam?"

"To him through you. You have his ear at the right moments. Don't allow him to let up."

"Let up?" I laughed. "Hell, Father, I couldn't *flail* him off with a bludgeon. He's staying with this campaign indefinitely."

"It's imperative that he keep boring in. It's a thing the population . . ."

A Goucher sociologist named Hoch was passing, and he jumped in quickly and said, "Did I hear you mention the population?"

"It entered the conversation," I said. "Dr. Hoch, do you know Father Baugh?"

"Distantly," Hoch said, "and population is something I wanted to talk to him about. It's my specialty. Everybody's worried about how we're going to feed the poor, starving people all over the world in a few decades. Do you know what I'm worried about?"

"You don't look worried," I said.

"It's just a figure of speech," Hoch said. "What I'm worried about is where all the people are going to stand in the year 2000. And the Catholic Church, Father . . ."

"I'll get Sam to pass a law," I said. "Standing room for

everybody, regardless of race, sex, creed or ticket price. Excuse me, I've got to check in with my employer." I left the sociologist belaboring the priest about the necessity of castrating the untouchables and wandered over to the group surrounding the senator, wedging in against Liz Ashton, a columnist for the *News-Post*, much favored by Bradford because she had both money and a voice.

Sam was well into his cups, but he saw me and his eyes focused and he said loudly, "All of you. Listen. If you don't know the man responsible for my success, here he is. Harry Dodge." He held up my arm as if I were a winning boxer. "I say the words, but Harry, he's the one that gets the facts. And don't you ever forget it. Jack, are you gonna forget it?"

Symington gave me a slight bow. "May I rot in hell," he said.

Sam put a beefy arm across my shoulders, in the process jostling aside several worshippers. "Harry, tell 'em what's comin' up next. Just tell 'em."

"Sensations on end," I said. "But I think we oughta make 'em wait for details. Not good policy to telegraph your punches."

"Damn right," Sam said. "Not good pol'cy. Make 'em wait. 'Meriano. 'Nother." He held up his glass and a brown hand emerged from nowhere, took the empty container and stuffed a fresh drink in the fist. I took advantage of the break to shake Jack's hand.

"How do you put up with all this riff-raff?" I mumbled.

He laughed heartily and started to reply but checked himself and said, "Just a minute. Here come the children." Meg was approaching with a cherub in her arms, maybe three years old, a boy of five or six at her side. A nurse in white followed at a discreet distance. The children had their mother's pure complexion, her dark hair. The boy's was cut European style, straight across the forehead, long at the sides. They were lovely little things.

"It's their bedtime," Meg said. "They insisted on saying goodnight."

"Madonna with children," Jack said proudly. He leaned to kiss the little girl on the forehead. "Good night, Sweets," he said gravely. The boy approached me tentatively, and I swooped him high in the air. When I put him down he turned to his father.

"Papa," he said. "'Night."

Jack chucked the boy under the chin. "Good night, Geoffrey."

The little man and his sister ran off, scrambling around the nurse. Meg watched them go. She turned and smiled maternally in our general direction and disappeared after them.

"Hard to get used to a new family," Symington said. "I have grandchildren older. What were we talking about?"

"I was just getting out of harm's way."

"Sam?"

"And I was asking where you dug up this odd conglomeration of people."

"Oh, campaign workers, mostly. Several of them own a little piece of Baltimore politics."

"Jack, why do you bother with it?" I waved my hand around, palm upward. "You've got all this."

"Harry, sometimes it isn't enough. You own the goose with the golden egg, but you get this urge to quack a little bit yourself."

"How did you get hooked up with Sam?"

"When he was on the bench, he did me some legal favors. We got fairly close. It went on from there."

"Would you rather own a senator than be one?"

"I wouldn't put up with all that horse shit in Washington for all the perquisites that go with office. It's enough to have my man over there." He saw a platoon of ward-heelers descending on us, and he said quickly, "Why don't you make for the buffet? I can't, but somebody ought to enjoy this party."

I patted him on the arm and had started to thread my way through the bodies when Liz Ashton laid a hand on my sleeve. "Was that true what you said back there?" she asked. "Nothing on where Sam is headed next? The phantom striking?"

"Tell you the truth, Liz," I said. "We don't know yet. But I can give you a couple things. Up to this point Sam has received almost a quarter of a million letters and telegrams. About one percent are abusive, and another one percent are from lunatics. But otherwise he has the support of ninety-eight percent of the American people in what he's doing. That can make you a paragraph."

"Hell," Liz said, "I can make a column out of that. Say, could I call you sometime and get a fill on the nut stuff? It would make interesting reading."

"Sure, I'll have Selma dig it out for you. But I think you ought to use phony names."

"Will do," she said. "And thanks."

As I headed for the dining room I had that slight guilt feeling that always grabbed me when I had lied to the press. I hadn't counted the letters. I didn't know percentages. But what did it matter? As I passed by the music room I saw Patricia on a sofa, a plate in her lap. Some shaggy type was leaning over her, trying to penetrate her decolletage, best I could make out. I caught her eye, raised my eyebrows, and she gave me a slight nod that said the situation was tolerable. Through many evenings in such gatherings we had worked out a complete set of signals, catcher to pitcher, third base to batter. The first rule of Washington cocktail parties is that husbands and wives do not visit with each other, but we had an understanding—we checked in at least every half hour.

The long dining table was filled with goodies and servants stood by unobtrusively to carve and pour. I got a load of finger things, a prime cut of rare roast beef, and a glass of beaujolais, then looked for a quiet place to enjoy it all in relative peace. As if on cue, Meg appeared at my elbow. "This way," she whispered. She snatched up an iced glass and a cheese trifle and led me through a series of doors to a dimly-lit sunroom that overlooked the valley. "I wanted to get out of all that smoke myself," she said. She closed the door behind her, and I went to the windows and put my plate on the broad ledge. She came and stood beside me, quietly sipping at her drink.

"Your children are precious," I said, attacking the cut of tender beef.

"Geoffrey liked you. His father doesn't play with him much."

"And your daughter?"

"Grace."

"Looks just like you. That same silkiness. Same nose. The very delicate features. She's going to be a charmer."

"Like her mother?" Meg teased.

I chewed elaborately and swallowed hard. "Very much like her mother."

"Thank you."

I looked out into the darkness, pierced slightly by dim lights from vague shapes. "These windows overlook the valley?"

"For miles."

"Must be beautiful in the spring. And in the fall, with the leaves."

"It's always beautiful." She stared into the distance, obviously seeing things that were hidden from me. "I bought that view," she said, almost to herself.

"But I thought—all right."

She had not heard me. "We stand at these windows and drink bloody marys and all our friends are here," she said in the same soft tone, almost unaccented. "When we have stood here long enough the riders in the Maryland Hunt Cup race flash past. The course runs down by the stream." She turned toward me. I had not picked up a napkin, and I took out my handkerchief and wiped my mouth and faced her. Suddenly Meg switched her glass from her right hand to her left, tugged at my zipper and had her hand all over my scrotum. Because of the unexpectedness of the invasion and the iciness of her touch, I jumped about three feet in the air. "Now, that was a strange reaction," she said, laughing.

"You took me by surprise."

"And I shocked you. You think I'm absolutely shameless."

"Not at all. But you could have warned me."

"I haven't figured that one out. How do you say to a fellow, 'Stand by; I am about to grab your dong'?"

"It would be a bit awkward. I've seen guys that'd jump right through that window—glass, screen and all."

"So have I. And I've seen others that would jump right on me, as if I had issued an invitation to rape. You have to know your man."

"And you know me?"

"I know you're very attractive. What are you, about five eleven?"

"In that range."

"A good, trim weight for a tall man. The dark features, high cheekbones. The little bit of gray at the temples. Very distinguished. And then there's that odd smile. It makes me melt."

"But this isn't something you go around doing all the time?"

"Only when I get horny. And you wonder why."

"It doesn't take much imagination, Meg. You're a young woman, and very beautiful, and utterly desirable."

"Which is a way of saying you're not interested."

"Interested? Jeezus, lady, a stone I'm not. But you may recall that I'm in consort with a little blonde wench out there, and that little blonde is a pistol. Really, she keeps me drained. But not without my consent and fullest cooperation."

"And you can't conceive of a time ever coming when . . ."

"Not at the moment."

She touched my face. "I admire fidelity in a man. I don't like it, but I admire it. Really, I do. But moments pass, Mr. Dodge, and the time will come. When it does, give me a call."

"I have your number."

"Not the house number. I'll send you my private number. You might call it my business phone. Monkey business. Fix your zipper."

"You fix it," I challenged her.

She dropped to one knee, fed the zipper into her mouth and pulled it up with her teeth. She patted me. "Comfy?"

"I just had a strange thought," I said. "A picture. If anybody had walked in, how would we have explained that particular operation?"

She laughed heartily and turned toward the door. "With your gift for invention," she said, "you'd have come up with something perfectly logical. Tell me," she asked as we walked, blinking, out into the light, "do you enjoy working for Sam?" I was examining myself and barely heard the question. "No lipstick smear," she whispered. "I'm very careful about that."

"Oh. Working for Sam," I said. "It's a job."

"I don't believe you. That wouldn't be enough. It would have to be something important."

"Do you think what we're doing is important?"

"I'm not always sure I understand it, but it may just be the most important thing in the world." She was terribly sincere.

"I'll let you in on a secret. Half the time I don't know what the hell it's all about, either."

"Don't tell Sam. Or Jack. They think you're a genius."

"What do you think?"

Her eyes teased me. "I think you're chicken, but it's not a final judgment. Now do me a favor. Two favors. I have to take charge here again. The lady of the manor. Would you go find that wench and make a big commotion about leaving? Somebody's got to start breaking up this soirée."

Patricia was wedged between Sam and a Bay realtor I vaguely remembered, and I nodded to her silently and we went around shaking hands and talking about the long drive back to Georgetown and how we had already imposed on Jack and Meg, whose hands we found conveniently outstretched.

On the road back to Washington, Patricia was strangely silent for a few miles, and I began to wonder if the lipstick had not indeed left a mark. "Chin up, love," I said tentatively. "Are you sulking?"

She shook herself, laughed, and moved over closer. "Not at you. It's just that Sam Bradford kept feeling my rump and I was hemmed in and couldn't get away and the next time he tries it, I'll cheerfully fracture his damn arm." Her hand dropped to my leg, and I knew she was herself.

I started to relate my experience with Meg, but I didn't, explaining to myself that it would change their relationship and that one or the other—Meg, I thought—would be the poorer for it. I had never kept anything from Trish before.

We talked trivia, and in the late hours of that night the thought of Meg did not cross my mind. In the days that followed I opened mail, read mail, sorted, filed, all impersonally, until from one of the bags I picked out a small white envelope addressed to me in an angular feminine hand that was almost childish. I slit it open and pulled out a note card engraved, "Mrs. John Taney Symington II."

There was no message. Just a telephone number.

I almost threw it away, but I caught myself and made an entry under "M" in a small book I always carried and then very carefully tore envelope and note card into tiny bits.

☆6☆

AFTER ABOUT A MONTH, Sam called me into his office and asked, rather cagily I thought, "What have you got out there?"

I guessed at what motivated him. He had been out of the headlines for two weeks, and for Sam, that was Siberia. The salt mines. He had to unveil new sensations, to make new charges, to keep his major thesis before the public eye.

"We got a lot," I said, rather conservatively.

"A lot of *what?*" he asked mildly, in a rather preoccupied fashion. He unlimbered from behind his desk, made for the bar and doled out a hefty shot of rye. He turned to me, sloshing the drink, and asked again, "*What* have you got a lot of?"

"Sit down, Sam," I said. "What precisely do you want? Sinai? The tablets of stone?"

He was in a mimicking mood, not a biblical one, and he mimicked me. "What *precisely* is available?"

"A whole damn lot. You can take off in sixteen different directions. We have indexed and cross-indexed all that stuff that came in—that's still coming in. Selma is so immersed in it that Communists are following her home at night. They are interfering with her goddamn sleep. It's all under headings. We have a whole file drawer full of Communist infiltration of the church. Right up from the local level to the National Council of Churches. Just as much on the Communist take-over of the public schools. Did you know that? The goddamn Communists are taking over the whole fuckin' public school system. And labor? You would not believe it. The unions are all controlled out of the USS and R. They are polluting our library system with the effluvium of Karl Marx. Moscow has this whole country by the balls."

Sam sipped at his rye and looked up at me mildly. "Are you tired?"

"You're damn right. I'm ready for the looney bin. I never knew before how close we are to utter oblivion."

"You're getting flakey. You sound like one of the fuckin' converts."

I grinned and shook myself. "I'm just trying to convey to you the sense of all that crap we've been getting. Sam, it is unbelievable. There are a lot of sick, suspicious people out there."

Sam shrugged and fingered his glass. "They don't matter," he said. "I don't give a fuck about the national malaise. What I want is a name. One name."

"I can give you ten thousand names. But I can't give you one."

"There has to be one. A biggie."

"I've got a name file. We were that careful. We set it up that way. But there was no single name that was recurrent. Not often enough. Mostly we got little fish."

"I need a big fish," Sam said. He reached in his breast pocket and drew out a folded slip of paper. "Does this name mean anything?"

I opened the slip. It read, "Leo Wiseman." I pulled up an armchair and sat down. "That's a name," I said.

"Who the hell is he?" Sam asked.

"He was in Skinner's file."

"Skinner?"

"Yeah. That funny little Pentagon colonel. Skinner had him."

"Would it mean anything?"

"If we said it often enough. He's big in the scientific community."

"Good. Those sonabitches are all suspect. What was he involved in?"

"Skinner says the Manhattan Project."

"Jesus!" Sam said.

"Yeah. Presumably he worked with Klaus Fuchs . . ."

"The guy who fed the atom bomb secrets to the Russians."

"One and the same."

"So presumably Fuchs got some of the inside stuff from Wiseman?"

"That's the connection Skinner makes. You see, Fuchs was a mathematician. That's all. He could do logarithms or what the hell and never know he was working up an explosive. So somebody had to clue him. The Russians needed more than a string of figures. Sam, where did you get this name? You haven't been reading all that crap out there."

The senator's face became stony. "Harry, you don't want to know. But after you leave here, I am going to make a telephone call. You don't want to know about that, either. And this afternoon, a package is going to be delivered here. All about Wiseman. Take Skinner and take the packet, and put it all together, and we'll tie a tin can on Leo Wiseman. We'll have what is known as a profile."

"The packet?"

"Don't try to figure it out, Harry. Will you do me that favor?"

I backed out of the door toward the public quarters. "No figuring," I said, "but, Sam, I know."

"No, you don't," he called after me. "You never had an inkling."

I closed the door and caught Selma eyeing me. "Do you

know," I said by way of explanation, "sometimes he thinks I'm stupid. He really does. Where the hell did we put that Skinner stuff? You know. The creep."

"In the locked file. Do you want it?"

"Drag it out. We're going to have a lynching bee."

"A what?"

"Selma, you don't go to the movies enough. You're a true believer, a red, white and blue."

"I should hope so," she said, without any apology whatsoever.

I had lunch at the correspondents' table in the Senate dining room, traded shots with a couple of Baltimore *Sun* writers and then went back to the Senate Office Building and tried to make some sense out of the Skinner papers. At about 2:30 a uniformed government courier delivered a thick manila envelope and Selma brought it over to me.

"This what you been waiting for?" she asked.

"I guess," I said. I turned the brown envelope over in my hands. There was no return address. I opened it carefully and dumped the contents out on my desk. All photostats. All photostats except one carbon on white bond paper. About twenty-four pound. I held it up to the light and the watermark was there, the Great Seal of the United States, authorized for use only by government agencies.

From the disorganized material—depositions, field reports, unauthenticated accusations—I put together a portrait of Leo Wiseman, physicist, one-time lecturer at M.I.T., personally known to (but not vouched for by) Albert Einstein, lender of his name to a dozen peace organizations, including the Friends of the Victims of Hiroshima. Mentioned without denunciation in a *Daily Worker* editorial. Representative of some obscure scientific organization to an "atoms for peace" conference in Prague. Married to a Russian Jew. Author of treatises in several learned journals. I would have to go to the Library of Congress to look them up. Pentagon consultant,

Cal Tech associations, means of immediate livelihood unknown.

Sam came off the floor just before five and thumbed me
into his office. He was pouring the ritual rye by the time I had
gathered my notes, and he lifted an inquisitive eyebrow.

"He'll do," I said.

"Would you say he is the chief architect of the Communist
conspiracy in the United States?"

"No."

"That's what I'm going to say. I have information that isn't
in those files, and that is the speech you're going to write for
me."

"I'll write it. But without conviction. You might be sticking
your neck out. I warn you. Lot to be said in the sonabitch's
favor. A whole stack of the FBI stuff—"

"You don't know where it came from."

"Right. A lot of the FBI stuff is rumor, unverified, un-
checked. He might be a very bad man, this Wiseman; he also
might be a very good man. Had that occurred to you?"

"No. The son of a bitch is vulnerable. On Friday he is
going to be a very bad man. Do you understand that?"

"Loud and clear."

"Without reservation?"

"Sam, it doesn't make any difference what I think. The
speech will be ready by Friday. Completely incriminating."

"All right. I trust you. And spread the word around that
Sam Bradford is going to make a major speech on the Communist menace. I am going to name the chief architect."

"Of the Communist conspiracy?"

"That, in a nutshell, is it."

I got up to leave, to leave for Georgetown and a small piece
of sanity. "Does it bother you, Sam," I said, turning to go,
"that it might not be true?"

"Do you read the Constitution?"

"Every day."

"Article 1. Section 6: 'And for any speech or any debate in either house, they shall not be questioned in any other place.' "

"I know. I read that last night."

I put all the stuff under the proper lock and key and put the key in my desk drawer and locked the drawer and got my coat and put it on and said goodnight to Selma and goodnight to Numeriano and goodnight to everybody I met in the hall who looked like a Congressional Clubber and goodnight on the elevator and went out to wait for the streetcar, on which no one would know me and I wouldn't have to say anything.

It trundled in, those blessings of old Washington, and I squeezed aboard and abided the stops and starts and oncomings and outgoings until we ran past the Seat of Grace on Pennsylvania Avenue, and it was time for me to debark for the short walk to Georgetown. There were transfer rights, but I didn't bother with them. The unlimbering after the day in the office always did me good, and even in the rain and snow and cold, I walked. Past the townhouses that once had been slums but had been redeemed and refurbished with gold, until Georgetown was becoming the "in" place to live, with little cafés that charged too much for transparent atmosphere and served appetites that were too small and had elegant wine lists, not showing a distinction between *Liebfraumilch* and *Liebfrauenstift*. Past the little artsy-craftsy places that turned junk into fashionable conversation pieces.

My pace quickened as I neared my own portal, because she always made it a surprise. One evening it would be off-white linen and red tapers and a Burgundy opened for an hour to breathe, and the next we might sit on the floor for sukiyaki. She might be gowned as for an evening out, or in tattered shorts. This time she had found an old pair of my dungarees, turned them up at the ankles and pleated them at the waist. Out of the laundry hamper she had scrounged a fading gray

William and Mary sweatshirt, soiled at the armpits from yard work. Whatever, regardless, she always sensed my mood, and when I turned the key and dropped the briefcase she eyed me momentarily and said, "A bad day at Tombstone."

"A bad day." I collapsed on the sofa. She got behind me and helped me out of the jacket and undid the tie, freed a few buttons and slipped her hands across my chest, nuzzling at the top of my head.

She held me closely, in warm welcome, and then she asked, "Wouldst have something?"

"Wouldst."

"Your pleasure?"

"Something out of the ordinary. Your father slipped me a bottle of Rebel Yell. A smidgen on the rocks."

She was back almost instantly, and she gave me the drink and sprawled on the sofa across my lap, her head on the arm rest, blonde tresses askew. She held a very pale one herself, and she tilted a sip, wetting her nose on the ice, and asked, "Are you in a rebellious frame?"

"No."

"Feel like yelling?"

"No. It's just good whiskey."

"But you are in a mood?"

I nodded. "Safe to say."

"What is it, liege?"

I put my hand under the sweatshirt, on her belly, splayed my fingers across the rib cage. She was not wearing a bra, and I palmed her breast, solely for comfort. "We are going to defame Leo Wiseman."

She put her hand on my hand, pressed firmly. "Who is Leo Wiseman?"

"A Jew."

"Sam's not getting into anti-Semitism?"

"Oh, no. Hell, no. I don't think it's even occurred to him. Wiseman is a physicist. He helped us manufacture that all-

American goodie, the atom bomb, with all its attendant blessings."

"I drink to Wiseman," Trish said, holding up her glass. "To victory and the forces of good. Or evil. To radioactivity. To doomsday." She drank shallowly.

"The Federal Bureau of Interrogation thinks he fed material to Fuchs. And Fuchs passed it on to the Russians. God knows what else."

"You are supposed to speechify him?"

"Out of his fuckin' mind."

"And Sam is going to denounce him from the Sacred Pit?"

"In that order."

The telephone rang distantly because we had muted it, and she disengaged herself. "You could have left one of those with me," I called after her. She twitched her buttocks fetchingly, swung the mane, picked up the phone at the foot of the stairs and refused to buy a vacuum cleaner. She came back with two ice cubes and the bottle, clinked, poured, rearranged herself as before. She took my hand and guided it back to the firm mound.

"I don't want to change the subject," she said.

"Yes, you do. What have you been at today?"

"I went at shopping, as I am sometimes accustomed, but I didn't buy anything except a sack of groceries. I came home, about 3:30, and I was changing clothes, and I looked at myself in the mirror, and I was naked."

"And you said to yourself, 'I am naked, and my Lord cometh, and I am ashamed. I will clothe myself in fig leaves.'"

"I started to clothe myself, but I was thinking dangerous thoughts."

"What were you thinking?"

"That I am a lustful woman, and that I needed my husband, right that very minute."

"You should have called me. By taxi I could fly."

"I didn't want to be so shameless. So I dug out these old things, the best substitute I had for you."

"When I last departed from that sweatshirt, I smelled like a goat."

"I propose now to depart from this goatskin. And I propose that you convey me forthwith to the marital couch and there have your way with me."

Under my fingers, the pert nubbin of erectile tissue suddenly had firmed, and a shudder passed through her, leaving muscles writhing. "Is there aught to burn? In the kitchen?"

"A stew simmers." She had the sweatshirt over her head and was wriggling out of it to the raw. "It won't be ready—until we're ready. Are you ready?"

"For my simmering bride, yes."

She clutched me with great strength. "I love you, Harry. Drown me. I want to drown."

In my arms she was a light, quivering thing as I took the stairs, and long before I had reached my peak the frenzy took her in great waves and she made guttural, animal sounds. Long after I had wilted she clung to me, her grip loosening as the passion subsided.

"Now that," she whispered, "was worth the wait." She snuggled, close, one arm around my neck and the other resting lightly on my chest. "Harry," she murmured, "will you tell me something?"

"Yes."

"Anything I ask?"

"Sure."

"How was it with you the first time?"

"You mean us? You were there."

"No. I know how that was, and where, and every last detail. But I mean your very first time."

"Well, the traditional way," I said. "My father was a great one for tradition. When I was eighteen years old, he told me,

'Today you are a man,' and he took me to a whorehouse in Norfolk."

"You lie, Harry."

I laughed. "Yeah, that was a bald-faced lie. It wasn't that way at all. Happened when I was about seventeen, I think my junior year in high school. I had a friend—his name was Rush Thomas. I don't know where the 'Rush' came from."

"Maybe Mount Rushmore."

"Undoubtedly. Anyway, one afternoon I went around to see him, and he wasn't there. It had slipped my mind that on Wednesday afternoons he took flute lessons. But his mother invited me in. She was about thirty-five, with a little babydoll face that she painted like a canvas, and she always wore sweet perfume. She offered me a Coke, and while I was drinking it she got behind me and put her arms around me and explored my chest. And then she let me explore hers, and in no time at all we were in the sack. So on Wednesday afternoons all that summer Rush and I both took lessons on the flute. And then he flunked flute, and she had him going out for football and basketball and baseball. He wasn't good at any of them and it damn near killed him. But he was game, and so was I. We got on a Monday-Wednesday-Friday schedule on the old mat, and my guilt feelings tripled, especially around old Rush. But my learning was increasing too."

"In what way?"

"Mrs. Thomas taught me how to seduce girls. The idea was to get the victim worked up pretty good and then thrust your hot, throbbing member into her hand. This was supposed to make her putty. The first girl I tried it on nearly passed out, and then she gave me a swipe that almost took off the top of my head. When I complained to Mrs. Thomas that her formula didn't work too well, she just laughed and said you had to develop a sense for the right kind of woman to play the trick on."

"Did you have a sense for me?"

"I had a yen for you."

"But you didn't try."

"I don't think it would have worked with you, either."

"How did this liaison end?"

"Well, I haven't told you all of it. The way it ended, she told me she was pregnant. I used to lie awake nights, praying the baby wouldn't look like me. But she had a husband, a construction worker with a lantern jaw, and when the little girl came, she had a lantern jaw. Grew up to be unbelievably ugly. Whole thing made me mad as hell, though. That woman had been cuckolding me all along with her own husband. Can you imagine that?"

"Sounds like she had quite an appetite," Patricia said. "Otherwise, was growing up as a boy pretty tough?"

"In the teens, yes. The high school years. You had this very strong sex drive that you didn't really understand and couldn't quite handle. Sometimes in perfectly innocent surroundings you'd get this god-awful erection. There was this one teacher we had in math. She had a nice chest and she used to wear tight red sweaters. I'm sure she didn't do it intentionally, but she taunted every boy in that class. And you'd be sitting there with this incredible hard-on, and that's when she'd call on you to go to the board to work out a problem. I never saw a single boy go to that chalkboard that didn't have his left hand in his pocket trying to keep that protuberance from showing. It was a rough year."

"Girls had problems of a different kind."

"I can imagine what some of them were like," I said.

"No, you can't. Oh, the wrestling matches with the boys, yes. But in the teens a girl's life revolves around her period. And unless she has a very sensitive mother, she doesn't fully comprehend it. And the stories that went around. I remember one of the first I heard, and it scared the daylights out of me. An older girl told me that if you got your feet wet during your period, you would die. Once I got caught in the rain, and when I got home, shoes just sloshing, I undressed and put on my prettiest gown and wrote a farewell note to my father and got in bed waiting for death. All I got was a bad cold, but I kept the note handy just in case that first escape was a miracle."

I turned toward her and stroked the long silken hair. "I'm glad the saints preserved you," I said.

"The worst part during your period was boys. You just knew you'd die if one of them found out. And there was supposed to be a dead giveaway. If you had circles under your eyes, that told everything, and we went to extravagant lengths to paint out dark circles—which actually did appear. And the funny expressions we had. If you had your period you 'fell off the roof.' Once there was a commotion at the house and my father came in and said he had to call an ambulance because Marsh, who was kind of a jack-of-all-trades, had been hurt. I asked him how it had happened and he said, 'Marsh fell off the roof.' I almost rolled on the floor laughing, and for a long time my father thought I had a very weird sense of humor."

"And you couldn't explain it to him."

"He'd have died of embarrassment. He could never get any further than 'female problems.' And I have to tell you that I'm a female with a problem."

"What troubles you?"

"The goatskin. Goats. Rutting."

"I am temporarily out of action."

"Think of Mrs. Thomas," she said.

"She doesn't work for me any more."

"The teacher in the red sweater." She massaged skillfully.

"I've outgrown her."

"And you're still growing. See. Now let me man the barricade." She was over me, quick with the insertion, operating furiously in seven different directions. At last she shuddered, stopped, and I moved to break the connection. "No," she whispered. "No." The sheet was damp and she leaned on me heavily and said, "Do we have to go to heaven?"

"There's an alternative."

"I don't want to go there, either. I don't want to go anywhere.'You are all I want of heaven—"

"And all you know of hell?"

"A little hell. There are demons."

"I know. When the tide takes you, the demon speaks in a strange tongue."

She giggled. "What do I say?"

"Nothing intelligible to the human mind. Wild groans, frantic, muttered syllables from some unknown place."

"Does it all mean anything to you?"

"Certainly. That you're somewhere—"

"—Over the rainbow?"

"Perhaps. In a land I can't share with you, even though I have taken you there."

"You're such a good conductor. I don't want it ever to end, what it is that we have. Sometimes I get wide awake at night and find myself trembling, afraid I only dreamed that I hit your car. Suppose it had been someone else's? Some little old lady who only drove on Sundays? Or some fat farmer's? And I would never have known you, and then I want to cry."

I moved her gently to my side and laced my fingers with hers. "You hit the right car, baby. It was predestined."

"I want it to be this way forever," she said fiercely.

"It will be," I said, little knowing then what a frightfully short time forever can be.

It was on a Friday in early March, 1950, that Sam Bradford rolled the heavy artillery into the Senate Chamber and began dismantling the Communist "conspiracy" that was "sapping the vitality" of the American spirit. It was a carefully choreographed performance. On the bulletin boards behind the press galleries of both houses I had posted notices that the Senator would make a "major" address on the theme which was so disturbing the American conscience, and to all entreaties for advance texts I had pleaded that the speech would be in process of revision up until the last minute, as new leads were being checked out. The truth is, we didn't intend to distribute any texts at all. The *Congressional Record* would not be available until the next day, and it, too, could be jimmied. Some of the choicest language ever uttered on the senate floor has failed to see print because the speaker afterward paid a discreet visit to the shorthand reporters' quarters. If there were conflicting reports in the Saturday morning papers on exactly what Sam had said, he would not be disturbed as long as the accounts were there, with his name, under big, black headlines.

Sam arrived on the floor of the senate at mid-afternoon with his drawstring duffel bag bulging, and an armload of manila file folders which for the most part contained outdated correspondence on trivial constituent inquiries. He bustled in with a great show in the middle of a discourse by a conservative Republican, Bourke of Iowa, on the evils of a pending foreign aid bill. Sam listened politely for a few minutes, conspicuously shuffling and arranging documents fumbled out of the blue bag, and then, by previous agreement, he rose and asked quietly, "Will the Senator yield?"

Bourke, whose eloquence could rarely be sustained for more than ten minutes, turned to Sam in relief and said, "I yield to the distinguished Senator from Maryland."

"Thank you," Sam said graciously. He had learned all the fine points in the parliamentary game played in the gentlemen's chamber, and he nodded to the vice president, presiding in a rare moment, cleared his throat and began. "Gentlemen," he said in a voice oddly soft but nevertheless commanding attention. "Gentlemen, I wish to bring before this forum a matter of utmost gravity."

"Mr. President," a voice broke in from a forward desk. Balding old Senator Royster, a crusty New Englander.

"For what purpose does the gentleman from Vermont rise?" the vice president asked.

"A point of order," Royster said. He was a mangled gnome of a man with a thin, piping voice. "Is the intelligence the gentleman from Maryland is about to bring us germane to the business at hand?"

Sam smiled his crooked smile, half contemptuous, and said, "Mr. President, we are debating foreign aid. It is my purpose to bring the Senators—and the American people—shocking evidence that some of our enemies at home have given entirely too much aid to our enemies abroad. I can't conceive of anything more relevant to our deliberations."

In the United States Senate, "relevance" is a very flexible word, and the vice president ruled accordingly. If Sam had wanted to talk about rat cheese he would have been declared in order. "The gentleman from Maryland may proceed," the vice president said.

"I thank the chair," Sam said, looking around at the well-filled galleries, "and I also want to thank the gentleman from Vermont. His tactics here illustrate the kind of obstructionism we are encountering in dealing with the Communist threat to our freedom. You all know me. You know that I am not given to spreading rumor or hearsay. On occasions before I have made certain charges here. To date not one of them, gentlemen—not one—has been refuted. But up to this point we have been dealing with little fish. Little fish can be dangerous, as witness the piranha. But they are not as dangerous as the big ones. Today I have brought a big one for you. A shark, no less."

Sam paused for effect, eyes taking in the entire chamber. I was standing at the back, near the main entrance, and I could see about eighty of the exalted immediately come to attention. In the press galleries the purveyors of sensation were scratching at their note pads, and in the adjoining visitors' loges there were murmurs and new arrivals. The word sweeps through Washington quickly, jumping over the Potomac into Virginia and across the District line into the Maryland bedrooms.

"In order to put this gigantic betrayal into perspective," Sam said, consulting his notes, "I have to tell you the stories of two men, one German, the other a native-born American. First the German. An odd fellow, born near Frankfurt-am-Oder in 1913, son of a Lutheran minister who was a Socialist. Bright, industrious, excelling sufficiently in his studies to win a scholarship at Heidelberg. There was a Marxist cell at the university, and he joined the Communist Party in 1930. When the Hitler regime began rounding up unreliables he went underground in Stuttgart, escaped to Paris, and from there, through church contacts, made his way across the English Channel to Dover. An English family, apparently well-placed, befriended him and got him a fellowship at Cambridge. There is no record of Communist Party activity, so we must assume that he was under secret orders from Moscow. Let's see. Doctoral thesis in 1937 in mathematical physics. Interned briefly in Canada in 1939, taken back to Cambridge in 1941 to do mathematical computations. Naturalized as a British subject in 1942. With a group of British scientists he arrived in New York in 1943 to work on the Manhattan Project."

Sam lowered his papers and looked around. "I know that I do not have to remind my colleagues that the Manhattan Project was the code name for the development of the atomic bomb," he said patronizingly. "It is probably safe to say that our German friend did not at first know the importance of his assignment. But with a little coaching from the right quarters, he learned. He learned even more when he was invited to view the test explosion of the first atomic bomb at Alamogordo, New Mexico, in 1945. After the war he returned to England to work in the British nuclear program, and last year he confessed that for years he had been feeding atomic secrets to Russian agents. Not just in Great Britain. Here, too. At present he is serving a fifteen-year jail sentence in England."

Sam paused again, and when he resumed his narrative he almost swallowed his words. "I don't suppose I have to tell you that I am talking about Klaus Fuchs, one of the most notorious traitors of all time." Sam looked around again, repeating the name for the benefit of the galleries: "Klaus Fuchs."

In the general hubbub the recollection evoked, Sam dug into his bag for a new set of references. "Gentlemen," he said, "such men cannot work alone. Fuchs was not in a key position, although assuredly it was an important one. He had to rely on information supplied by others. Or by another. And I would like to present to you another biography, somewhat more pitiful because it involves the best this country has to offer. Picture this: youngest son in a family of five in Salem, Oregon. Not deprived. His father was a wealthy mortician, his mother prominent in social circles. During the Depression, when many were scrabbling for bread, he was a student at M.I.T. Why would such a man, so blessed with the bounty of his country, turn to Communism? We don't know. That he was drilled in Marxist theory we do know, although that knowledge has come to light only recently. An atomic scientist, drawn early into the Manhattan network, feeding to Fuchs every scrap of calculation for transfer to the Soviet Union. Because of this man's monstrous perfidy, Moscow was never more than two weeks behind New York in solving the atomic puzzle. That's on paper, of course. The Soviets lacked the hardware, they had only the design. And it was not until last year that the Soviet Union was able to detonate its own atomic bomb. Without the leak from our own traitor through Fuchs, the U.S.S.R. would have been delayed for at least ten years, and we would not now live under the threat of atomic collision, of global extinction. And yet this man, out of Oregon and M.I.T., continues to this day as a consultant to the Pentagon, as a party to the President's directive for the development of the hydrogen bomb. While Fuchs languishes in jail, he roams free, no doubt funneling this nation's most precious secrets to agents of the Soviet Union. That, gentlemen, I call high treason."

Sam stopped and sagged. He had delivered himself of his most direct assault to date, and it had drained his energy. Or so it seemed. From down the aisle once more came the voice, in plaintive tone, of Senator Royster. "Does the distinguished Senator from Maryland plan to name this culprit, or must we, as in the past, be left in the dark as to the identity of the accused?"

"I resent the Senator's tone," Sam said, "although until now I had counted him a friend. Yes, I will give you a name. The chief architect of the Communist conspiracy in the United States, the architect of our national downfall, is Dr. Leo Wiseman."

Uproar broke out immediately in the Senate chamber. Wiseman was a respected scientist, acquainted with many senators on both sides of the aisle. He had testified on defense appropriations bills. Over the head of the presiding officer, at their front-row panels, the wire-service reporters grabbed their phones and started gabbling frantically into them, on the long lines of the AP, UP, and INS linking the name of one of the nation's foremost scientists with that of a convicted traitor. There were gasps of chatter in the diplomatic balconies. No doubt Wiseman had been a dinner guest in the homes of some of the befurred matrons.

The vice president rapped his gavel and recognized Senator Royster. "I would say to the gentleman from Maryland," Royster said when order had been restored, "that he sets forth charges that cannot be ignored. I suggest that Dr. Wiseman, whom I know personally, is due the courtesy of response. I therefore move that Senator Bradford's charges be referred to the Internal Security Subcommittee, chaired by the distinguished gentleman from Delaware, Senator Miller. And I would incorporate in this motion a suggestion that hearings be scheduled at the earliest possible moment."

"Is there a second?" the vice president asked.

Sam was again on his feet. "I would be privileged to second that motion, Mr. President," he said, "and in doing so might I ask that I be allowed to offer such evidence as I have at my disposal?"

"That would be your privilege," the vice president said. "Do I hear dissent? There being none, it is so ordered." He rapped his gavel, and debate on the foreign aid bill was abandoned for the day and Senator Bourke was allowed to sit down.

Senator Bradford, the bloodhound baying on the trail of malodorous Communists, was not, of course, abandoned. He made bulletins in the late afternoon papers, led the network newscasts at 6 P.M., and was still good copy at 11 P.M. He made the front page of every morning newspaper in the country, and he arrived at the office with the happy expression of a sated vampire. He greeted everyone cheerily, even stopped to buss Selma, called me to follow him into his lair, slapped the newspapers freshly piled on his desk and said, "We did all right, didn't we?"

"We taxed the headbones of every grubby headline writer on the globe. You struck a nerve, I think. The scientific community has been a kind of sacred cow. Above reproach."

"Not any more. We will have all the shit-eatin' doctors of science quaking in their fuckin' boots."

"Did you see the shirttail on the *Post* story?" I asked.

"Nah. I don't read the jumps."

"The AP tracked Wiseman down in Brussels. He said he welcomes the inquiry, and he dares you to repeat your charges off the floor."

"They all say that. He 'welcomes the inquiry.' Like he welcomes a rattlesnake. That mother is going to squirm."

"Can you really substantiate any of that stuff? I know Skinner had some pretty raw material, but we didn't have time to check any of it out. The bastard might have made it all up."

"It checks. And wheels are turning."

"What wheels?"

"Wheels that grind exceeding small."

I looked at Sam with new respect. He had made some high-level contacts. He had impressed somebody. And I was not about to dismiss the F.B. and I. or the CIC. Or any of the other wheels within wheels that we pay our tax money for and get no accounting from. He had impressed somebody. I groped for the key in what I knew was a very crude fashion. "This guy Wiseman," I said slowly. "Is he expendable? Can he be thrown to the lions?"

Sam was guileless. "The lions, shit," he said. "These pinkos, they're all expendable. Wiseman is sucker bait. Really. There is not one soul in the whole establishment who is going to come to his aid. Do you know what that means?"

"Not really."

"He's a turd."

☆ **7** ☆

THE INTERNAL SECURITY SUBCOMMITTEE had set the Wiseman hearing for a Wednesday in early March, and promptly at 10 A.M., the respectable hour at which all Washington hearings begin, I walked with Sam past the waiting spectators into the red-carpeted Caucus Room which was a showpiece of the Senate Office Building—spacious, ornately figured, fitted with rare and costly draperies. Senator Miller, a Delaware Democrat with a fixed mind and pursed lips and who had been quoted in the interim as saying that he would make Bradford the "laughingstock of the nation," was flanked to the left by the Democrats McIntyre of Georgia and Grauen of Rhode Island and, in the minority on the right, Bourke of Iowa and the aristocratic Cabell of Massachusetts.

Sam shouldered his way past the press table, chaffing good-naturedly with AP and INS reporters, and approached the long, polished committee table along the front wall. He had no right to sit there, but a committee staffer courteously surrendered a chair to him. Sam rested his bag at his side and I stood behind him, leaning against the gleaming beige paint. Wiseman was already seated at the witness table, a new briefcase and a fresh pitcher of water before him. He was a short, grey man, his eyes unfocused behind thick convex lenses. He turned the glasses on Sam, staring, steeling himself. He twitched slightly when the chairman banged the gavel, betraying a slight case of nerves.

"The Committee is in session," Miller said. If he had been a college professor all his students would have hated him. "You all know why we are here. Certain charges have been made against the witness by the gentleman from Maryland, and this Subcommittee has been directed to inquire into them. The chairman will make no opening statement—why we are here has been made abundantly clear—but he reserves the right to make closing remarks, and a summary if that is necessary. I would remind the spectators that strict decorum will be observed here. There will be no claques, either in support of the accuser or the accused. Dr. Wiseman, you are not on trial here. This is not a court of law, but you are entitled to legal counsel. Are you so represented?"

Wiseman started to speak, gurgled and cleared his throat. "Mr. Chairman, I saw no necessity for that."

Miller was not a man to abide a direct answer. "You have no legal consultant?" he asked.

Wiseman shook his head.

"For the benefit of the record, you must give oral answer to all questions."

"No. No. I am without counsel."

"The record will show that. I told you that this is not a court of law and you are not on trial, but in a matter whose nature is this serious, it is necessary that you testify under oath. Do you object to that?"

Wiseman started to shake his head again, caught himself and said, "No, of course not, although I would give the same answers in any case."

"All right. Will you please rise?" Miller said. Wiseman struggled awkwardly to his feet, and the chairman intoned the sacred writ, uttered God only knows how many times in that sacred chamber, "Do you solemnly swear that the statements you give to this subcommittee will be the truth, the whole truth, and nothing but the truth, so help you God?"

"I do," Wiseman said, the phlegm once more clogging his throat as he sank into his seat.

"Now," Miller said prissily, "are you aware of the accusations that have been made against you by the Senator from Maryland?"

Wiseman cut his eyes at Bradford, looked back at the chairman and replied, "Yes. I have read the newspapers, and I have been supplied with the appropriate pages of the record."

"Do you wish to make any statement at the outset?"

"If I may." Wiseman reached into that gleaming alligator briefcase and drew out a thin, typed manuscript. He leaned into the microphone, held the print about six inches from his eyes, and began reading with calm assurance, as if he were delivering a restrained scolding to a class of moderately unruly schoolboys.

"Gentlemen," he began, "while I am always happy to cooperate with a committee of congress, and have willingly done so many times, I must tell you that on this occasion I am wasting time which for all of us could be spent with greater profit on other duties of far more consequence. I myself was in Europe on a series of strategic conferences when these ugly charges were made public. I am aware that slanders have been whispered about me before, but I never expected to hear them repeated on the floor of the United States Senate, for which body I have the highest regard.

"Let me just briefly review my record. I was, indeed, born in Salem, Oregon, in 1910, of German immigrant parents. My father was a mortician, although he called himself an undertaker. He learned the trade while working at lowly wage with a funeral director in Chicago. He was a self-educated man, with little formal schooling, and he besought for me more than he had for himself. I was born—and I say this in all modesty—with a gift for science. Even in high school I was performing advanced experiments in physics, and I could read and understand the papers of Albert Einstein, who was then my hero and who was later my friend. I did not live off the fat of the land, as has been alleged. My father mortgaged his house, and in the Depression lost it, to send me to the best technological university in the country. Later, when I had won honors and was offered a teaching position at M.I.T., I bought the place back for him."

I looked down at Sam, who was watching Wiseman without interest, barely listening, appearing to take notes but actually doodling arrows and stars on a scratch pad in front of him. Occasionally he would bow his head, cover his mouth with his left paw and yawn in boredom.

Wiseman continued, his voice now more of a hurried monotone. ". . . And on occasion my work would take me to Princeton, where I met Professor Einstein. Through him I met other important scientists, and later he told me of the note he had written to President Roosevelt suggesting massive research in atomic physics. In the meantime I had been visiting lecturer at several other universities, had published a number of papers and several texts, and I was among the first physicists recruited for the Manhattan Project.

"I might say parenthetically that I was never 'drilled in Marxist theory,' as Senator Bradford recklessly suggested. I had the usual college student's acquaintance with *Das Kapital,* which, of course, I could read in the original. Marx interested me, because he was German, but politics was not a subject that claimed much of my attention." Wiseman looked up apologetically. "Forgive me, Senators. I know politics is uppermost in your minds, and I don't mean to minimize its importance. But I was involved in science. It was my life, and has been my life as a loyal American. That I 'fed' classified information to Fuchs is a lie. To the best of my knowledge, and I have thought through this very carefully, I never met him. Many people, in many places, were at work on the atomic bomb. There was no little club or inner clique that chewed over the subject at lunch or at cocktail parties.

"Since the war I have been fortunate enough to be in great demand as a university lecturer, I have been a paid consultant to the Pentagon, and my services have been utilized in the field of advanced weaponry we are now developing."

Wiseman put down his text, took off his glasses and polished them elaborately with a white monogrammed handkerchief. He was no longer hesitant or casual in speech. He blew on his glasses sharply and buffed the lenses, continuing extemporaneously. "Gentlemen of the Subcommittee, I am a loyal American. I deeply resent being called a traitor, and I am pleased to have the opportunity to clear my name. If you have questions, I am at your disposal." He poured himself a glass of water and drank deeply.

Chairman Miller beamed at him. "Dr. Wiseman, you give a good account of yourself, and the country owes you a debt of gratitude for your services. For the benefit of Senator Bradford, let me pose the critical question. I know the answer, and I don't mean to insult you. But for the record: Are you now or have you ever been a member of the Communist Party?"

Wiseman laughed as if at a joke. "Most certainly not," he said.

"What is your party registration?" Miller asked.

"Forgive me, Senator, but I have none. I think of myself as an independent, but truthfully, I am so devoted to my work that I generally forget to vote. Except in the case of the President. I voted for him."

"And stayed up until all hours to see whether he was elected?"

"I'm afraid not. I went to bed at nine o'clock."

"I wish I had had your optimism," Miller said. "I lost a lot of sleep that night. But then, of course, I had no bomb to occupy me."

Wiseman smiled good-naturedly.

Miller said, "I have no further questions at this time." He looked to his right. "Would the senior minority member care to interrogate the witness?"

"Just one or two things," Senator Bourke said. "Dr. Wiseman, I'm curious. Why did your parents leave Chicago for Salem?"

"Well, of course, that was before my time," Wiseman said. "But as I understand it, my mother came from a small town in Germany and was never comfortable in a large city. When my father felt ready to establish his own business, my mother persuaded him to seek a new location."

"Salem has a certain connotation in American history," Senator Bourke said with a half-smile. "Were there any witches in Salem, Oregon?"

"I hope that question is jocular," the chairman broke in.

"Certainly," Bourke said.

Wiseman smiled back at him. "Not to my knowledge, Senator," he said.

"I leave further questioning to my colleague from Maryland," Bourke said. "Nothing further at this time. Reserving the right . . ."

"Of course," Miller said. "Senator McIntyre?"

In the deep, flat accents of South Georgia, balding McIntyre, a most respected member of the Inner Circle, began. "Dr. Wiseman, I want to offer you my apologies for the circumstances that bring you here today, and to tell you that it is an honor and a privilege to be seated in the same chamber with you. I think that in your biographical account, you have been unduly modest. Is it not a fact that you have received the highest honors of your own country and distinguished awards from others?"

"Well," Wiseman said gratefully, "I didn't feel it necessary to bring all that out. I am a Fellow of the National Academy of Science and have been elected to several offices in that organization. I hold the Medal of Freedom, the French Legion of Honor and the Order of the British Empire."

"And you were nominated for a Nobel Prize in physics?" McIntyre continued.

"I was, but nominations don't mean a whole lot."

"To the contrary, Doctor. For our purposes, I think they do. Even a nomination speaks highly of your standing in the international scientific community, and I congratulate you. Thank you, Mr. Chairman."

"Senator Cabell?" Miller said.

"Dr. Wiseman," Cabell began, in an accent different from McIntyre's, "I have here a clipping from the Communist *Daily Worker,* an editorial commending the American government for honoring you with the Medal of Freedom. Don't you find that a little strange?"

"I never saw it," Wiseman said. "What is the date?"

"April, 1946, I believe," Cabell said.

"I can only conjecture," Wiseman said. "At that time we were still ostensible allies of the Soviet Union. There remained an aura of good feeling. I suppose the editorial was written in that spirit."

"Strange," Cabell said. "Half a dozen other Americans received the medal at the same time, but the *Worker* doesn't mention any of them."

Wiseman put his hands out in front of him, palms upward. "I'm sorry, Senator," he said. "I can't explain it. Perhaps their work was in different fields. I don't know. But I can assure you that I never had friends at the *Daily Worker.*"

"That's all, Doctor. And I thank you."

"Senator Grauen?" Miller said. Senator Grauen, a Yankee approaching his eighties and noted for his dapper approach to night life, was asleep. Chairman Miller shot a quick glance at him, ignored the babble of amusement in the audience and addressed the witness again. "Dr. Wiseman, Senator Bradford, of Maryland, whose charges initiated this hearing, has obtained unanimous consent of the senate to participate in these proceedings. He is not a member of this subcommittee, but he has been accorded the same privilege that would be granted any colleague. He is next in line to question you. Do you feel like continuing now, or would you like a recess for lunch?"

"If it's all the same to you," Wiseman said, and now rather cockily, "I would prefer to get this whole thing over with. I'll be glad to respond to any questions Senator Bradford may wish to ask."

"Well, then," Miller said, "the chair invites the Senator from Maryland to examine the witness at such length as his conscience requires."

Sam ignored the barb. "Thank you, Mr. Chairman," he said quietly. "Dr. Wiseman, you do, indeed, give a good account of yourself. The perfect picture of a true, loyal, patriotic American. You have been rather selective, though, in the material you presented so casually to the committee, haven't you?"

"I didn't wish to . . ." Wiseman began.

"Take the last few days, for example," Sam went on. "You didn't cover them. You arrived back in the United States— when was it, Friday?"

"About ten Friday morning. The plane was late."

"Your fellow travelers can appreciate that dilemma," Sam said. There was just the slightest emphasis on "fellow travelers," and Wiseman pursed his lips, fully aware of the innuendo. "Was there anything unusual about your arrival?"

"Not particularly."

"At immigration?"

"No. I was readmitted to the land of my birth."

"All routine."

"Yes."

"Isn't it a fact," Sam asked cagily, "that your passport was confiscated?"

Wiseman took a long drink of water. He smacked his lips and nodded. "Yes."

"Isn't that unusual?"

"It never happened to me before, and I suppose I have you to thank for it."

"You overestimate my influence, Dr. Wiseman," Sam said. "But the net result is that you can't travel outside the United States anymore, can you?"

"Not until my passport is restored."

"Do you anticipate that it will be?"

"Until I came here today," Wiseman said, "I did. Now I'm not so sure."

Sam allowed himself a shadow of a smile. "You described yourself as a consultant to the Pentagon," he said. "Does that mean that you *are* or that you *were*?"

"Senator," Wiseman began, and he was beginning to look a little hounded, "I don't think you would ask that question if you were not aware that as of Monday of this week that relationship was terminated."

"Were you given any reason for that?"

Wiseman gulped and reached for the water glass again. "For reasons of security," he said. "That's what they told me. And again, I suppose I'm in your debt."

"Does that mean that you no longer have security clearance? Access to classified documents?"

"I'm not allowed even to look at my own files," Wiseman spat out bitterly. "Theories that I myself postulated and tested I can't review. But, Senator, the Pentagon can't deny me access to my brain."

"Pity," Sam said. "But you have always been good at carrying things in your head, haven't you? Photographic memory. You do have one, don't you?"

"I have a good memory."

"Then let's go a little bit more deeply into some things that will test your memory. Your total recall. Your childhood, for example. Would you say it was happy?"

"Reasonably so. Yes."

"Despite the fact that your mother was committed to a mental institution in 1920?"

"I don't see what this . . ."

"Where she died in 1927?"

Wiseman appealed to the chair. "Mr. Miller, is this line of questioning really pertinent?"

"Mr. Chairman," Sam said, still low-keyed, "the witness promised us . . ." He looked at the stenotypist. "Go back to the beginning of my interrogation. Give us exactly what the witness promised."

The stenographer was a bleached blonde who did not like to have her routine interrupted. She lifted up a few of the folded tapes, scanned them, and said, "The witness said, 'I'll be glad to respond to any questions Senator Bradford may wish to ask.' " She let the tapes fall back into place.

"That was my recollection," Sam said. "Now I ask the chair, is the witness to be allowed to choose the questions he will answer?"

"Really, Senator Bradford," Miller said testily. Then he paused and said in resignation, "The witness will answer the question."

"All right, yes. My mother died in a mental institution," Wiseman said.

"Was her condition ever diagnosed?" Sam asked.

"No. But she required constant care."

"And at times had to be restrained?"

"Yes, yes," Wiseman said angrily.

"Dr. Wiseman," Sam said, "there is no need to get histrionic about this. You are a scientist, right? Looking back now, in the light of modern medical technology, how would you describe your mother's condition?"

"I'm not a psychiatrist."

"I'm not either. But she was schizoid, wasn't she?"

"I suppose."

"I'm not too familiar with that manifestation. It's a split personality? One person at one time, something entirely different at others?"

"I told you, I'm not medically trained."

"I remember. Would you know whether schizophrenia is congenital?"

"I resent the implication."

"What I mean is, would it be possible for a person, a scientist, say, to be a loyal, patriotic American at one moment and at another to betray his country?"

McIntyre broke in heatedly. "Mr. Chairman, the Senator from Maryland is abusing the witness."

"Let it pass," Sam said, "but I can assure you that we are going to develop some evidence of scientific schizophrenia. Dr. Wiseman, in talking about your education you said that you were only vaguely familiar with Marxism. I believe you said you had read *Das Kapital*. In the original, if the notes I have made here are correct."

"Yes."

"Do you remember for what college course you read that work?"

"No. I'm sorry, I don't."

Sam buried his hand in his duffel bag and brought out several dark pages, white on black. "I have here photostats of your academic record, your transcript," he said, waving the papers. He flipped through them. "You really loaded up on science," he said. "Very high marks, except for a 'B' on World Literature. But that wouldn't have included Marx, would it? How about Survey of Political Systems? Do you remember that?"

"Just vaguely."

"Do you remember who taught it?"

"No."

"Does the name 'Fodor' mean anything to you?"

"I remember Professor Fodor."

"Pretty good prof, wasn't he?"

"He was popular with the students."

Sam nodded. "Didn't he used to have little soirées in the evenings at his apartment?"

"If you say so."

"I say so. And I say that you attended. Regularly."

"How can you know that?"

"Because I have here the depositions of six of your fellow students who remember your attendance."

Miller inserted himself impatiently. "Senator Bradford, where is all this leading us?"

"To a very important connection. Professor Fodor has been identified as a member of the Communist Party, and according to the statements I have here, the evening sessions at his apartment were for the purpose of student recruitment. I would like to offer these depositions as part of the record. You may read them if you wish, Dr. Wiseman."

"No, thanks. I have no taste for loaded accusations."

"Loaded?" Sam said with the ghost of a smile. "Are you suggesting that I coerced the deponents?"

"I'm not suggesting anything."

"I'm sorry," Sam said. "I thought you were. These statements, collected by agents who I assure you are reputable, describe you as being very enthusiastic about Marxist doctrine."

"Then they lie."

"There are lies and lies," Sam said tolerantly. "Would you like us to bring Professor Fodor here to testify about his star pupil?"

"But that would be imposs . . ." Wiseman began quickly and then tried to reach out and pull the words back and swallow them.

"Exactly," Sam said maliciously, "and you know that. Of course it would be impossible. Professor Fodor is now chairman of the political department of the University of the Ukraine. In the Soviet Union." There was a wave of babbling in the spectators' section, and Chairman Miller rapped his gavel for order. "Incidentally," Sam continued, "when you were telling us about your awards, you neglected to mention that the Soviet government had decorated you with the Order of the Red Star. Just oversight, I suppose?"

Wiseman said nothing, but he was beginning to perspire. With the handkerchief that had buffed his glasses he now mopped his brow.

"There is another little matter," Sam said, flipping through another manila folder. "I pick out at random here half a dozen letterheads, all of suspect movements, all listing your name as sponsor. Was that with your consent?"

"I don't know the organizations you refer to."

"Let me list some of them for you," Sam said, turning the pages. "The Oder-Neisse Society, The East-West Friendship League, The Fellows of World Peace, The Association . . ."

"I never heard of any of those and have no idea what they stand for. It's impossible to prevent organizations from using your name. It happens to all prominent people."

"It never happened to me," Sam said, "but then I'm only a United States Senator and not what you would call prominent. Did you ever protest their 'borrowing' of your prestige?"

"Senator, I never even knew about it until now."

"Let me ask you about one organization in particular. Were you a member of the World Consortium of Atomic Scientists? Answer carefully. I have the membership roll here, and you are still under oath."

"I was a member," Wiseman admitted. "Until recently."

"And you attended their meetings? In Prague, Warsaw, Belgrade, other places?"

"Some of them."

"How many meetings? Three? Four?"

"A dozen, maybe."

Sam looked at him in feigned astonishment. "Do I hear you right? A dozen?"

Wiseman nodded uncomfortably. "Yes."

"Were you aware that it has been listed by the Attorney General's office as a Communist-front organization?"

"Not at first. When it was brought to my attention, I resigned."

"And you were at that time an officer?"

"Second vice president. There were five . . ."

"Are you familiar with Executive Order 9835, dated March 12, 1947?"

"No."

"It provides for the dismissal from government service of any person who has held 'membership in, association with, or sympathetic affiliation with any organization, movement, group or combination of persons designated by the Attorney General as subversive.' Actually, Dr. Wiseman, you have been working illegally as a Pentagon consultant, haven't you?"

"That might be one interpretation. I'm sure it's yours."

"Well, about that you're certainly right." Sam furrowed his brow and looked sternly at the witness. "And I'm sure that would be the interpretation of the Pentagon legal staff. Not only would be." He smiled without humor. "*Is.* Else why would your security clearance have been withdrawn? Do you think that I, as a Senator, and a junior one, could have forced such action?" He looked at Wiseman as if he expected an answer, and there was none. His tone changed, became more confidential. "Let me pursue a different line of inquiry. You haven't told us about your marital status."

Senator McIntyre again interrupted, this time more heatedly. "Mr. Chairman, in good conscience, hasn't the Senator from Maryland harassed this witness enough?"

"Mr. Chairman," Sam said. "Mr. Chairman, I think my friend from Georgia chooses his words ill-advisedly. I have not been harassing this witness. I have been establishing some very important evidence, perhaps even suggesting a basis for a perjury citation. It is in that evidentiary sense that I ask permission to proceed. We have not yet turned over all the rocks."

"You may proceed," Miller said resignedly. "Dr. Wiseman, I believe the question was about your family situation."

"I am a widower," Wiseman said.

"Your wife is dead?" Sam asked.

"Yes."

"And you were married when?"

"In 1936."

"Your wife's name was Anna, I believe."

"Yes."

"Any children?"

"Unhappily we were not blessed with children."

"When did Mrs. Wiseman die? I know this is painful for you."

"About a year ago."

"Can you be more specific?"

"Last April."

"April 11, wasn't it?"

Wiseman was counting his fingers. "Yes."

"Would you care to tell the Committee how she died?"

"She took her own life." Wiseman wiped his eyes with the back of his hand, a curled finger slipping in behind the lenses. "Sleeping pills," he said chokingly.

"On April 11. That was the day that Klaus Fuchs was arrested in Great Britain for espionage. Don't you find that coincidental?" Wiseman stared mutely at his inquisitor, and

Sam forced his hard smile, the one that always accompanied the thrust of the bloodied knife. "What was your wife's maiden name, Dr. Wiseman?"

The scientist's voice was barely audible. "Fodor, Anna Fodor."

"Anna Fodor," Sam said. He made a pretense of speaking sadly, as if troubled by what he had found. "Anna Fodor. The sister of the university professor whose name you had so much trouble remembering. The sister of the Communist recruitment agent, of the turncoat. And I suppose you don't know why your wife committed suicide?"

"She left no note," Wiseman said.

"Did she have to? Isn't it pretty clear that she was afraid Fuchs would disclose his relationship with you?"

"I didn't know Fuchs. I've told you that. I didn't know him."

"You didn't meet him at Alamogordo?"

"No."

"Not even casually?"

"No. Not to my knowledge."

"And you didn't attend a birthday party for him in New York in February of 1946?"

"No."

"Nor say goodbye to him and other British scientists at the airport in May, 1946?"

"No."

Sam dug once more into his duffel bag and brought out a large brown manila envelope. "Perhaps I can assist your memory," he said. "It seems to suffer from convenient lapses." He ripped open the sealed flap and drew out some crisp papers. "I have here some photostats of pages in your appointment book for 1946," he said. "A notation in February shows 'Party for F.' and gives Fuch's 57th Street address in Manhattan. An entry for May 17 says, 'LaGuardia, 6 P.M.,' which was the departure time for the British Harwell team. One additional item: here is a picture showing you at the plane. In the photograph your head is circled. You are shaking hands with a man, whose head is also circled. The second man is Klaus Fuchs. Now I haven't had the time or the resources to explore your exact relationship with Fuchs, the times and places when American secrets were passed along for transmission to the Soviet Union, with incalculable damage to this country which has sheltered you and honored you. I have certainly proven that a relationship existed, despite your dissembling tactics. The ingrate Fuchs was very clever in his 'full confession' to British intelligence. He gave only the names of those informants who were either dead or beyond the reach of Western authorities. He didn't name you, Dr. Wiseman. Or your wife, who may have been the conduit. What I have done here is prove that you have lied to this Committee, and I accuse you of being not only a liar but also a traitor to your country. A liar, sir, and a traitor." Sam put his full malevolence into a stare at the witness, and he said, very softly, "That's all, Mr. McIntyre. That's all, Mr. Chairman."

We edged our way out of the Caucus Room and started walking down the corridor of the Senate Office Building, around the big circle, uniformed guards holding the crowd at bay. Still, one woman, fiftyish, broke through the cordon, ran up to Sam and dangled her handbag in his face. It was a tiny replica, drawstring and all, of the Senator's worn carry-all. She had decorated it with red, white and blue tape, and Sam grinned and said, "Bless you," and patted her and made her day, if not her life.

Neither of us talked until we were safely in the inner sanctum with drinks in our hands, and then Sam asked, "What do you think?"

"You did a job on him. I felt sorry for the poor little bastard. He was so cocky there at first, a big, important man, and you burst his bubble."

"You know," Sam said, "I felt a little sorry for him myself.

All the while it was happening. But he was such fair game."
Sam threw down his rye and favored himself with another.

"Where did all that stuff come from?" I asked. "Skinner
only had pieces of it. Nothing hard. Somebody had access to
Wiseman's New York office. The appointment photostats.
And the medical records. They aren't easy to come by." I
knew I wouldn't get a straight answer.

"All that stuff's been kicking around," Sam said. "There
had to be a leak, and Wiseman was the most obvious one."

"The picture, too? That was the most damaging. And all
that stuff about his wife."

"Wives can be a liability. Actually, I think she fed the stuff
to Fuchs. He was protecting her. And the picture? From file
shots."

"Whose files? And you know damn well that photos can be
doctored. Wiseman could have been a thousand miles away.
All but his head."

Sam laughed and evaded the direct question. Instead of a
substantive reply, he said, "What was it Miller was going
to make me? The laughingstock of the nation? Who's laughing?"

"Hold off, Sam," I warned. "They've got some blood-
hounds on that staff, and Miller'll turn 'em loose. No telling
what the report will say."

"Fuck the report," Sam said. "What do you think the papers'll say tomorrow?"

"Pretty predictable. 'Bradford Shafts Wiseman,' and variations on the theme. The *Post* will have an editorial saying that
you raise some important issues about government employment and asking how the eminent doctor slipped through the
loyalty screening. *The Times* will counsel a thorough inquiry
by the Justice Department. The *Chicago Trib* will lead a lynch
mob waiting to hang the bastard from the nearest yardarm.
And all shades of opinion in between. Nothing very favorable
to Wiseman, except maybe in Salem, Oregon. And who the

hell ever heard from Salem? You'll get coverage. The clipping service will work overtime."

"What kinda shape do you think I'm in for reelection now?" Sam asked. It was not so much a question as a boast.

I answered it anyway. "Hell, Sam," I said, "if you keep shooting from the hip, keep plunking away, nobody in his right mind would run against you. It'd be like campaigning against God. Who the hell runs against God?"

Sam nodded, but he wasn't listening to me. He was musing. "You know what I think I need?" he said.

"What?"

"My own investigating team. Oh, the regular agencies are all right, and they help. But I want some guys, bright guys, who can turn over the rocks."

"They wouldn't have any official standing."

"Oh, hell, I'd make 'em official. Print up some identification cards. Great Seal in the background. 'Special Investigator for the United States Senate.' With pictures, thumbprints. You can design it."

"And who pays them?"

"It comes out of the war chest. We'll set up a special account, and I'll pass the word that we need some big bucks. I mean the big figures."

"Texas money?"

"A lot there, and it's easy to tap. Maybe something from the Church. Get started on it, will you?"

"Right away."

The headlines and editorials were what we expected, and they trickled in for two weeks. But the Internal Security Subcommittee report on the Wiseman inquiry, signed by the Democrats but with angry demurrers from the two Republicans, was a frontal assault on Sam Bradford, his character, his motives and his methods. It covered not only Wiseman but also all the anonymous characters in governmental departments who had been Sam's targets. Bradford's charges, the report said, "represent the most disgraceful campaign of half-truths and untruths in the history of this republic. In essence, Senator Bradford has perpetrated a fraud and a hoax on the Senate of the United States and on the American people. We have seen in his official deportment the personification of the vilest technique known to man, one which we had hoped had been forever discredited, the 'big lie.'

"With respect to Dr. Wiseman in particular, Senator Bradford promised to prove that his victim was the 'chief agent of the Communist conspiracy in the United States, the architect of our national downfall.' This eminent scientist, the Senator from Maryland charged, fed to Klaus Fuchs, a convicted espionage agent, 'every scrap' of information about the atomic bomb 'for transfer to the Soviet Union.' Given full opportunity to prove that allegation, the Senator from Maryland presented no evidence whatsoever. Instead, he indulged in a cruel invasion into his victim's private life, dredging up painful but irrelevant information about Dr. Wiseman's mother, who died in a mental institution, and about his wife, who, suffering from terminal cancer, took fate into her own hands.

"The single piece of hard evidence Senator Bradford presented linking Dr. Wiseman to Klaus Fuchs was a photograph, which on close examination we have found to be a montage. It was a cruel forgery. Dr. Wiseman's services to this nation, of worth incalculable, have been prematurely ended by the heartless accusations of a headline hunter, and the country's strength is thereby eroded. Our colleague has done no service to this country. Rather he has sown discord and division at a time when we most need union."

The Republican minority report, signed by Senators Bourke and Cabell, said that the Committee, through its staff, had made no attempt to substantiate Sam's charges but had bent all its efforts to discrediting a colleague of respectable standing in the United States Senate. "Surely, the Senator's revelation that Dr. Wiseman was married to the sister of a defector from the United States bore further investigation," the Senators said. "Questions have been raised here which cannot be brushed aside by expedient politics. The Committee abdicated its responsibility. It sought only to discredit Bradford, not Wiseman, and we are constrained to assert that Senator Bradford presented evidence sufficient for a full investigation, if not by the Committee, surely by the Justice Department."

In the Senate the opposing reports brought forth arguments of every stripe, most of them partisan, but the commentary that was historically significant was made by Sam Bradford himself.

"The Chairman of the Internal Security Subcommittee, Mr. Miller," he said, "has shown himself unwilling to accept the certain fact that this country is under grave threat from communism and from Communist sympathizers. One who is unwilling to confront that danger is unfit to serve in the United States Senate. Unfit. I serve notice on the gentleman from Delaware that I always pay my debts, and I always collect them. I advise the gentleman to enjoy the pleasure of this company while he can, because after the next election, in which his seat is at stake, he will not return. And may I say this further word. In the annals of the United States Senate, the name of Senator Miller of Delaware will be completely forgotten. In this illustrious body, which I hold in such high esteem, it will be as if he had never existed. Never existed at all."

☆ **8** ☆

MILLER OF DELAWARE did not return.

In the 1951 campaign, Sam turned loose his newly formed investigative team, operating out of a suite in the Congressional Hotel. Every day of Miller's life was laid bare, and he had not been blameless. Sam blanketed Delaware, and to recall his attacks on Miller, it appears that Miller had been a tool of the DuPont interests, that all his life he had been "soft on Communism," and that his voting record had been inimical to the best interests of the American people. In his bravery, clothed in the toga of the Senate, Miller had affronted the voice of the people, the anointed of the Pope, the High Priest of anti-Communism. Senator Miller made feeble efforts, but he was outclassed, outgunned, outfinanced. Bradford turned his whole energies to bringing down the Chairman of the Senate Internal Security Subcommittee, and when the smoke had died down, Miller was a distant, lonely runner. He had no claim to distinction, he had no charisma on the podium, he had no cause, no advocates.

He was only one of the many Democrats to fall in the popular sweep of a Republican hero into the presidency. Sam humbled Miller, and was responsible for the humbling of others, and for his triumphal contributions to the campaign, which returned a Republican majority to the senate, Sam Bradford was rewarded with the chairmanship of a Select Committee on Investigations, which, in effect, gave him *carte blanche* to pursue his Communist witch-hunt wherever it might lead. It also took a load off the "war chest." Sam immediately transferred his special task force to the staff of the Select Committee, employed glamour-boy counsel, and catapulted into the most vicious game of cat-and-mouse this country had ever witnessed.

The beginning was a sifting of the agencies of government, and the Select Committee, meeting on a daily basis, challenged the patriotism of employees ranging all the way from under-secretaries to garbage men in every executive department. And after those excursions it was a screening of the armed services, with gumshoes making forays even into overseas establishments. And as the months passed, the weeding out of enemies extended to the schools, the churches, the labor unions—every facet of American life. Sam Bradford now had his forum, his pontifications were reported daily, no one dared rise up to challenge him. If he condemned, the victim was damned, if he forgave, forgiveness was national.

I was not a part of that. We had enough to do, in the office, answering the swell of mail, keeping the ship afloat for the most powerful politician in the land. His target was a natural, and he was a natural for his target. How, one might ask, and one can be answered only in the context of the times. The United States had suffered through the Berlin blockade, when ultimate might was on our side; it had survived Hiss and Chambers, and emerged bewildered as to whether justice had been done. It had seen the Soviets explode the bomb on which we had a patent. It had tolerated officials with strange global views, and the formation of a United Nations which we seemed to be underwriting but for which we got no international credit. And here was Sam, black against white, right against wrong, fighter against the Red Menace, at home and abroad. Sam Bradford reduced very complex equations into simple, understandable answers, and so the peddlers of trivia sold the duffel handbags at $4.95 a throw, uniting the buyers into what came to be known as the "Bradford Brigade," and it seemed that the complex world had been reduced to an understandable formula.

If your soul were pure.

To the impure, or the resisters, it was a nightmare. Simply to be suspected of impurity, or to argue for tolerance, or in any way to question the dicta of the Select Committee, was to make one an immediate outcast. Security clearances were denied to people in the smallest places, applying for the most menial jobs, simply because one could be judged guilty by association, or judged guilty simply by having a name that was like that of a suspect. Neighbors were turned against neighbors, parents against teachers, congregations against church leaders. To be a "Bradfordite," to believe in "Bradfordism," one could prove simply by carrying the Bradford duffel bag, or by wearing in the lapel a small gold replica of the senator's trademark. In the smallest towns, prudent store owners displayed Sam's picture as prominently as the president's, as proudly as the flag. In a way that even the White House did not, Sam stood for the flag and gave it new meaning, a corruption of the tradition of freedom.

As I say, I was not a central part of the inquisition. "You run the shop," Sam told me, and Selma and I ran it. "Running the shop," of course, required that I daily familiarize myself with the interrogations, because the one thing that Sam still relied on me to produce was the speeches. "You know my style," he said. "No one else can capture the flavor better." And when there were speeches to be made, and there were many, I ground them out, lacing them liberally with the tar and feathers with which Sam rode his victims into oblivion, or worse.

I tested my own briefing by spinning it off on Patricia every night. She listened in silent disapproval, her sympathy for the halt and lame greater than her pride in my association with the most powerful Senator who ever basked in Washington's easy glory. The great debates, the ringing resolutions of the past were overshadowed by this demon bent on his great crusade, to rid the national fabric of the taint of communism, remarkable in its many manifestations. He found it in people, in institutions, in movements. He could stumble over it on his way to the garbage cans.

So I knew it was not out of interest in the peregrinations of Senator Bradford that Patricia called me, tears in her voice, on a late October afternoon in 1952. "Can you come home? Please?" she begged.

I did not at first recognize her agony, which shows perhaps how submerged I was in the office routine. "Are you wearing my sweatshirt again?" I asked lightly. She had about worn it out.

"Harry!" she protested, and she sounded close to hysteria.

"I'll be right there," I said. I knew my wife, as well as one person ever gets to know another. She might summon me, but not on a fool's errand. "Domestic crisis," I told Selma, grabbing my coat. Numeriano was lounging at his desk. He could be quicker than a taxi, and I asked him, "Where's the Cad?" Obviously floor matters had adjourned the committee, or Numeriano would have been shadowing his boss.

"At the curb," he said. Nobody ticketed Bradford's limousine. "Where you want to go?"

"Take me home. Urgent."

We made it in ten minutes, totally disregarding speed limits, red lights, rights of way and other minor considerations. Numeriano loved it. I thanked him and slammed the door and ran to the carriage house and burst into the living room. Patricia was huddled in a small ball, and she jumped up and flung her arms around me and I held her very close and patted her. The tears came, and I stroked her hair in a comforting way and didn't intrude. After about five minutes, I picked her up and carried her to the couch, and she wiped her eyes with a dab of tissue.

"Can you tell me now?" I asked.

She looked at me tragically and said with a breaking voice, "It's Father."

I was immediately concerned, because the old man meant a lot to me. "Is he ill? A heart attack or a stroke or something?"

She lowered her head and shook it, and the words came out in fragments. "He's been—indicted. By a federal grand jury."

"Your father? That's idiotic!"

"It's true. Something about Commonwealth. Misappropriation of funds, whatever that is."

"There has to be a mistake. Your father wouldn't play around with money. He has all he needs. Do you know anything else about it?"

"No. His lawyer called. An old family friend. Herbert France. He said he'd fill us in when we get there. I tried to call Father. He's in such a state of shock he can't talk. He must feel so—alone."

"We'd best get down there. I'll call Selma and tell her to let Sam know I'll be gone for a while." I dialed the office, and when Selma answered I said, "Is Sam off the floor yet?"

"Just came in," Selma said. "Stand by."

When Sam came on, I said, "I gotta run down to Richmond. Family problems."

"Anything I can help with?" Sam asked.

"I don't think so. It's Patricia's father. You remember him, don't you? From the wedding? He's under indictment for some kind of savings and loan foul-up."

"When will they stop persecuting good, decent Americans?" Sam said. "Take all the time you need. And keep me posted."

We wheeled out the Studebaker and crossed the Fourteenth Street Bridge and headed down Highway 1, a strip of commercial roadway I have always loathed. I made a few passes at conversation, but Patricia answered in monosyllables and I gave it up. When we finally hit the Richmond bottleneck, after what seemed an interminable drive, I vented my frustration in curses. It was about eight in the evening when we finally negotiated the James River road and pulled into Mason's Bluff.

Late as the hour was, Peyton was still on duty. He came out to the car and gravely took the bags and said quietly to both of us, "Miss Trish, your father is in the drawing room. He ain't et nuthin' ."

"Thank you, Peyton," Patricia said. "I guess we'll be using my old room. And you could make us some sandwiches and hot coffee."

We went into the house, to the drawing room fire, and Stanwick B., who was slumped in a chair, stood and greeted us with a show of hospitality. But he was not as erect as before, not as full of life. He gave me a limp hand, chided me for keeping his daughter away so long and complained that Patricia was thin.

Trish hugged the old man, kissed him on both cheeks, and came directly to the point. "Father," she said, "what in the world is it all about?"

Colonel Mason sagged into his wing chair. "I have been sitting here, trying to puzzle it all out," he said. "I don't understand, not at all. I have done nothing wrong. You make loans, and some of them turn out bad. You expect that. You have a reserve built in for it. I really can't . . ." Plainly, he was quite confused, and for the first time I caught a hint of senility.

"It's all right, Father," Patricia said. "We're here. We're going in to talk to Herb tomorrow. I'm sure it's all a mistake."

"I have done nothing wrong," Mason repeated.

"We know that, Mr. Mason," I said. "There was probably some oversight on a regulation. Lord knows, there're too many of them. We'll get this straightened out."

Peyton came in with sandwiches and coffee on a silver tray. "You must eat something, Father," Patricia said. "Peyton has brought a feast. Roast beef sandwiches. Ham. All the things you like. I'll fix you a plate."

"I had no appetite before," Mason said as she busied herself. "But now that you and Harry are here, I'm ravenous. Do I have to get indicted by a federal grand jury to get my children home?"

"Hush," Trish said. "And eat. Here. Harry, help yourself."

I dug in and sat looking at the fire. It made strange designs that I couldn't read.

"Your Senator is kicking up quite a stir," Mason said, and he was eating.

"He's busy," I said.

"And he keeps Harry busy," Trish said. "I never see him. I have a part-time husband."

Mason was chewing meditatively. "You know," he said, "I don't think I like him."

"With the Masons, it's in the blood," Patricia said. "Sam Bradford is a menace to organized society. An outrage. *He* should be indicted."

"He does seem a bit much," Mason said. "Harry, how can you tolerate it? You don't believe all this Communist stuff, do you?"

I lingered reflectively over a slice of very sweet ham. "It's pretty heady," I said. "All that attention. It's like being part of a hurricane."

"You like that?" Mason asked. "You need it?"

"I must," I said. "I married your daughter."

"Oh, what a low blow," Patricia said. "And just for that, the weather will be rather chilly tonight."

But it wasn't. In her own room she lived out the fantasies of girlhood, of a teenager's wild imagination, of first awareness, of yearning, of desire, making absolute demands. But I think it was not release, but a tension created by this first serious assault on the bastion of her childhood security. Except through the flesh, there was no other way to find her deliverance. We didn't sleep until the glow of day breaking lighted the windows to the east. Funny thing about Patricia, at that particular point in our relationship. She could indulge to unfathomable excess, rest for a very few hours and awaken refreshed. I, on the other hand, was as grouchy as a bear roused from hibernation.

I had barely recovered my pajamas from the far recesses where she had thrown them when Peyton was rapping at the door, calling us to breakfast.

Fortified with grits and redeye gravy, we drove into Richmond, parked the car in a multilevel deck and walked to the Bank of Virginia Tower, where Herbert France, attorney at law, had his office. We planted ourselves on bright plastic and aluminum until he was free and then marched somberly into his office.

"What is it all about, Herb?" Patricia asked.

France was a grey, lean Virginia-firster. "I wish I could make it easy for you, Patricia," he said. "But it's an airtight case. The FBI had all the goods to present to the grand jury, and—I wish there were some better way to say this—your father is probably going to spend some time in a federal penitentiary. Oh, we'll plead him not guilty, but we haven't got a case. This is what happened. About fifteen years ago your father bought a tract of land in Henrico County, about 120 acres. Times were hard, and he picked it up for a song. He just sat on it, like a lot of other properties he accumulated during that period. You have no idea, Patricia, how much land your father holds title to. A lot of real estate. About a year ago a promoter approached him, supposedly a land developer, a real sharpie. In his prime, when he had all his faculties, your father would have thrown the man out of his office. At least he would have checked a little closer. Fellow by the name of Graham. He's been one jump ahead of the law in land frauds all the way from Florida to Texas. He offered your father a good price on the Henrico property. It wasn't a windfall. Land out there has escalated in value tremendously, so your father wasn't lining his pockets. Where he made his mistake was to loan Graham the money to close the deal. Ethically, he should have sent the buyer to some other financial institution. Commonwealth shouldn't have figured in the transaction at all. Once in possession of the property, Graham applied to Commonwealth for a development loan. He was going to build G.I. housing, Mason Ridge, he was going to call the tract. Again, your father approved a transaction he shouldn't have been involved in. He approved the construction loan, which was to be made available in installments. Installments, because the borrower has to show that he is meeting a development timetable. Graham moved some grading equipment out there, and he made a pass at laying out streets. On paper, there's a Patricia Avenue, but it never got off the blueprints. Your father was completely taken in by Graham. He read the developer's faked reports, sent no inspectors out to check their veracity, and Graham swindled Commonwealth out of three-quarters of a million dollars. The FBI has it all, in very carefully documented depositions and reports. Commonwealth is a federal lending institution. That's how the Hoover people got involved."

"Will the depositors lose money?" Patricia asked.

"Oh, no. They're protected by the Federal Savings and Loan Insurance Corporation. And, of course, the land can be put up for resale. There'll be some recovery there."

"It can't come close to making up the loss," I said.

"Oh, no. The feds will squeeze Graham. They'll uncover anything he's got stashed away. But these fellows have a way of hiding assets. And Graham didn't show much that was convertible. Flew a leased plane. Even bilked the heavy equipment people. When one of these slick fellows comes on the scene, he's got all the angles figured out, even to the probability of a vacation in a federal dormitory."

"So what are we going to do?" Patricia asked.

"All we can do is go through the motions. We'll make the usual plea at the arraignment, and at the trial we'll play up the lack of criminal intent. If he could make restitution . . ."

"How much?" Patricia asked.

"He's got all that land he could sell off. And the James River property, if necessary. Mason's Bluff. But he'll probably come up short a couple hundred thousand."

"I have some money," Patricia said.

"I know," France said. "From your mother. Taliaferro money. He wouldn't want you to do that, even if you could help him, bail him out. I know your father, and stripping you of your mother's inheritance would hurt him more than public humiliation. Don't even suggest it."

"But . . ." she began.

"No, I'm serious. Your father would put a gun to his head before he'd let this scandal touch you."

"So he goes to jail? And we sit by? And there's nothing we can do?"

"We can delay. Appeals can take years. But ultimately, unless there is some miracle . . ." France shrugged.

Patricia put her hand in mine, and I patted it. "I feel so helpless," she said.

We stood up to go, shaking hands around. "I'll let you know about the arraignment," France said. "But don't let it get to you. Falling apart now won't help your father."

We retrieved the car and drove glumly out the river road. As we turned into the entrance, Patricia reached over and turned off the ignition. She sat, looking down the tree-lined drive toward the magnificent house, perched on its proud knoll overlooking the river. "I can't believe we might lose this," she said. "It has been in the family since before the Revolution, way before."

"I know," I said miserably, although I didn't know.

"You don't know how it got its name, do you?" Patricia whispered.

"I can guess. A Mason house. On a river height. 'Mason's Bluff.' All very logical."

"That isn't the way it was at all. One of my ancestors—I think his name was Malachi, Malachi Mason—won it in a card game. On a busted hand. So it became Mason's Bluff, in commemoration of a poker game."

"I don't think you'll lose it," I said without conviction.

"Oh, we will. My father puts honor above possessions. And I don't know why he got into that Graham business. He didn't need the money, and he wasn't a speculator in land. I remember stories about the Depression, whispered as family secrets. Foreclosures. He really skirted the law to avoid them. Not a hardhearted banker, and if character witnesses would help, we could round up a thousand. Peyton. He gave Peyton a piece of this land that his sons now work. And when Peyton's wife died—her name was Amanda—she was buried in the Mason cemetery, off to the right over there. All my people . . ." She broke into muffled sobs.

"Maybe I should come back and reactivate the business," I said miserably.

She didn't hear me. Her mind was wrapped up in family, in tradition, in the proud history of Virginia. "It isn't so bad that he'll lose the bank," she said. "That was never a part of all this." She spread her hand futilely, in a despairing gesture that encompassed the whole horizon.

I started the engine again, but Patricia opened the door on her side and got out. "Go ahead," she said. "I want to walk. I never knew before how much I love this place." I eased away, and in the rear-view mirror I looked back at her, a tiny, bundled figure, scuffing at the gravel, plodding along the strip that horses and carriages had graced. I myself could only marvel at such association with the historic, at what that association instills. I had no such imbedded roots, but I could respect and weep for the loss felt by that tiny girl trailing behind me, representing as she did the last of that particular Mason line. She had wanted—she had told me—to give this place to her own sons, yet unborn, as a legacy of that past in which she took so much pride. I cursed my own helplessness. And I cursed my father-in-law; he had no right to bring such grief to my blond angel. I looked once more in the mirror, and I couldn't see her.

It was with leaden spirit that I had to leave Patricia there, my joy, my reason, as I thought then, for being. She would stay with her father through the first round of the legal maneuvering, and we would play it by ear from then on. At the next weekend I would bring her car down, and perhaps thereafter, depending upon how the colonel was bearing up, she would slip up to Georgetown for a few days at a time. It would be our first real separation, and I dreaded it, came to hate it as I got back to work. I had not realized before that the hours at the office were such drudgery, that I previously had left home in the mornings with the certain knowledge that no matter how bad the day, no matter how revolting, the evening would come, and with it the togetherness. I tried to bury myself in the routine. I tried chumming it with Sam and his team of conspirators, but the constant strategy sessions, the chortling over the next victim, the zealousness with which they went about the national purification, made my stomach queasy. The only really pleasant interlude was an evening with Selma.

I picked her up at around 7:30 at her Capitol Heights apartment, a modest little efficiency. She was in a party dress, but for Selma, party dresses did nothing.

"Pretty dress," I said, biting my tongue.

"I've been saving it," she said, swirling grotesquely. "Let me get you a drink."

"I'll have a light . . ."

"I know." And she came to me with a Jack Daniels, chokingly strong because she didn't know how to mix drinks. She held a thimble of clear liquid. "Zubrowka," she said. "Polish vodka. Is 100 proof strong?"

"It's bracing," I said.

"I don't want to get tipsy, Mr. Dodge."

"Selma, don't 'Mr. Dodge' me. We're both on Sam's pay-roll. You can call me Harry."

"All right. But only outside the office."

We finished the drinks with shop talk, and then we went out in the street and hailed a cab.

"Where to?" Selma asked.

"A very special treat. The National Press Club."

"I've heard about it. All those muckrakers."

"They're very nice people," I said, "maybe the only real people in Washington. Flesh and blood, I mean. Everyone else is made up of echoes and shadows. And the Press Club is something to see. Stag bar. Wire tickers. All the action of the greatest capital in the world. Some of the press people love it so much they never leave it."

"What would Mrs. Dodge say if she knew you were taking a secretary to dinner?"

"I talked to her this afternoon. Since she knows who the secretary is, we have her blessing."

"You're so lucky," Selma said. "Mrs. Dodge is like—I don't know—some beautiful painting I saw once in a book. In per-son she's charming, and she's absolutely devoted to you. What else is there?"

We had arrived at the Fourteenth Street entrance, and we debarked and walked in through the massive doors to the elevator bank. "Scared?" I asked.

"A little. What if I use the wrong fork?"

"I'll tell the waiter to bring only one. Then you can't miss. Selma, I'm afraid we've neglected you."

"No, you haven't. I see you every day."

We got the express and were whisked upwards. I waved at the deskman, passed through the corridor with its impressive stereotype mats of the great front pages, and checked in with the headwaiter. He seated us immediately. A party of *Daily News* and *Tribune* men—a most unlikely New York-Chicago combination—had themselves and their wives bibbed up for lobster, and they hailed us drunkenly. I stopped, chatted, met wives impressed with the "Sam Bradford" password and saw that Selma was comfortably chaired.

"How about escargot?" I asked.

"I don't even know what it is."

"Snails in garlic and butter sauce. In the shell. But they cheat. The snail doesn't get the shell he grew up with."

"I'll have no part of such thievery," Selma said. "A shrimp cocktail and the small steak. Is that horribly expensive?"

"Not here."

"Were you joking about the snails in their shells?"

"You'd be surprised. Would you like wine?"

"If you would."

I ordered a Beaujolais and the shrimp and the steaks with side orders of whole mushroom caps, and while we were waiting, over the first glass, I asked, "Selma, are you happy?"

"I never thought I could be so happy."

"You like working on the Hill?"

"If, when I was a little girl, I had fantasized about what I wanted to be when I grew up, it wouldn't have been so wonderful."

"How do you spend your evenings? We see you so little."

"But you've had me to parties, and Mrs. Dodge has always been so kind. Nothing put-on about her." She looked at me levelly. "You love her very much, don't you?"

"Out of my mind," I said. "But isn't there any madness in your life?"

Deftly, the black waiter slid the salads in front of

us, and I had forgotten about the forks, and Selma watched me covertly and matched me and settled into her greenery.

"No madness," she said. "But I have good friends. The Capitol Hill Club has something going on every week, and I've met some Polish-American people. We have a little circle."

"Do you get down to Richmond much?"

"Not as much as I should. But there's something I'm very proud of. You know I make a lot of money?"

"Well, you're not getting rich, but it's a fair salary. More than I could ever have paid you if we hadn't all come to Washington."

"I know I owe you for that, and I still think of you as my employer."

"I didn't mean it that way, and, of course, it's not true. You are employed by the United States Government, through its agent, the United States Senate, through its most highly touted member, Sam Bradford."

"But you didn't have to make a place for me."

"Sam had to have a staff."

She buttered a rye cracker. "What I started to say was, I don't need all that money. I have some, but I'm helping my father pay off the mortgage. He always had to scrape, and it's easier for him now. You don't know how good that makes me feel."

"Yes, I do." The steaks had arrived, and we made a pretense of checking them for doneness, and I motioned the waiter toward Selma's empty wine glass.

"Not too much of that for me," she giggled.

"Afraid I'll make a Polish wino out of you?"

"No. There's something wrong with my metabolism. Two glasses of wine, and I get a headache."

"You don't have to get a headache with me."

She was an earthy person and she laughed, knowing the

tired old joke. "I don't think I'd ever have that kind of headache."

"How do you know? Do you have a special boyfriend?" I cut into the meat and watched the red juices flow.

Selma placed her cutlery on her plate carefully, and I prepared for a serious confidence. "Mr. Dodge. *Harry.* It's the one thing missing. I know that I am not a pretty girl." She waved aside my protestations. "I know that. But I want a man, a real man-to-woman relationship, the kind of trust you and Patricia have. Is that too much to ask? There are some men who aren't so beautiful. And somewhere there must be a gentle, understanding man for a homely Polish girl."

"Eat, Selma," I said. "That man is out there somewhere, and you'll find him. Or he'll find you. Have I ever lied to you? Eat. Keep up your strength. But forgive an impertinent question. Does Sam still give you goose bumps?"

She reddened slightly. "I can't explain it," she said. "Whenever he's around, I get all—gooey—inside."

"Mystifies me," I said. "He's not really a very nice guy. He swears like no man should in front of a lady. He hits the bottle at all hours of the day and night, half pickled all the time. Everything you disapprove of. Why should you feel that way? Have you tried to analyze it?"

"No. It's just that, from the first, I've seen the little boy in him. A little boy, more or less helpless, that no one really liked. And my heart goes out to him."

"He was a pretty damn mean little kid."

"Mr. Dodge . . ."

"Harry."

"I forgot. Harry. Sometimes I get the feeling that you don't really like what he's doing."

"It's not supposed to show."

"But it's true?"

"Yes."

"Why? Don't you think it's important?"

I couldn't tell her that it was all an act, a charade dreamed up out of desperation by some half-crocked strategists not six blocks from where we were sitting. I poured myself more wine and sipped it slowly. I speared the last brown mushroom and savored it. "I don't like smear campaigns," I said finally.

"But isn't there something—a basis of truth—in what he says?"

"Just enough to make the whole campaign viable. He has grown a whole forest of oaks from a single, worm-infested acorn."

"But communism is a threat, isn't it? Those people would sell out this country, wouldn't they?"

"They'd never have a chance."

"Poland . . ."

"Poland was overrun with tanks, and the Polish people don't like the Russians any more than they did the Germans."

"Still, where there's smoke . . ."

"That's an old cliché, and it's not necessarily true. I could mix together a few chemicals and fill the whole Press Building with smoke, but with not a sign of fire."

It was not until we were leaving and I was helping her with her coat that I noticed that Selma was carrying an elegant blue and gold evening bag, petite, but cheapened by the tiny drawstring. If it was nothing else, it was fashionable.

In the days that followed, Patricia and I burnt up the telephone lines. I wanted to go down to Richmond for the arraignment in November, but Patricia flagged me off. "Herb says it's so cut and dried it won't take but a few minutes. He's going to plead Father not guilty and ask for a trial without jury. Just the judge. I'll be there with Father, and he really would be just as happy if you didn't come. He finds the whole thing humiliating."

And so I stayed in Washington and sweated, agonizing for that aristocratic old gentleman, agonizing for my child bride who was having to make the sometimes startling discovery that no human being is without fault. You can believe that, you can die believing it. But if our faults were all laid bare, to public perusal, there would be no innocents left. She, of course, would never concede that her father had committed a crime, as he could not. What she did know, and yet could not accept, was that he had exercised wretched judgment. But that is not always a crime.

Late on a Friday afternoon she called about the first appearance in formal court, and there was but one cheering note. France had moved for a severance, and Stanwick B. Mason would not go to trial at the same time as the swindler Graham. "Did Herb say anything about a change of venue?" I asked.

"Graham's lawyers did," Patricia said, "but the motion was denied. And Herb didn't want a change of venue. He thinks Father's reputation in the community will work in his favor. And so do I. Masons are not criminals."

"Has a trial date been set?"

"Yes, and in a way that works against us. Herb is kicking himself around the block for not requesting a speedy trial. Graham goes to court the second week in January, and Father's trial starts the 19th. That's a Monday."

"So Graham will already have been convicted?"

"That's the bad part, and I really don't care if they execute him. But the earlier trial will have been a kind of precedent."

"Same judge, too?"

"Houston. A friend, but not enough of a relationship for there to be a taint of conflict of interest. Father thinks he's a fair man. Even if he was a Roosevelt appointee."

"Well, we don't want a New Deal, just a fair deal."

"Harry, I don't even want justice."

"No?"

"I'll settle for mercy."

"And how are you?"

I shouldn't have asked, because her voice faded and was far away when she said, "I'm holding all the pieces together."

"Hold them together," I said lightly. "I like every single piece. Crooked toes. Fingernails. Belly button." She hung up, and I had no way of knowing if she knew that I meant it, that I did, indeed, treasure every morsel of that incomparable woman.

The holidays were a grim time. There was little doing at the office, of course, and I left for Richmond in mid-December, the Studebaker loaded with my clothes and the ones Patricia had asked for. At about Fredericksburg I ran into snow and crawled the rest of the way to the Virginia capital. The salt trucks were out in Richmond, but the James River bridge was slick, and on the back road along the river there had been no clearing. The snow tires barely gave traction, and what should have been a three-hour drive lengthened into six.

Peyton was out though, in gum boots, a fur hat and a worn navy coat. He pulled me from behind the wheel, almost carried me to the porch, and said, "You go on in, Mistuh Harry. Miss Patricia, she got somethin' waitin' in there to take off the chill."

She threw herself at me. "I was so worried," she said. "There were reports of accidents all over the state." In the long living room the fireplace was throwing out its warmth, and as I backed up to it, Patricia thrust a glass into my hand. "Hot rum punch," she said. "Peyton's idea. He's had it warming for two hours."

I let the warm liquid trickle down my throat, still holding onto Patricia. "Peyton is a man to be admired," I said.

"More?" She ran for a decanter, warming over a candle in a wrought-iron stand. I held the cup out. "Us flatland Virginians can't cope with snow and ice," I said. "We panic. Go bananas. How is your father coping?"

Patricia pulled me down into a sofa positioned in front of the fire. "He's resting now, but he's not coping. He's in a constant daze. He gets up every morning to go to his office, and he can't go there. So he wanders the grounds, walks by the river. I'm almost afraid he may wander off and not come back, so I keep a close eye on him."

"Patricia is coping?"

"Just barely," she said.

"I have a complaint. I have been here five minutes, and you haven't blessed my lips."

"But I have," she said. "According to an old family formula. When frostbite—or snakebite—strikes, bless the lips with rum until the blue has faded, until circulation is restored. Then carry on."

"Carry on, woman."

She gnawed at me, and her bravado died, and she clung tightly. "Harry, it has been so terrible. Knowing I had to be here, wanting to be with you. Missing you every waking moment. Have you missed me?"

"Not really," I said, nuzzling her right ear and palming her right breast.

"So many pretty girls on the Hill?"

"Just reach out. A plateau of tits."

"I'd fracture your tibia."

"That's in the leg."

"So you couldn't walk. Fibula?"

"Same general area."

"Then I'd be less anatomical. I'd fracture your damn elbow."

"Now you're getting on track. Would you like to try for my neckbones or the cranium?"

"Ah, Harry. My beautiful man. Fractured or not."

I seized her fiercely. "I missed you. I spent the nights in an empty bed."

"What did you miss most?"

"You're baiting me. Was it the flesh, or the spirit? Do you want anatomy? I have memorized all the parts."

"Not necessarily."

"That wasn't it, anyway. Anatomy is very important. But not the be-all and end-all. I just missed your being there when I got home, or in the night, to reach out and know that you were there. A tactual reassurance. My cup was empty."

Within forty-eight hours, as is the case in Virginia's December, the snow had melted and we could tramp the woods. We took a bow saw and went into the woods and spent a half day rejecting Christmas trees. Finally, she was satisfied, and I sawed at the base until it toppled. We dragged it to the house and she found the stand and the ornaments, and we set it aglow. "You understand why we have to do this, don't you, Harry?" she asked.

"Sure, like the old days. Nothing has happened to interfere with the eternal routine."

"He'll appreciate it, and God knows where he'll be next Christmas."

"Wherever he is, we'll be there."

"You promise?"

"Cross my heart."

But the words were empty, and we both knew it. The one bright spot in that cheerless holiday season was a trip we both made a few days before Christmas for dinner with Selma's family, the Gadowskis. They lived very humbly, south of the James, a modest house on an acre of farmland toward Midlothian. When we drove up we heard song and merriment inside, and we would have left had not Selma herself flung the door open and hustled us inside. Selma's mother sat in a rocker, a frail woman of the old country, unbelievable as the mother of this large daughter and three large sons, the consort of Justin Gadowski, a big, lumbering chunk of a man.

"Let me take your coat," Selma said to Patricia, and stroked the white fur adorning the blue leather.

"Selma," I said, "I haven't got goodies for everybody, but I have a present for you, and you have to open it." I handed her a slim package and she broke into it, bringing forth a silver bracelet with small replicas of the Washington Monument, the Capitol, Lincoln brooding in his chair. She smiled at me and said, "My mother wishes to say something," and we listened to the old woman rattle in the mother tongue.

I looked at Selma questioningly. "She just wants to express her thanks," she said, "that you have placed me so highly in the American government."

"Is right!" Justin roared, and we all toasted the moment in Polish vodka. Then we repaired to the dining room, which was flowing over with strange delights. We started with *nozki w galarecie,* a strange concoction of pigs' feet in jelly, then came a clear beet soup, *barszcz z' uszkami,* which had delicious little wild mushrooms in it. That was followed by the main course, *bigos,* which contained eight kinds of fresh meats and sausages and took, Selma told us, three days of heating and reheating to prepare. All of this heavy fare was topped off with a dessert called *szarlotka,* a kind of apple pie. Every course was washed down with Zubrowka, and with all the food and the toasting my bride and I were forced to retreat lest we fall down. Justin fawned on me as if I were an emissary of the emperor, his respect growing with every shot of the bison's vodka, this craggy old man with a wholly gentle soul. When the time seemed appropriate I nodded beseechingly to Selma, and she got Patricia's coat and was helping her with it when she noticed the bag I had bought my wife, a carry-all in soft brown leather.

"So pretty," Selma said. "Mr. Dodge always gives the perfect gift."

"Thank you," Patricia said, "and thank you for keeping him away from all those Washington vamps while I've been gone."

"We had a nice evening together," Selma said.

"He told me," Patricia said. "I scolded him. He never takes me anywhere and plies me with strong drink."

"He didn't . . ." Selma began. And then she stopped. "You're as big a tease as he is."

We were hailed off the premises, Justin roaring from the doorway, and I couldn't help thinking how much more perfect the simple life sometimes is. Justin, with the companion of all his days, the three strong sons and the daughter who was placed very highly in government circles. A place to call their own. Surely the dream of all immigrant families.

But the holidays waned, and the New Year came in, and within the first ten days of the new year Harvey A. Graham, late of Texas, Florida, and other points of notorious misdeed, had been sentenced to six concurrent prison terms of ten years each for the big swindle. I missed the proceedings, having returned to Washington, but Patricia kept me briefed with clippings from the *Times-Dispatch* and the *News-Leader*. The testimony covered a period of three days, and Judge Joel Houston did not temper justice with mercy. With Graham's past machinations paraded prominently across the record, the Judge visited upon him the wrath of God.

I was piddling in the office on Friday the 16th, getting ready to leave the next day for the Mason trial, when Sam came in. He didn't have to. Congressional proceedings were at the pace of a snail, and he had no hearings scheduled in January. He tapped me on the shoulder and said, "Come on in and stop farting around out here." I followed him and he made us drinks and as we settled down, Sam asked, "How does it look?"

"With Mason?"

"Sure. That's what's on your mind, isn't it?"

"Pretty damn bad," I said. "The other guy got ten years."

"Yeah, but that cocksucker was a crook. A fuckin' operator. He ought to be locked up. But Mason?"

"Oh, he was a patsy. A naive fall guy."

"How's your wife taking it?"

"She's hamburger. All chewed up."

"It's always hard on family. I remember from my days on the bench. The wives. The kids."

"I don't think anything has ever hit Patricia so hard. Maybe the death of her mother, but I wasn't around then. And there was time to prepare. She had leukemia."

"She was First Family, too, wasn't she?"

"A Taliaferro. Big name down there."

"I know the name. Never could spell the damn thing, and I still don't see how they can get 'Tollifer' out of it."

"Goes back to the Revolution. Chummy with Patrick Henry."

"Everybody in the whole fuckin' State of Virginia goes back to the Revolution. Freshen you up?"

"Why not?" I handed him the glass and thought how idiotic it was to be getting an edge on at 11 A.M. "I don't think the Dodges go back that far. Or if we do, we were probably Tories."

Sam brought me the renewed drink. "I may have to investigate your ass," he said. "The Tories were the Communists of their day."

"You're not going back that far?"

"With all this stuff runnin' around loose? Christ, I've already got enough to do for two lifetimes. That's the damn trouble. There's not enough time."

"You've got time."

"Not the way I got it figured." He swirled his ice and said pensively, "You know what I worry about?"

"I didn't know you worried about anything. I mean, real worry."

"Well, I do. I worry that some bastard is gonna shoot me."

"You're a natural target," I agreed.

"Some lowdown, creepy, Communist sonofabitch is going to shoot me. Or some screwball who wants his name to go down in the history books. And that's why there's not enough time." He shook himself. "Well, I just wanted to tell you, if there's anything I can do . . ."

"I'll keep you posted."

"You don't have to do that. I've arranged for a guy on the *News-Leader* to cover the trial for me."

I was bowled over. "Why the hell would you do that?"

"Because, Harry, anything that affects you affects me. We fought the war together."

I heard him, but I wasn't convinced.

Promptly at 10 A.M. we took our seats in the Federal Courtroom in Richmond. France had sent a car for Mr. Mason, and he with another member of France's law firm was sitting at the defense table with Stanwick. Mason was not in good condition. For these last few months he had been withdrawn, little aware of what was going on around him and little caring. I don't know that he knew he was in a court of law. He was dressed meticulously in tweeds—Peyton had seen to that—but he could have been lounging in the Generals' Club or listening to a classical concert.

The door leading to the Judge's chambers was flung open, and the bailiff began the ritual chant as we all rose. Judge Joel Houston, once dean of the illustrious University of Virginia School of Law, rapped his gavel. He nodded to the clerk, and that official read off some numbers and statutes in a monotone and the crowd of spectators stirred restlessly. From the front row, I stole a couple quick glances around, and in large part I could detect only an air of somberness. There seemed to be few of the sensation-seekers that a juicy murder or a divorce scandal would have brought out. If anything, the mood was one of quiet sympathy toward the defendant.

Judge Houston looked toward the defense table and in a

voice not at all unkindly said, "It is my understanding that the defense has waived trial by jury."

"That is correct, your Honor," France responded.

"Then would the defendant please rise?" The lawyer took my father-in-law by the arm, and the two stood together. "Mr. Mason," the Judge said, "you are accused of some rather serious offenses involving breach of trust. I'm sure you're aware of their nature, but I'll repeat them for the purposes of the record. The counts are four in number: that you misappropriated the funds of the Commonwealth Savings and Loan Association, of which you were president, in the sale of a certain parcel of land in Henrico County to one Harvey A. Graham for your own personal gain, said transaction involving the sum of $178,000; second, that you did unlawfully and without due respect for the regulations governing your Association make available to the aforesaid Harvey A. Graham the sum of $500,000 for development of the said property; third, that you failed to exercise the supervision required by law in providing development funds to Mr. Graham; and fourth, that you did illegally conspire with Harvey A. Graham to defraud the depositors of Commonwealth Federal Savings and Loan Association, in contravention of Federal statutes governing the Association and its officers. Does the defendant understand the charges?"

Mr. Mason said nothing and Herb France nudged him and Mason nodded and said, "Yes, I understand."

"And how does the defendant plead?" the Judge asked.

"Your Honor, the defense pleads not guilty," France said.

"Does the prosecution wish to make an opening statement?" the Judge asked.

The District Attorney was a thin young man, Vince Johnson, who had gotten a good press on the Graham conviction. He was not a spellbinder or a trickster. He simply relied on his staff to assemble the materials, to interpret the law by the book, to protect the interests of the United States. He stood angularly and deferentially. "Your Honor," he said, "we have been through this once, you and I, with the trial and conviction of Harvey Graham. Much of what transpires here will be repetitive, but since the court allowed the severance of the cases, that is unavoidable. Much of the substance of the allegations we have proven once, in Graham, and we will prove it all once more." He looked toward the defense table and said pointedly, "Make no mistake about that." He addressed the Judge again and said, almost wearily but very deliberately, "The Government stipulates that Stanwick B. Mason, president of Commonwealth Federal Savings and Loan Association, sold a piece of his own property to Harvey Graham and loaned him the money to buy it; we shall prove this by deed registries and by the testimony of qualified accountants. We shall further prove that once the land transaction was completed the defendant agreed to loan Graham, and did loan him, a half million dollars in development funds for the stated purpose of building G.I. housing on the Henrico tract. By photograph we shall show the extent of that development, or perhaps I should say lack of development, and we have from agents of the Federal Bureau of Investigation testimony regarding the negligence of the defendant in supervising that loan. The sum total represents a conspiracy that bilked the depositors of Commonwealth of almost $700,000. The depositors, of course, will not suffer loss, since the Federal Savings and Loan Insurance Corporation protects their investments. By extension, therefore, the losers are all of the people of the United States, and it is the duty of this court to protect their interests."

Judge Houston broke in, chiding Johnson mildly. "I don't think it's necessary for counsel to remind this Court of its obligations."

Johnson reddened slightly and said, "I didn't mean to imply . . ."

"Get on with it," Houston said.

"What I want to emphasize," the attorney said, "is that

there is fraud here. We shall prove it, as it touches upon every point in the indictment. I shan't go into the morality of this case. We intend simply to present the evidence. I believe the Court will find it beyond challenge."

"Mr. France, is there anything you wish to say before we go into the evidentiary aspect of this proceeding?" Judge Houston asked.

Herb did his best, and his best proved the legal axiom, when the facts are against you, rely on rhetoric. "Very simply, your Honor," he said, "in this litigation we are dealing with a case which never should have come to trial. We are dealing with the law, but we are not dealing with a lawbreaker, a criminal. Mr. Mason was duped by a confidence man. Duped. That has already been proven. There is not a dishonest bone in this man's body, and if he erred, it was out of age or ignorance, not out of greed. If one is duped, your Honor, is he in fact guilty of a crime? I think not. And the truth is that had Mr. Mason been presented privately with the facts of the indictment, he would have seen to it that no depositor, no bonding company, no government agency would have lost a red cent. We have pleaded not guilty to the charges, your Honor. We do plead guilty to human fallibility. But if all of us who are fallible were put behind bars, there would not be enough jails to contain us." France stopped and smiled at the Judge. "And with all due respect to this Court," he said waggishly, "there would be no one left to try us." He had gotten away with something Johnson couldn't have.

I fancied old Herb then. He had stood up for integrity, for decency, for honor and humanity—qualities which I have always held to be outside the jurisdiction of law.

Johnson first called an expert in real estate and paraded him through a gallery of the Henrico County property, taken recently, showing rude slashes through the scrub pine but no houses, not even foundations.

"Can you tell us," Johnson asked, "when Mr. Mason acquired that tract?"

"The registry of deeds shows 1934," the realtor said. His name was Charles Asbury and he had a broad Southern accent and a known fondness for corn whiskey, although no one ever implied that the weakness incapacitated him in any way.

"And Mr. Asbury, do the deeds show how much Mr. Mason paid for that acreage in 1934?"

"Yes. He paid $38,000."

"And does your study of the registry show whom he sold the property to?"

"Harvey Graham Enterprises."

"For how much?"

"For $178,000."

"So that Mason made a profit of $140,000?"

"Well, it wouldn't be all profit. He had to keep up the taxes, and . . ."

"Would a profit of $125,000 be close?"

"Around that."

"I have no more questions. Mr. France?"

Herb had a nice courtroom manner, easy, never antagonistic, and he was friendly with the realtor. "Chuck, uh, Mr. Asbury, you have been in real estate in Richmond—how long?"

" 'Bout as long as you've been practicin' law, thirty-five years. Thirty-six."

"Then you probably know every foot of real estate within one hundred miles of Richmond."

"That's a lot of territory," Asbury laughed, "and I sure wouldn't say that. But I was called as an expert witness. I guess I'm an expert."

"And I know you're a thorough one. Let's talk about these records a little bit more. Do they show who Mr. Mason bought that property from?"

Asbury consulted his notes. "From the estate of Francis B. Witherspoon."

"Do you know who Frank Witherspoon was?"

"Just vaguely. Never did any business with him."

"Old Virginia family. Dealt in stocks and bonds."

Johnson broke in. "Your Honor, is this relevant? We're hearing ancient history from counsel."

Judge Houston shushed him. "History is important in Virginia, young man. Counsel may proceed, although what he is saying might better come from a witness."

"We can produce witnesses, your Honor, and we will. A flock of 'em. But I wanted to set this in perspective. Does the prosecution object to perspective?" He looked at Johnson, and Johnson was silent. "When the market went out the window, so did Witherspoon. I mean literally. He jumped from the sixth floor of the Virginia Bank Building. It was very simple. He had lost everything he had, and he killed himself. Mr. Mason bought this property to save Mr. Witherspoon's family. Would you say that he paid a fair price?"

"On that scrub pine in Henrico? In 1934, it was going for $100 an acre. If you could find a buyer."

"So a fair market price would have been—we're talking about one hundred twenty acres, aren't we?—well, $12,000?"

"He could have had it for ten. Ten thousand."

"Why do you suppose he was so generous?"

"Objection," Johnson said.

"Well taken," Houston said. "But I'd really like to hear the answer."

"Well," Asbury said, "some are good businessmen and some aren't. But I know what you're driving at."

"Mr. Mason was a much younger man then, and shrewd," France said. "He was performing an act of charity. Would you accept that?"

France looked at Johnson, expecting an objection, but the prosecutor let it pass. "I would accept that," Asbury said.

"Then let's come down to more modern times. We have the same one hundred twenty acres, but we don't have the same market. Mr. Mason sold that property for less than $1,500 an acre. Was that a windfall?"

"No, it wasn't. Single plots in Henrico are going for more

than $5,000 now. Of course, this was a large parcel, and it had to be developed. If Mr. Mason had wanted to subdivide it, put in a few roads, do a little judicious landscaping, he could have gotten half a million for it. Easily."

"A half a million?"

"On that order."

"But he didn't do that. I wonder why?"

Johnson came on quietly. "I must object to that now, your Honor. Counsel is asking the witness to speculate. He can't know what was in Mr. Mason's mind."

Sustained. Proceed, Mr. France."

'Thank you, your Honor. Let me approach this from a different direction. Do you know of other real estate transactions in which Mr. Mason was involved as a principal?"

"He's turned over some property. Henrico. Chesterfield, and within what are now the city limits of Richmond."

"What happened to most of that land?"

"G.I. housing developments."

"Has there ever been any suggestion that Mr. Mason was profiteering in any way?"

"No. I can say truthfully, nobody ever even hinted he was out for the buck."

"Would it accord with the facts to suggest that Mr. Mason's sole interest has been in seeing that housing was provided for veterans at reasonable cost?"

"I would . . ."

"Objection."

"Sustained."

In the afternoon the FBI came on. I never knew agents before to travel in packs, but they were coming out of the woodwork. First they established that the con artist Graham, who was sole owner and proprietor of Harvey Graham Enterprises and other fictions, was a no-good, lousy, dirty, rotten sonabitch. Herb France didn't object to any of that. He wanted Graham to look as black as sin, in comparison with his snow white Virginian. And for an interminable period we heard detailed accounts of Graham's transgressions over most of the populated areas of the South and Southwest. He had a way about him, but of course phony ways do not sustain one forever and his ways were going to land him in the pokey as soon as the appeals ran out. At about four o'clock, when the feds got into piecing together the Commonwealth scam, Judge Houston asked the prosecutor how long he expected to go on with that, and when Johnson replied, "For hours," the court was recessed until the next morning.

We were not a very cheerful bunch at Mason's Bluff that night. Peyton prepared an extravagant dinner, the things he said Stanwick loved best, but the old man only picked at his food. He was more attentive to the wine decanter, and after dinner he had a hefty shot of brandy, but he excused himself shortly and retired. Patricia and I were left with the fire and each other. Under normal circumstances we would have asked no more, but the spectre of prison bars was heavy in the great living room.

"It takes so long," Patricia said once.

"A moment in time," I said philosophically.

She was in no mood for philosophy. "A moment in time," she repeated. "Some moments drag out to infinity. I feel like we've been in court forever."

"Chin up," I said. "So far, your father has come off as a pillar of the community. Wait until they trot out the sordid stuff."

Johnson did that the next day. After the FBI guys had done their thing, he got into the technical details, calling officers of the Savings and Loan Association to support the charge of negligence. The comptroller's testimony, given precisely by a junior functionary named Harold Spivey, was the most damaging. He took the stand in the afternoon, an automaton, responding as the prosecutor pressed the right buttons, volunteering nothing but answering the direct questions fully and completely.

"The burden of your testimony," Johnson said in summary, "is that you were directed to write checks to Graham by the president himself—the defendant."

"That is correct."

"And normally you would have received certain supporting documents?"

"That would have been the routine procedure. The inspectors would have certified that the building program was on schedule, and a loan officer would have stipulated that a certain advance was in order."

"But in this case you got no validating papers?"

"None."

"Then how did it work?"

"I simply got a note from Mr. Mason directing me to prepare a check in a certain amount for his signature, drawn to Mr. Graham."

"Did you protest that the appropriate documents had not been filed, that there were none of the progress reports normally accompanying such a request?"

"No, I did not."

"Why not?"

"Mr. Johnson, I am not high in the chain of command at Commonwealth. I was employed by Mr. Mason. I served at his pleasure. It would not have been appropriate for me to challenge any directive I received from him."

"You were in a box, weren't you?"

"I was uncomfortable, to say the least."

"But to your knowledge, the checks were drawn and negotiated?"

"Yes."

"In what amount?"

"The books show eight vouchers, totalling $500,000."

"Thank you. Your witness, Mr. France."

Herb strolled over to the tight little man in the tight little box. He began in a confidential tone that didn't last very long. "Mr. Spivey," he said, "Colonel Mason has told me that you are one of the most valued employees at Commonwealth. Did you know that he regarded you so highly?"

"He never told me."

"But he paid you well?"

"Quite well."

"I have told you what your employer thought of you. What were your feelings toward him?"

"Correct, I think."

"Just what does that mean?"

"I respected him."

"Did you like him?" Herb's voice was rising, and each question carried a little more edge.

"Mr. France, I am not an outgoing person. I tried to do my job."

"You didn't hold a grudge against him?"

"Certainly not."

"You just did your job, as well as you could?"

"Yes."

"In the Graham transaction, do you think you did your job well?"

"I followed orders."

"That doesn't answer my question. Did you, in fact, carry out the duties of your office?"

"No, I didn't."

"In what way were you remiss?"

"I did not insist that proper procedures be followed."

"Why?"

"Because I didn't want to lose my job."

"You were aware, though, that there were some oversights?"

"Oh, yes."

"And yet you didn't bring them to Mr. Mason's attention?"

"No."

"Why?"

"I think I explained that. Mr. Mason was president of the association."

"What did you think of the irregularities?"

"I tried not to think about them."

"But they bothered you?"

"Yes."

"How did you account for them?"

"I couldn't."

"Were you aware that prior to the Graham loan Mr. Mason had suffered a mild stroke?"

Johnson was instantly on his feet. "Your Honor, there has been no showing of physical disability on the part of the defendant."

"Mr. France?" Judge Houston asked.

"Your Honor," Herb said, "the defense is prepared to present medical evidence. It will show a period of impairment. May we proceed on that assumption? If the prosecution isn't satisfied with the testimony of Mr. Mason's doctor and the records of the Medical College of Virginia, the defense will be the first to insist that this portion of the record be stricken."

"Mr. Johnson?" Houston said.

"Agreed. But I think this line of questioning could have been reserved until later."

France continued. "Did you know that Mr. Mason's health was impaired, that perhaps his mind was not clear, at the time of the Graham transactions?"

"No," Spivey said.

"If you had known, would you have called the discrepancies to his attention? Or to that of someone on the board of directors?"

"I don't know."

"Then let's take it completely out of the context of your employment. If you had known that the president of your association was not absolutely physically fit, that he was functioning strangely, *should* you have done somewhat more than you did?"

"In the abstract, yes. But you are not going to pin negligence on me!"

"Mr. Spivey," Herb said in dismissal, "if you were a donkey, I wouldn't pin a tail on you. Thank you."

In the late afternoon, the prosecution rested, and Judge Houston addressed France. "Would the defense like to adjourn until tomorrow morning?"

"Yes, your Honor. We have more than one hundred character witnesses and expect to occupy this Court for some time. But first, we would like to make a motion."

"Can't it wait until tomorrow?"

"Yes, but I thought the Court ought to hear it now, perhaps for reflection overnight."

"All right."

"On the evidence, the defense moves that the fourth count in the indictment be dismissed. There has been no showing of conspiracy."

Johnson rose up at his table. "Your Honor, the people would lodge strong objection. Mr. Graham has been convicted of conspiracy to defraud the Commonwealth Federal Savings and Loan Association. One cannot conspire with himself."

"The motion is denied," Judge Houston said. "Until ten o'clock tomorrow morning." He banged his gavel and swept toward his chambers.

I spoke to France on the way out. "Much of a setback?"

"No," he said. "Just making points for the record. The prosecutor went a little light on that charge. He never showed Colonel Mason and this fellow Graham sitting down and saying, 'We're gonna clean out the Savings and Loan.' He has to prove intent, and he didn't do that. Don't take any comfort from that, though. We can't win. The record is clear that Commonwealth suffered a loss, and Graham didn't come in with a gun and hold the place up."

"Can't we put a gun in the bastard's hand?"

France laughed. "I'm afraid not."

"Are you really gonna put a hundred people on the stand?"

"Nah, that was for the record, too. I want to get that medical evidence in, and we'll call five or six character witnesses. I'll read off a list of people who would appear if necessary, but actually we'll be through by noon and probably have a verdict. I've gone over it with the Judge. He wants a couple hours, and the sentencing will come sometime tomorrow afternoon. You better warn Patricia. I didn't expect it to move this fast."

"It hasn't been fast for her," I said.

Herb picked up his briefcase. "No, I guess not."

There was a skinny little guy standing near us, face like a bowl of oatmeal, whom I had noticed at the press table, unusually busy with his comings and goings. He dashed off as soon as he heard Herb's prediction, and I assumed he was already on the line to Washington from one of the pay phones in the hall. Sam would have twenty-four hours to prepare his condolences.

We went on back out to the River, and Patricia waited until we were in the house with drinks in our hands before she lit into her father. "Why didn't you tell us you had had a stroke?" she demanded, fire in her voice.

"There wasn't much to it," the Colonel said. "A little impairment on the left side, but nothing lasting. It cleared up in a few days."

"So you kept it to yourself?"

"There was no reason to bother you. I wasn't dying. And you would have been down here with nurses around the clock, and all that fussing. Wasn't worth it."

But the testimony of Dr. Ebenezer Manners the next morning was somewhat grimmer. Stanwick B. had had a stroke, which he explained in interminable medical detail; there was some permanent damage, and Mr. Mason actually should have retired. The stresses of the financial world could have brought on something more serious, but the Colonel was determined to do business as usual.

"And in your professional opinion, was Colonel Mason in full possession of his faculties in the period of time we are considering?" France asked.

"Most decidedly, he was not," Manners said. "I have treated the Mason family for more than thirty years. At no time in those thirty years were the colonel's physical and intellectual powers at a lower ebb."

Johnson asked only one question on cross examination. "Was Mr. Mason responsible for his actions, Doctor?"

"Yes, but at an impaired level."

"Thank you. You can step down."

And then Herb France brought on the farm contingent, white and black. The substance of their testimony was what Patricia had already told me, that during the Depression they couldn't meet the mortgage payments on their property, that Mason had personally handled the foreclosures, that with his own money he had paid off the indebtedness, that he had allowed them to maintain possession and use of their land, and that when times had improved he had allowed them to pay off their indebtedness, without interest. I was mighty proud of that broken old patrician.

"If Colonel Mason is sentenced to prison," one overalled old farmer said, "I ask that I be allowed personally to serve his term."

Herb smiled. "There is no provision in the law that would allow that," he said, dismissing the witness, "but I thank you for your testimony. Your Honor, we would not presume to take up the time of this Court on testimonials which might all sound the same. But if we may, we ask that we might enter into the record the depositions of about thirty other landowners whose farms were saved through the intervention of Colonel Mason."

"The depositions will be received," Judge Houston said. "Do you plan to present character witnesses from other areas?"

"Again," France said, "in the interest of time, only the depositions. We have them here from legislators, educators, ministers."

"They may be accepted as part of the record," the Judge said. "Anything further?"

"The defense rests."

There was a murmur in the courtroom. Oatmeal dashed out. The Judge said, "I suppose there are summary statements. Mr. France?"

"Your Honor," Herb said, "we have not much to add. We plead that this entire transaction was entered into in good faith, in the interests of adequate housing for veterans, a cause for which the colonel, an old campaigner himself, has always fought. We plead that there was never any intent, on the part of the defendant, to defraud Commonwealth Federal Savings and Loan. Colonel Mason is an old man, and his faculties are not what they once were. I don't think we should make it a crime in this country to become old. The Colonel has tended to be trusting, to believe that all men are as honest as he. We know that is not true, because Mr. Mason is the very model of decorum. But he slipped, and he slipped badly. Your Honor, a buyer has been found for the Henrico property, and we have a firm commitment for a $300,000 sale. We have recovered some slight principal, in the amount of $60,-000, from Graham. My client has closed contracts for other properties he owns which bring the total recovery to around $578,000. He is prepared to put his estate, Mason's Bluff, on the block, and from the proceeds he will make up the remaining deficit, something over $100,000. There will therefore be no call upon the bonding company or the federal insurance agency. Full restitution will have been made, at great sacrifice on the part of the defendant. We therefore ask the court to clear the name of this good man, Colonel Stanwick B. Mason."

Judge Houston nodded, pondered, looked toward the District Attorney. "Mr. Johnson?"

Vince rose and looked compassionately toward the defense table. "Your Honor," he began, "before the initiation of this trial we did not know Colonel Mason. We knew his name, that of an old and honored Virginia family, and we have been persuaded in the course of these proceedings that he is a man of great integrity. But your Honor, good men do bad things, and the evidence has shown that a bad thing was done here. Mr. Mason is culpable. He did business with a scoundrel, he abused the good faith of his depositors, he contravened the law. The law, your Honor. It must apply to the lofty as well as the lowly, and in good conscience, in spite of extenuating circumstances, this Court must obey the dictate of the law. Mr. Mason's guilt has been established here, beyond the shadow of a doubt. And is that not what justice is all about? We concede that he did good things; we have proven that he did bad things. Therefore, this man, in whom so many reposed such trust, must be found guilty and incarcerated. Not in vindictiveness, your Honor, but as a bulwark to that cement which holds the republic together—the law of the land." Vince sat down.

"Anything more from either side?" Judge Houston asked, and waited. "No? Would the defendant care to speak? No?" Houston took off his horn-rimmed glasses and rubbed his eyes. He polished his lenses with the sleeve of his black robe and positioned the frame over his nose again. He drank from a glass of water, set the glass down, licked his lips and looked out over the courtroom. He looked meaningfully at the bailiff and his armed deputies. "This court is prepared to rule," he said, and took up some papers. "On the first count, of misappropriating funds of Commonwealth Federal Savings and Loan for his own personal gain, we find the defendant not guilty. On the second count, of illegally providing funds to Harvey A. Graham for the development of that property, we find the defendant guilty. On the third count, of failing to exercise due vigilance in the disbursement of those funds, we find the defendant guilty. On the fourth, the conspiracy charge, we find the defendant not guilty. Ladies and gentlemen, we have had a long morning and it is now past noon. The Court wishes some time for reflection, for looking at certain sections of the transcript. We therefore will adjourn until 3:30 P.M. and reconvene at that time for sentencing." Houston rapped the hardwood and was gone. And my father-in-law stood convicted of two felonies which could mean that he would spend the rest of his life in a federal penitentiary, notwithstanding the loss of the James River estate which had been in his family for more than two centuries.

We didn't drive back out. We repaired with Herb and the entire entourage to the Generals' Club. From the colonel's locker—over-the-counter whiskey sales being illegal—we sampled fiery libations, and we lingered long over a luncheon that started with bluepoint oysters on the half shell. Stanwick tried to joke. He dunked an oyster into catsup laced with grated horseradish, downed it, and said, "Not much grub like that in the pen."

"You won't go to the pen, Colonel," Herb said. "We can keep this thing going for years on appeal."

Mason dunked another oyster, swirling it liberally in the sauce, and said, "Herb, no appeal. This has been a fair and proper trial, and I will pay whatever penalty the court prescribes. Incidentally, I think you were first-rate. You had no case at all, but you made it appear that you had. And all those old farmers you dug up. I had forgotten most of them, but they're the salt of the earth."

"And they're walking around free," Patricia protested. "And they have their land because you bent a few rules for them."

"They should be free," Mason said. "Not one of them, not a single one, reneged on me. But, Herb, you know that old guy who wanted to serve my term? Send him up to see me when they put me in the hoosegow. He won't be so easy with the answers once he sees what bars are like."

We lingered over roast wild duck, and I spit out a few shot. We made the strong, black coffee last until the pot was cool, and we had a good snifter. And then it was time to go back to the courthouse.

It was not a long walk, and the colonel led the way, just as, I imagined, he had marched in front of those boys in France, leading the charge against the enemy. I was dragging Patricia, because she wanted to cry. But she didn't cry when we took our seats, and she didn't cry when Judge Houston's door burst open and he glided, robe slightly askew, to the mercy seat. We all stood for the mumbling, and then we sat down in silence.

Houston began his monologue. "I have reviewed the evidence," he said, "and I have talked with the probation officers. They told me nothing I didn't already know." He stopped, looked up and frowned. There was commotion in the corridor, and then the courtroom door opened smartly and a commanding presence strode down the aisle. I glanced over my shoulder and froze.

It was Sam, in all his senatorial splendor.

"Your Honor," Sam said, "might I approach the bench?"

"The distinguished Senator from Maryland is always welcome in this Court," Houston said.

The bailiff held the swinging door, and Sam faced the judge. "Your Honor," he said slowly, "I appreciate the consideration of the Court in allowing me to say a few words here. Obviously, I am not disinterested. My chief assistant, the man who helped me launch my campaign against the Communist conspiracy in this country, is Colonel Mason's son-in-law. It was my honor and privilege to be best man at his wedding to Patricia Mason, that beautiful young lady sitting out there so bravely and with such concern for her father's future. I have followed the proceedings here carefully and know every detail of the testimony, so I don't speak out of blind ignorance. Whatever the circumstances which have brought him here, Colonel Mason, that fine old Virginian, whose family has served this country as ably as any you could name, is typical of the best that our society has to offer. The very best. There has not been a showing here that there is a dishonest bone in his body. Or a disloyal one. Your Honor, this man is pure gold, unalloyed, a compassionate man, a sensible man, a man who has quietly helped forge a Virginia society which knows no equal. I would remind this court of the Shakespearean lines, uttered by Portia, ringing down through the ages: 'The quality of mercy is not strain'd/ It droppeth as the gentle rain from heaven/ Upon the place beneath: it is twice blest;/ It blesseth him that gives and him that takes.' And there is another line in there, not quite so well known. It says that mercy is 'an attribute to God himself.' And so I would encourage this Court, in passing sentence this afternoon, to be 'a Daniel come to judgment.' Those lines I address to the bench, but I would speak also to the defendant, in words enshrined in holy writ: 'Blessed are the merciful, for they shall obtain mercy.' That is the promise of the Redeemer Himself. Here we have Colonel Mason, brought low, humiliated, his reputation demeaned, the infamy of this trial to weigh upon his shoulders the rest of his life. But as the testimony has shown, without dispute, he has been, all his years, a merciful man. Merciful. I don't think he should have to wait until he reaches the streets of gold to claim his reward. He should obtain mercy now."

Sam shifted gears, looking around him, back toward the spellbound spectators held in thrall by this man with the magic name, and then he began again. "There is a little matter here," he said, "that can easily be cleared up. I have made inquiry, and the shortfall of Commonwealth Federal Savings and Loan now stands at $122,000. Colonel Mason proposes to make up that loss by selling Mason's Bluff, the estate that has been in his family for generations. Your Honor, over a period of a few hours I have canvassed a number of the Mason family's friends—important people who drive Cadillacs, simple folk who drive tractors. They would be unhappy if the result of all this were to take the Bluff out of the hands of the Mason line. So they have made up a kitty." He reached into his inside coat pocket. "I hold here," he said, pronouncing each word distinctly, "a certified check in the amount of $122,000, which I offer to the Court, representing full and complete restitution. If it should not be enough, more will be forthcoming. We want Colonel Mason to live out his days at home, and for his heirs by Harry and Patricia to follow him if they wish. And I hope this check will take a little of the sting out of this ordeal for my very good friend." Sam stopped again, fingering the check and weighing the moment. "Your Honor," he continued, "I don't think I really have to say anything more, except to point out that in the eyes of Colonel Mason's friends, this piece of paper represents his acquittal." Sam nodded to the Judge and went over and took a seat at the defense table. His gesture filled the room with babble.

Judge Houston signaled for order, and when the chorus had died, he said, "I thank the Senator from Maryland for his remarks. He is skilled in jurisprudence, and this Court attaches a great deal of weight to what he has said here. It has, in fact, slightly altered the Court's thinking in this case. Accordingly, will the defendant please rise?"

Herb France stood up, again pulling Colonel Mason to his feet, and Sam Bradford flanked the old man on the other side.

"On the charge of illegally providing funds to Harvey A. Graham, this court sentences the defendant to two years in the Federal Penitentiary." There was a cry of dismay from the spectators, and Houston resorted once more to the gavel. "On the supervision count, the court sentences the defendant to a concurrent term of two years in the penitentiary." The Judge quickly held up his hand to quell the anticipated outcry. He lowered it slowly. "On condition that the defendant sever all connection with Commonwealth Federal Savings and Loan and never again take up a position of trust in a financial institution, and out of consideration for the fact that full restitution has been made, the sentences are suspended." The Judge looked down at the defense table and smiled. He was smiling not at Mason but at Sam Bradford.

That exchange barely registered with me. I was assaulted by a blond demon, her arms squeezing my neck. Patricia ungracefully climbed over the railing and hugged her father, who was crying unashamedly, hugged Herb France, hugged Sam Bradford and bussed the senator on the cheek. I somewhat more decorously went through the wooden gate, shook hands all around, even with Vince Johnson, and whispered in Sam's ear, "You're a damn liar, but it was in a good cause."

He looked at me in wounded innocence.

"You didn't talk to anybody," I said. "That check came out of the war chest, didn't it?"

He grinned. "Have I ever lied?" he asked.

"No matter," I said as we tried to break through the mob. "We all appreciate it. If you hadn't shown up, I think the colonel would have gotten an active term."

"I was led to believe that," Sam said.

"By whom?" I asked. "Oatmeal? That skinny kid?"

"By the Judge."

In a small, broken party we shouldered our way into the corridor, down the hall, out the front door and down the stone steps. The Cad was at the curb, Numeriano lounging against the fender. "Give anybody a lift?" Sam asked. We demurred, and he walked smartly to the limousine and was borne away amidst a squeal of tires.

Patricia watched him go, and she asked the question that was large on all our minds: "How can we ever repay him?"

☆ **9** ☆

TOWARD THE END OF January we returned to the carriage house in Georgetown. It was good to be home, to feel ourselves in the midst of the small things we had come to love—a vase, a flask, an end table, an old clock—but in the back of my mind there was a nagging worry about Patricia. Normally so outgoing, she was preoccupied, held within herself, restrained, remote, not so easily caught up in sexual rapture. I supposed that it was the after-shock of the trial agonies, and I made no comment, although it involved some personal discomfiture.

The work had piled up at the office, with letters, the details of bills, the usual office procedure. But things were not percolating as usual. On a Tuesday Sam called me into his office, and his mood, normally so easy to read, was unfathomable. On his desk were two cases, and he showed them off proudly to me. "A little belatedly," he said, "but the Navy has seen fit to honor me." He picked up one case: "The Distinguished Flying Cross." And the other: "The Air Medal with four stars."

"What in Christ's name for?" I asked innocently.

"I jogged them a little," Sam said. "Reminded them of my

heroic exploits during the war. Of which you were a part. The Navy doesn't want to be investigated. So I have these handsome medals. Good politics."

"We'll get out a release," I said.

"Nah," Sam said. "The Navy PIO is doing that. Better it should come from those fat asses. They haven't got anything better to do. But we have. There's more serious business. Have you seen the *Record* for Friday?"

"I glanced through it," I said. "Dull stuff."

"Did you happen to look at the appendix?"

"I never wade through all that crap. Should I have?"

"This once, yeah. Becker slipped one in. He submitted some editorials."

"We got ten thousand editorials."

"Not like this. There's a little place called Sanford, Ohio."

"I never heard of it."

"Neither did I. But Sanford, Ohio, has a rinkydink newspaper called the *Sanford Herald.* And the editor of the *Sanford Herald* thinks I'm a shit."

"Does the *Sanford Herald* have national distribution? Does the son of a bitch think he's William Allen White on the masthead of the *Emporia Gazette?*"

"Wouldn't make any difference. But the editor of the *Herald* has written some very bad things about me. 'Charlatan.' 'Chameleon.' 'A veritable danger to the fabric of American life.' Now you know I have never made a frontal assault on the press. And largely because you counseled me not to. But I don't like this stuff the *Herald* editor wrote."

"I wouldn't suspect that you would be his most ardent subscriber."

"I wouldn't care too much if he were sounding off only for Sanford, Ohio. But these things got into the appendix of the *Record.* Which gives them some stature."

"So what do you want me to do?"

"I want to crucify the mothuh."

"And I'm anointed to be the crucifier?"

"You heard right. I want you to go out to Sanford, Ohio —wherever the hell that is—and put this bastard out of business."

"Destroy him?"

"That's the idea. Can you do it?"

"Sure. I know how to murder a small town newspaper. If it were *The New York Times,* we couldn't do it. But in a small town, population 236, we can do it. There will be a matter of a minor cash flow."

"No problem."

"How much am I allowed?"

"Harry, there are over two million dollars in the war chest. Obviously, I don't want to deplete it. But how much will it take? I mean, to rub this sonabitch's nose in the goddamn Ohio turf? As a kind of object lesson?"

"We won't even scratch the surface. I think I can do it with twenty-five thousand. Forty at the outside. No big goddamn deal. But, Sam, I won't enjoy it."

"I ain't askin' you to have a ball. I'm askin' you to do a job."

"I can do it."

"Then, get out there."

I went back out to the reception room and told Selma, "Find out where in God's name is Sanford, Ohio, and figure out how to get me there."

"Official biz?" she asked.

"From the throne of grace."

She consulted her charts and the astrological signs, and after a while she came over to me and said, "The best way to get there is to fly into Cleveland, rent a car and drive about a hundred miles due west."

"Well, get it rolling. Lay on the flight and the rental and

book me into the best hostelry in Sanford and sound as official as the Angel Gabriel. I want Sanford, Ohio, to know that a really big wheel is rolling into town."

"Aye, aye, Big Wheel," Selma said. "Are there any Communists in Sanford, Ohio?"

"You wouldn't believe. They are an affront to the nostrils of all right-smelling Americans."

Selma booked me on an Eastern flight, and I picked up the Hertz Ford on a bright Wednesday afternoon and drove over toward Sanford, which wasn't too far off Lake Erie. I had reservations at the Sanford Buckeye, an old hotel in the center of town, and when I checked in a female clerk with dyed red hair and a nasal twang said deferentially, "You are the gentleman from Washington?"

"That's right."

"Will you be here long?" She tried a crooked smile which showed her bad teeth. "Don't mistake me. We can accommodate you."

I shook my head. "I'm not really sure how long I'll be here. Just try to put up with me."

"That shouldn't be too difficult. Is there anything special I can help you with?"

"Yes, thanks," I said. "I kinda need to get my bearings. Where do I find the bank?"

"There's a branch of Central Ohio a block down the street."

"Fine. And could you put me onto a printer?"

"There's a job shop two blocks over on State Street."

"State Street. Okay. The public library?"

"Certainly. On Independence Square. Open nine to twelve." She rummaged in a drawer and pulled out a simple city map. "Let me mark these things for you."

"Very kind of you," I said. "One last question. Does the hotel have hot and cold running water?"

"Oh, yes—but you're joking, aren't you, Mr. Dodge?"

"A little bit. But I've stayed in hotels that had no hot water."

"If there's any problem, call me."

She tinkled an old-fashioned bell with the palm of her hand, and a 120-year-old bellhop in a faded uniform came for my bag. We took the rickety elevator up to Room 304, and I gave him a dollar and his heart almost failed him.

By the time I had put my shirts away and hung up the spare suit I was feeling hunger pangs, and I went down to the coffee shop and waited to be seated. No one came to do it, so I took a table overlooking the street. The place was almost empty, but the chubby waitress in soiled white took her time finding me, at the moment being absorbed in a comic book.

"I didn't mean to interrupt your reading," I said. "I like to see people improve their minds." She was chewing gum and she stopped in mid-chomp and gave me a very strange look. "What's the specialty of the house?" I asked.

"I been working here on the late shift five years," she said, "and that's the first time anybody ever asked me that."

"What would you recommend to your best friend?"

"To go somewhere else."

"I'll remember that next time, but tonight I feel like gambling," I said. I studied the worn menu she handed me. Most of the flocking had worn off the cover and the gold buckeye was barely distinguishable. "What's the soup du jour?"

"Green split pea. Always green split pea."

"I'm not into peas much," I said. "I'll settle for a tomato juice, a rare Delmonico and a baked potato."

"Anything to drink?"

"What did you have in mind?"

"We have an extensive wine list. Two reds, two whites, and a rosé."

"I think not. I'm a prohibitionist."

"Sorry. I didn't know. Could I bring you some water?"

"I hope so. And maybe a carafe of coffee."

She shuffled off, working at the gum, and eventually brought my dinner. It was adequate.

When I passed the desk, the redhead was still on duty. "Could you send me up some ice?" I asked.

"I was sure you mixed your drinks with hot water," she said. "Something will be coming up to you."

I went on up to the room, and in about fifteen minutes there was a tentative knock at the door. *"Entrez,"* I said.

She had brought the ice herself, in a styrofoam bucket. "I'm on my break," she explained.

"Then maybe you'll have one with me," I said. I dug out the Jack Daniels and started icing two of the spotted glasses, but she said, "I'll take mine neat. But not too much. I might do something foolish." I poured her one and did something light for myself with the ice, and when I handed her her glass I said, "What is the most exciting thing in this town?"

"Besides me?"

"Well, otherwise."

"Lover's leap," she said. "It's the dead end of a road, and people actually have killed themselves."

"Have you ever been there?"

"Not for jumping-off purposes. But I've been there a lot of times."

"I don't mean to offend you," I said, "but I don't go to lover's leaps. Or neck in parked cars."

She put her glass down and excused herself and went to the bathroom, and I could hear water running and various rustlings. When she came back out she was naked except for her shoes. She wasn't a glamorous specimen. Her thin breasts drooped and there were stretch marks on her bulging abdomen. "Don't get me wrong," she said. "I'm not play for pay."

"Honey," I said, "we've got so much loose stuff floating around Washington that we have to export it. Foreign aid. Finish your drink."

She sat nude in the worn chair and said, "I'm sorry. I misjudged you."

"No offense intended, but I'm married to a pretty exclusive dish. You've been married too, haven't you?"

She touched her belly, fingering the marks above the scraggly yellowing bush. "It wasn't anything very serious. I had a little girl. Stillborn." She tossed off her drink with finality and stood up, a rather forlorn creature. "It was worth investigating," she said, heading for the bathroom, and as she dressed she called out, "Thanks for the drink, and if you change your mind . . ."

"I know where to find you," I said, ushering her out.

I made myself another Jack Daniels, and set the alarm for 7 A.M. By 7:30 I was up, bathed, shaved, and ready for breakfast. The bacon was rancid and the eggs were cold and I longed for some grits, but I buttered the English muffin and spread it liberally with marmalade, washing it down with very weak coffee.

At a little after nine I strolled into the library and went to the newspaper rack and sorted through the *Plain-Dealer* and the *Blade* until I found the thin version of the daily *Sanford Herald*. There was a whole week of reading, and I had not come to browse. I made notes on the display ads, calculating the linage of the Bestway Supermarket and the Great Northern Ohio, GNO for short. There were two major auto dealerships, three dry goods stores and an assortment of electrical, sporting and automotive equipment dealers. There were not many classifieds, and real estate companies showed up in only two display ads. The news hole was about fifty percent, which was a very bad ratio financially. To my mind, from what I could see, the newspaper was skirting the thin edge. For its economic health, a newspaper ought to be about seventy percent ads and thirty percent news.

I put the papers back on the rack and walked down to the

Central Ohio Bank not far away. I avoided the tellers and found a receptionist who seemed to be running interference for some very important personage. I handed her my card. It was one of those beauties that I had had made up, with the picture and the United States seal and the "United States Senate" in bold Garamond type and the signature of the most famous man in the United States.

"I was hoping to have a few words with your boss," I said.

"Mr. Prestwick?"

"If he's the president."

"Nearest thing we've got. Executive vice president. He owned the bank before it merged with Central Ohio ten years ago."

"He'd be my man."

"Let me check." She pushed an intercom button and spoke briefly, and then she said, "You can go on in."

I pulled the door open and went into the inner office with my card in my hand. "Mr. Prestwick," I said, "I'm Harry Dodge. Washington. I've been talking to some people at Ohio Central headquarters in Cleveland, and they said I could confide in you."

Prestwick fingered the card as if it were gold. "Did they say that?" he said, seemingly delighted. He was a short, fat man whose coat strained at the buttons.

"I hope you can understand that I'm here on some rather sensitive business," I said. "I'd rather that our talk be just between us."

"Oh, I understand that," he said. "The United States Senate. I never thought . . ."

"It happens," I said. "We're interested in Ray Emmons."

"Emmons?"

"Yeah. Your crusading editor."

"Not my crusading editor. A pain in the ass, if you'll pardon the expression."

"My sentiments exactly. Now, in general terms—and I'm

not asking you to reveal confidential information—what is his financial situation?"

Prestwick hedged. "I can't go into that," he said. "There are rules in banking."

"I know there are," I said, "and I think I should tell you that there is a great deal of interest in banking in Washington. Senator Bradford is very close to the Banking Committee and—what day is this, Thursday?—I think by next Wednesday I could have a whole platoon of auditors in here looking at every cent you've got. And then there could be difficulties with the Internal Revenue boys. I don't think you want to go through all that."

Prestwick's face had lost all its color. "No, I don't," he said. "And you could make all that happen, too, couldn't you?"

"I promise you I could. So why don't we talk a little bit about Ray Emmons?"

The banker was suddenly eager to cooperate. "Well, Emmons is in a rather shaky financial position."

"How shaky?"

"Well, let me run over it with you, without mentioning specific figures. He came here about three years ago. Had been an editorial writer in Detroit and wanted to run his own newspaper. They say . . ."

"Every newspaperman wants to do it eventually."

"Yeah, so I'm told. The *Herald* was a weekly then, not much of a rag, but it carried the town gossip. Who had Sunday dinner with whom, who was visiting in town. We were all comfortable with it and didn't expect more. Everybody took one of the big papers for the hard news. Emmons picked it up for $23,000, an estate sale. We loaned him about eighteen. Couldn't lose. It was a good property. Only outlet for local advertising. And he's been good credit. Comes up with the dough on time. But he got in over his head. Had it in mind to turn the *Herald* into a daily. Needed money for a new press, really a used offset, and he came back to us. Took a second mortgage on his house. And then he had kids going to college. It's really touch and go now. And he hasn't got any liquid assets. Everything is in the paper."

"How old a man?"

"Forties."

"What don't you like about him?"

"Well, Sanford's no Detroit. About 7,000 population. And we didn't need an editor kicking everybody's butt."

"Real hell-raiser?"

"Nose into everything. Some of it none of his business. You know. Race stuff. Schoolbooks. New library. Pave everything. We don't need that kind of annoyance."

"If he fell behind, couldn't come up with the ante, would you call his paper?"

"Well, normally, little town like this, we'd try to work something out. Give him an extension. But if we had a good reason . . ."

"I'm here, and I'm after his ass. Isn't that a good reason? Emmons has been writing some bad things about Sam Bradford."

"I read that stuff. Sounded like Communist talk to me. But I wouldn't think anything in the *Herald* would percolate all the way to Washington."

"It did. Even showed up in the *Congressional Record.* Sam didn't like that."

"Well, hell, why doesn't Bradford investigate him?"

"We'd rather ruin him. Take away his paper. That would hurt him more than anything else."

"How long you think it'll take?"

"Well, we're in February. He won't meet his March payment."

"All right, we'll call his paper."

"Thank you."

"And will you tell Cleveland I cooperated?"

"I sure will."

I nodded to him, winked at his receptionist, and walked over a couple blocks to State Street. The Star Printing Company was on a corner next to an overgrown vacant lot, and there was no one at the long counter when I walked in. I could hear machinery clanking behind the false wall, and I went around the counter and pushed open the door to the shop. A wiry fellow of about fifty was sitting at a linotype, and he looked up at me through his green eyeshade. "Girl's got the flu," he said.

"Lot of that around," I said.

"Doin' some church bulletins," he said. "Got about another stick here. Can you wait a minute?"

I nodded and walked around the shop, grateful for the warmth of the molten lead. Besides the one linotype, which appeared to be a Mergenthaler original, he had an old flatbed that had seen little recent use, a Ludlow, a paper cutter and various other pieces of hard-worn equipment associated with job work. Along a rear wall there were carelessly arranged stacks of supplies. I heard the last slug fall and the power checked, and I followed the printer to a scarred old oak desk piled high with copy and layouts.

He turned and held out an inky hand. "Name's Benson," he said. "I hope you brought me some work."

"Might have," I said. I handed him the identity card and he looked at it and scrambled through a drawer for a pair of glasses and looked at it again before handing it back. "Don't get many visitors here from Washington, Mr. Dodge," he said. "I'da known who you were I'da washed my hands." He threw some papers off a straight-backed chair and said, "Set down and tell me what's on your mind."

"You know Ray Emmons?"

He shifted the plug in his mouth and missed the cuspidor and said, "Too well."

"No love lost?"

"None 'tall."

"Mind tellin' me why?"

"Nope, unless you come down here to investigate me. Wouldn't find out much. 'Cept that I'm a cranky old man."

"Nothing like that."

"Well, tell ya. He beat me out of the *Herald.* I got this wuthless son-in-law over in Elyria thinks he's a journalist. When old man Gramley died—it was his paper—I had it in mind to buy the *Herald* and install Marvin over there—Marvin's muh son-in-law—as a real journalist. Works over in Elyria now. Chases fire engines, best I can tell. He's dumb, but he's not too dumb to run the *Herald.* Nobody is. But Emmons, he come along and offered the heirs more'n the paper was wuth, 'n I got left out in the cold. You see, if I coulda brought Marvin over here, I coulda put up with him bein' a asshole just so I could of had Brenda and the grandchildren with me. Wife's dead. All the family I got. An' that's why I got no use for Ray Emmons. In a nutshell."

"Well, I think we can get Marvin over here, and Brenda, and—how many grandchildren?"

"They's three. But I ain't followin' you at all. An' I ain't dumb, Mr. Dodge. I can still put the square pegs in the square holes."

"With what you've got here, could you publish a newspaper?"

He looked around him and shook his head. "I don't think so."

"I don't mean a real newspaper. I mean about eight pages of advertising twice a week."

"I could maybe do a tabloid. But where'n hell would I get the ads? Everybody goes to the *Herald.*"

"They're gonna stop."

Benson looked at me appraisingly. "You gonna steal the *Herald's* revenue? Old Sam Bradford musta got pretty hot under the collar."

"We propose to make an object lesson out of Ray Emmons. How much would an eight-page tabloid cost?"

"Oh, couple hundred. Ad revenue'd take care of that."

"No revenue. The ads'll be free."

"Then who pays?"

"I do."

"For how long?"

"Long as it takes. A month. Six weeks. A year."

"So when do we crank up this Trojan Horse?"

"I'd imagine the *Herald* has its advertising lined up for this week. Why don't we shoot for the first issue Monday, with a Monday and Thursday schedule? Can you round up twenty or thirty kids for the distribution?"

"I'll turn out a couple Boy Scout troops."

"I haven't talked to the advertisers yet."

"You flash that card, they'll shit their pants."

"It'd be my idea to stay here about a week or ten days to get things rolling. Could you bring Marvin down here to take over? On salary, of course."

"I think Marvin's makin' 'bout fifty bucks a week on the police beat over there in Elyria. Would you go seventy-five for him? Not that he's wuth it."

"Sure. But one thing you have to understand. Once you're in control of the *Herald,* we're out of it. Marvin'll have to make it on his own."

"I'm not lookin' for no subsidy."

"And we'd be obliged if our part in this little . . ."

"Sabotage?" he put in craftily.

"That's right. We wouldn't want it to be broadcast."

"It won't get out from me. But there ain't no secrets in this town. Was one of Ray's problems. He tried to uncover skullduggery where there warn't none. No secrets here." He chewed his tobacco thoughtfully. "Tell you the kinda thing I mean. I'll lay you odds that redhead over't the hotel, Irma, tried to crawl in your sack last night."

I was slightly shocked. "She did indicate her availability for that purpose," I said.

"Pathetic case," Benson said. "Used to be as prim an'

proper a lady as ya'd expect to meet anywhere. Kind of a straw-colored blonde then. Married to a construction worker, pretty nice chap. One night he drove his car into a tree. Kilt him, kilt the woman that was with him. Irma was about seven months along, an' she lost the baby, an' somethin' in her snapped. Ever since, she's been the town party girl. Ya see, no secrets."

"Sorry about Irma," I said. "'Fraid I didn't treat her very gently."

"Good thing you didn't treat her at all. Prob'ly give you a dose. That's rumor, too."

"Well, I don't care if my business is rumored. But I wouldn't take it kindly if Marv did an in-depth analysis of the palace revolution on the front page of his first issue."

"Mr. Dodge," Benson said, "I don't like to badmouth nobody, especially my own kin, but Marvin, he couldn't analyze the operation of a kitchen match. When can you get me the first ad copy? An' I gotta order newsprint from Cleveland. That'll take a spot of cash."

"Suppose I advance you five thousand? You can receipt me on it."

He looked at me in amazement. "You carryin' five grand on you?"

I laughed. "Letter of credit," I said. "I'll bring the first ad copy around in the morning. One other thing. Work up an announcement. For the period of the emergency, we'll accept classifieds free."

He nodded, dug in a drawer of his desk and brought out a pint and two paper cups. "Would you have a dram with me to seal the bargain?" he asked.

"Best way I know," I said, and he doled out two good shots.

"Drink it fast," he said, downing his at one gulp. "The alcohol in this stuff melts the wax. No tellin' what it does to your stomach." I tossed it off, and it was red-hot. Coughing, I turned to leave.

"Hey, what we gonna call this thing?" he boomed after me. "Gotta have a flag."

"You think of something," I said. " 'The Sodomite,' or some other appropriate nomenclature." I could hear him chuckling after me.

The approach to the advertising community did not bring on quite the epidemic of diarrhea that Benson had predicted, but there were a lot of tight sphincters in Sanford, Ohio. My reception ranged from outright genial, as at Central Chevy-Olds and Crossroads Ford-Mercury, to the suspicious, at the Great Northern supermarket, where the manager and butcher, Teddy O'Toole, had to call the regional office in Akron for clearance before succumbing. When he mentioned Washington, however, his face all of a sudden lost its hamburger ruddiness and, white with apology, he stuttered his agreement. Akron wanted no part of a collision with Sam Bradford. By the end of the week I had hit every business in town, the two realtors, the florist, the radio shop, three restaurants and all the apparel outlets, a dealer in office supplies and baseball bats and the combination auto supply-hardware that also sold feed and farm implements. For good measure I called on the mortuary, an ice-cream parlor and a few other specialty operations that didn't normally advertise.

Ray Emmons must have wondered what blind alley he had wandered into on Monday afternoon when his *Herald* hit the streets with only two national ads and the small layout of classifieds, to be followed an hour later by the tabloid blanket, the *Sanford Index,* which carried more than his usual display of local advertisers.

Marvin Foust, the printer's son-in-law, was a pleasant surprise. He was not the dumb-ass old Benson had led me to expect. A small fellow, about five six, educated at Kent State, studious, but no good with machinery. "Trouble is," Benson complained, "he ain't got no common sense. He can't even saw a straight line." But you don't saw with a typewriter, and

I sensed that young Marv would make a reasonable, conservative editor for the *Herald*. He wasn't much help with the *Index*, except as a proofreader, but we needed one. Benson didn't give a damn about spelling. And the younger man supervised the kids in distributing the tabloid. He knew the town well and wasted no copies on the shacks where ads are not read.

By Thursday, after what seemed like ten days on the Sanford job, I was ready to leave, and I phoned Sam and gave him a complete report. The *Herald* was going to expire within a month, the town would be left with a good paper, and there would be no more potshots at royalty. "Would you ask Selma to call Trish and tell her I'll be in tomorrow?" I asked.

"Hell, I'll call her myself," Sam said. "Always glad to be the bearer of good tidings."

I rang off and went down to the coffee shop for a leisurely dinner, lamb chops with mint jelly and some fresh asparagus. I had returned to my room, read awhile, put on my pajamas and brushed my teeth when I had a sudden urge to call Trish. I gave the operator my Georgetown number, and there was a faint ringing at the other end. By the sixth ring she hadn't answered, and I was wondering vaguely where she might be when there was a rap at my door. I flung it open, half expecting to see Irma giving it one more try, and there stood a nondescript man, puffed pockets of worry under his eyes.

"Are you Dodge?" he asked.

"Yeah."

"Do you mind if I come in? I'm Emmons."

I motioned him in and asked, "Can I offer you a drink?"

"Not if Sam Bradford paid for it."

"It's Jack Daniels. Black Label. I bought it myself."

"Then I'll have one."

I made two drinks and thrust one at him, and he gulped it as if booze were on the rationed list. I made him another and handed it to him, and I asked, "What can I do for you?"

"Tell me why. I'm a small-town editor, and you come in and wreck my paper."

"That's about the size of it," I said.

"The First Amendment guarantees a free press in this country. Where did that go?"

"You interpret the Bill of Rights a bit liberally. A free press, yes. You can say anything you want to. But that doesn't insure you against retaliation."

"But I thought . . ."

"You didn't think, did you? Not really. You wrote those editorials denouncing Sam Bradford. That was your right. And you sent cuttings to anti-Bradford senators. Nobody restrained you. And the editorials were read into the *Congressional Record*, as a malicious attack on Bradford, who is my boss. Big deal, to be reprinted in the *Record*. But the Constitution doesn't protect you from lawful reprisal. It doesn't order your advertisers to spend their money with you. We have a free press. And you made the most of it. But the free press has to be ready to stand on its own."

"Bradford is an evil man. Don't you understand that?"

"I work for Sam."

"How can you do that?"

"It pays the bills."

"Do you know what this paper means to me?"

"I think I do."

"Then how can you be a party to what is happening? I have a wife, kids, expenses."

"Did you think about them when you sat down at the hot keyboard and wrote all that stuff about Sam Bradford?"

He shook his head. "Can I have another?" He held out the dirty glass, and I sloshed it full. "I didn't think about them," he said. "I thought about myself as a responsible editor, as a devout American."

"And now, for the sake of your integrity, everybody pays the price."

"Honest to God, it never entered my mind that Bradford would turn his hand to a little editor in a backwater town."

"But in circulating what you wrote, you must've wanted some kind of recognition."

"I was proud. They were well-reasoned."

"So what did you want?" I said angrily. "The goddamn Pulitzer Prize?"

He collapsed. "I suppose so."

"So was it worth it? Was it really worth it? You dumb-ass. You didn't get the Pulitzer Prize. You got the Bradford Shaft. And where are you? How much better off?"

"It was a mistake in judgment."

"And for your fucking mistake, who pays? The wife and kids. Don't come bleating to me."

He stood, unsteadily. "I didn't expect any compassion," he said. "I just wanted to see what kind of man you were, who could do this to me. You're not a Fascist. You're not even a Bradfordite. I mean in ultimate persuasion. Sooner or later, it will touch you, too."

"It well might," I said. "But I won't come around pleading for mercy."

"It will touch you."

"Get the hell out. Go home to your wife and kids. Tell them you goofed. Not me, for Christ's sake."

He shuffled out, and in all my life I have never felt sorrier for any man.

Except once.

I GOT BACK INTO Washington at about 1:30 Friday afternoon and went straight from National Airport to the office. I stowed the suitcase in a corner and turned, and there was Selma, sniveling, her eyes red, looking as if she hadn't slept in forty-nine nights. I went over to her and chucked her under the chin familiarly and said, "What in the hell is the matter with you? You look like the walking dead."

My attempt at humor only brought on fresh tears, and I saw that something serious was troubling her. I took her face in my hands and said, "Selma, this is your old boss talking. Why are you coming unglued?"

"I don't want to talk about it," she said.

"Talk about it."

She girded herself. "Last night," she said, gulping like a bowled fish, "the Senator called me. He wanted me to bring some papers out to his apartment. I've done it before."

"Don't tell me the bastard seduced you?"

"N-no. I got the papers, and I took a cab out to the Tower and went up on the elevator and knocked on his door. He was in his bathrobe, with nothing on under it, and he acted as if he had company."

"So he had a broad. It's not the first time. He's an adult male."

"I don't want to tell you this."

There was something in her voice that made me feel small flutters of alarm, but I said, "Tell me."

"I went inside. You know, to put the papers down. And Mrs. Dodge's bag was there, and her coat."

It was the one thing I was not prepared for, and I temporized. "A lot of women have a bag like Patricia's. And a coat."

"I know. I know," Selma whimpered, "and I kept telling myself that. But I went out in the parking lot and I wandered around until I found a black MG, like hers."

"Go on."

"And I know it was wrong, but I stayed there, huddled against the cars—so cold—until about 4 A.M. And then Mrs. Dodge came out and got in her car and drove away. Very fast. I'm so sor-r-y." And then she went to boo-hooing again.

I patted Selma on the head, comforting her, but I couldn't control the great ball of wrath I was feeling in my chest, a giant bubble waiting to burst. I went over to the Senator's door and flung it open. He was there, drinking rye, and I stared at him, a stare of about two million volts that would have laid most men out. Sam greeted me with a smile, and the smile faded as I stood there. The scowl came on, and he put out his hands defensively. "Harry," he said, "you know me. I always collect my debts. Cunt is cunt, and every woman has her price."

I advanced a step into the room and said, "I ought to punch you into the middle of next week." But then a blind rage paralyzed me. I slammed the door, got my bag and motioned to Numeriano, who was totally bewildered. "Get me out of here!" I said.

"Sure, Lieutenant," Numeriano said. I followed him to the Cadillac and I didn't sit in front with him but in the back and I told him to take me to Georgetown.

I almost took the door of the car off at our place on N Street, and I told Numeriano to get the hell out and I stormed into our carriage house.

It was empty and cold.

I put the bag down, with its dirty clothes, and stalked through the premises, so chilling, and I didn't see the note until I had made myself a big drink and plopped down on the sofa. In the neat, round hand, with the circles for dots over the i's. "I have had to go away to sort out my life. Please do not follow me or attempt to get in touch with me. Believe me, truly, when I tell you that I love you with all my heart and soul."

She loved me. A strange way to show it. I have said that I felt sorry for Emmons, because he lost his paper. I had lost something infinitely more precious to me and I now felt sorrier for myself. I made myself another drink and sat reflecting. No doubt she had gone to Mason's Bluff, the well-spring of her line. I could find her there, and shake her, and shake her, and shake her. But there was her injunction: "Please do not follow me or attempt to get in touch with me." I should give her that comfort. Follow her? A cuckold? That would be the day. I had turned up the heat, and I whipped off my coat in preparation for one grand binge. Out of my breast pocket came the little book. I opened it to "M" and under "M" the name "Meg" appeared. And a number I had written down in all carelessness.

I picked up the book, went to the telephone, dialed the operator and gave her the Valley number in Baltimore County. In the distance, a hundred miles away, a phone rang. It rang and rang, and I was about to hang up the instrument and settle for solitude and Jack Daniels when the voice came on the line, very cool, very remote, "Hello." It was absolutely neutral.

"Meg?" I said.

"Yes?" Still distant.

"Harry Dodge."

She expelled her breath huskily. "I knew you would call."

"I'm calling."

"And . . . ?"

"Could we meet somewhere?"

"Do you want me to come to Georgetown?"

"No." Puritan principles.

"What do you have in mind? An hour? A day? Or some more extended period?"

"Nothing short-term."

"Then I think our place on the Bay. Do you know where Mayo is, down below Annapolis?"

"No."

"It's 214 out of Washington. Take it all the way, and when the road ends, you'll be in Mayo. Go through town and take a dirt road to the Bay, about a half a mile. It's the last house on the right. If you get lost, ask anybody where the Symington Roost is. But it's about twice as far for me, so give me time. I can't be there before six this afternoon."

"Okay, I'll try to make it about then."

"Don't give me out. And Harry?"

"Yes."

"Thanks for remembering."

I had some time to kill, and I wandered through the rooms. There were all her things, the little knick-knacks and curios she had collected, some as a girl, the walls she had rollered, her scents in the bedroom. I slid open her closet, and all the gear of the female was there, the old, familiar things, the sheer nighties, neatly arranged. She was not extravagant with clothes, and I knew every piece, had helped with zippers and catches. I stared at the telephone. It would be so easy to call Mason's Bluff and to say that I shared her hurt. But I wasn't ready for that, nor, apparently, was she. My own gorge rose at the thought. I threw a few things in a bag and wheeled out the Studebaker. It responded sluggishly, and I made a mental note to have it tuned. And the MG, too. Patricia thought oil lasted forever. She had no concept of maintenance.

The map in the glove compartment showed 214, and I drove back up past the Capitol, around the House side, hit Independence and turned off toward Capitol Heights to pick up the highway. I drove rather aimlessly, slowly, taking in the landscape of Prince Georges and Anne Arundel, which was not remarkable. I tried to remember who the hell Anne Arundel was to get a Maryland county named after her, but nothing came to me. More pressing was the certainty that I was going to get laid in Anne Arundel, by a blueblood probably more regal than the dam of this turf. I rolled into Mayo at about 5:30 and it was rush hour and there were two cars on the streets. The road went on toward Beverly Beach, and I wondered if Meg had steered me wrong. I knew she wouldn't do that intentionally, and I stopped at a Gulf station and bought some high test and had the oil checked, and when I was paying the man, I said, "I'm looking for Jack Symington's place."

"The Roost? That dirt road down there to the left," he said, and gave me change for a ten. "Don't nobody go there much this time of year," he volunteered. "All them summer places is closed up."

"He gave me the use of it," I said, and pulled away and turned off on the dirt road until it dead-ended in a turnaround overlooking the Bay. I killed the engine and got out and looked around, and the breeze off the water was fresh and I buttoned up my heavy jacket and was glad I had worn gloves. The Symington place as right there, done in weathered shingles with a boathouse down the hill and a Chris-Craft chained up out of the water. I went down there and looked at it, and there were only the gulls and me and *Gracie,* which was stenciled on the stern of the boat, reminding me that Meg had children. I was looking in at the depth finder when there was a purr of powerful machinery on the turnaround. I two-stepped up the grade as Meg was getting out of the car, a black tank the likes of which I had never seen before except in pictures.

"What in God's name are you driving?" I asked.

She got out of the car on the wrong side, her trim black slacks tight under a red parka. "It's a London cab," she said. "See the glass divider?"

"How on earth did you come by that?"

"We had hailed one near Buckingham Palace one day, and I happened to say to Jack how much fun it would be to drive one around Baltimore. He bought it on the spot and had it shipped home. Only trouble, we have to fly in parts if anything goes wrong. It's got over two hundred thousand miles on it. Here, take the grub."

I loaded myself with two Food Fair bags and she got out a small suitcase and a cosmetics kit and we climbed the steps to the front porch of the house. The key was under the doormat. "I should have told you," Meg said. "You could have gone in and turned up the thermostat. It'll take an hour to make the old Roost livable." She swung open the door and I edged past her with the groceries.

"Let me get my stuff," I said. I ran to the car, extricated my bag and ran back in. I flipped open the suitcase and rummaged for the bottles. "I couldn't remember your drink," I said, "so I brought you gin and scotch. Or you can share my sour mash."

"Scotch," she said, "but there's plenty here. In that cabinet over there. Jack doesn't believe in going dry, not anywhere."

"Then I propose we take some of the chill off the bones."

"There ought to be ice cubes. Maybe a little old. Glasses over the sink." She had tinkered with the furnace controls and I could feel the rumbling in the basement. "One ice cube for me," she said, "and don't stint on the hooch." I made her a double and a long, strong one for me and took them in to where she sat on a plastic sofa rubbing her hands. We clinked glasses, and she said, "I had about given up on you."

I took a deep draft and said, "Your last words were 'moments pass.' You were right."

"Let's don't go into the painful part of it just yet. Later, maybe. For the moment let me enjoy the fact that you called me, for whatever reason." She sat up straight and looked at me with utter seriousness in the dark eyes. "You didn't call anyone else first, did you?"

"Meg," I said, "I speak truly. There is no one else I would have called. I would have gotten soused and had one dilly of a hangover about the first of July."

She dipped her tongue in her drink and wet her lips. "I propose to give you a scotch kiss."

I put my sour mash on the glass-topped coffee table and turned to her, and in our outerwear we were very bulky. But we made the connection, and her tongue licked out and it was eighty proof. I pulled away after a reasonable interval and said, "You know, a few rounds of that and a guy who didn't touch the stuff would be falling down."

"Don't fall down."

"No, I'm fairly tolerant of the alcohol part of it. How long does it take for the heat to come up?"

"Isn't your heat up yet?"

"I don't function too good at zero degrees."

"It takes about two drinks. The radiators will start to hiss pretty soon." She tossed her drink off. "You can make me another."

I gulped mine, took her glass and tended bar. When I turned around, movement outside caught my eye. A dirty black panel truck with small round windows had pulled up in the turnaround and two guys were getting out with fishing gear. "Who the hell would fish this time of year?" I asked as I settled down beside her.

"There are nuts along this shore all the time," she said. "There's nothing out there but sting nettles, but they keep coming." She had wriggled out of her parka and had removed the heavy shoes, and she was down to the black slacks and a vivid red blouse. The combination was feminine, but it was not very suggestive. I handed her the drink, took off my to-boggan and the pea-coat and slouched beside her.

"How long can you stay?" I asked.

"As long as you have need for me."

"What about . . . ?"

"The children? I have a theory about that. The raising of children is best left to professionals. To nannies. I check in with nurse twice a day. She knows where I am. She can reach me at any time."

"What about . . . ?"

"Jack?" She put her fingers to my lips. "No explanations yet, huh? I haven't asked you. We'll have plenty of time for talk. But first, the bedroom is through that door." She motioned with the scotch.

I nodded and took my drink and cigarettes through the door and encountered a massive bed with a pair of night-stands. I placed the drink and the smokes beside the bed and was down to my skivvies when Meg passed me on the way to the adjoining bathroom. I heard water running and the commode flushing and small bottles clinking, and I stretched out on the playground and lit a cigarette.

She came nude out of the bathroom in soft light, and she eyed my softness and said mockingly, "A gentleman should rise when a lady enters the room. This looks like something I'll have to take in hand." But she took it in hand only briefly, with a few deft motions, and then I could feel her lips and the tongue playing indescribably over the glans and the restraining string, and I felt a quick erection, and she came up to me snuggling and said, "You see, you do know your manners."

"I want to start over," I said, the rapidity of the transformation startling me. "Go back to the bathroom and come out again, very slowly." She padded back and I sat on the edge of the bed facing her and watched her emerge, the long, dark hair falling over the shoulders, the full breasts upturned and challenging, the hips most gracefully harp-like. "I think," I

said slowly, "that you are the most beautiful woman I have
ever seen. Or imagined."

"Are you a qualified expert?"

"I think so. I've seen a lot of naked men, with their pot
bellies and the rolls of fat. And women are generally disap-
pointing, the breasts sagging, the belly protruding, the thighs
too heavy. You have none of those faults." I leaned toward
her and with my hands gently traced the lines of the torso.
"There is not a single flaw," I said. "Not one. It's a sight I had
never expected to behold. Uncanny."

"How do I stack up with the Pistol?"

"It's not a fair question. She's got it all, but in miniature. I
have never seen anything more—more full-blown."

"And what is your pleasure?"

I reached up and cupped both of the magnificent breasts,
burying my face in her flat belly. "My God," I groaned.

She inched in beside me, and I took a nipple in my mouth
and stroked the long thighs, walking up to the pubic triangle.
I found her vagina and teased it with light, probing touches.

"Whenever you're ready," she said calmly.

I rolled over on top of her, and she guided the dart expertly. I gave it a few tentative, experimental thrusts, testing
the lubrication, and then I assaulted her with full force. She
pushed me away. "You are angry and hurt," she said, "but
you are trying to peg me to the bed. That isn't the way. I
wasn't part of the other. Now, nice and easy, huh, until we
get a reading?"

With slightly subdued alacrity I rolled over, penetrated
and began a more circumscribed rhythm. "Easy. Controlled.
And I'll tell you when to hit the high notes."

She didn't have to tell me. I sensed the quickening in her,
the fixed anticipation, and I thrust with power and urgency
and she let loose a long, shuddering sigh and the whole galaxy
exploded, in all its wondrous separate parts, and I rolled away
and put my hand on her, and she rose to it, tensed, relaxed,

and I knew that I had made it for her as I had for myself. We lay in silent communion for five minutes, the tide gently ebbing.

"You are very good, Harry," she whispered.

"The right time, the right place," I said.

"You paced it with a perfect touch. Or stroke."

"You were ready. It wasn't my doing, except for a small encouragement."

"God help me," she sighed, "I'm always ready."

I was stroking her, all that perfection, calming her. "You can't be ready all the time." She was recumbent, surrendering, and finally she said, "We have to eat something."

"I don't want to eat. Can't we go on like this?"

"To keep up our strength. A marathon is quite demanding."

"I wouldn't know. What did you bring?"

"I'm not a cook. I never had to do it. So I go for what is simple. Filet mignon, and you can do the salad."

"With filet mignon," I said, burying myself in her breasts, "we don't need a salad."

"The right salads are aphrodisiac."

"It must be the dressing. I think rocquefort is horny."

"We're in business."

She got up and started searching for clothes, and I said, "Nothing opaque," and she settled for a black see-through negligée that left absolutely nothing to the imagination and went into the kitchen. I slipped on the bottoms of my pajamas, and when I got to the kitchen island she was picking bacon to the steaks. I moved in behind her and skipped my hands up the black lace and found her breasts and she placed the toothpicks very insecurely. She put the grill under the broiler and followed me to an armless chair and sat on my legs until my penis found her, and she said, "If they char, it's your fault," but she was already into the rhythm and took it up until she moved violently to shuddering release. "Wiggle,"

I said desperately, for I had not yet climaxed, and she threw her ass into action and I was delivered very quickly.

She disengaged herself and said, "Spinach salad," and pointed me in the direction of the bowl, and while she was in the bathroom I shredded a mass of greenery and doused it liberally with lumpy rocquefort dressing. She had four filets in the broiler, and she whipped up some frozen hash browns and discovered a bottle of French red and we moved most elegantly even if thinly clad into the shank of the evening. We loaded the dishwasher with all the mess, and I put my arm around her waist and urged her back into the bedroom. She allowed me to lead her, fluffed her pillow on end and said, "All right, now tell me what this is all about. The Harry Dodges of this world—and their number is few—don't hide away for a weekend with the Meg Symingtons, whose number is legion."

"Meg, I'm in the dark." I put my hands behind my head, elbows out, and sprawled out for the serious talk. "Really. I was out of town for ten days or so, and when I came back Trish had had a rendezvous with Sam Bradford, and she departed for parts unknown, saying that she wanted to be by herself."

"Oh, my God," Meg said.

"Why are you oh-my-Godding?"

"Sam. If she was with Sam, she's decimated. But she'll have to tell you."

"You had a go with Sam?"

"One evening. One is all it takes."

"What . . . ?"

"Is he like? Trish will tell you, when she's ready. I won't take the edge off it, and I suspect it was a lot more difficult for her. I will tell you that it's a shattering experience. Nothing more, and for good reason. This weekend, you belong to me, and I'll use you."

"Use *me?* You're a goose. I'm using you."

"Well, then, let's say we're in a mutually agreeable pursuit. Let me tell you about Jack and me. It's an explanation I don't generally make."

"I've wondered."

"So have a lot of other people, and the hell with them. I got married when I was twenty-two. Or got married off. Jack was fifty-four, a widower. For the exchange, he settled a million dollars on my mother, in a trust, the residue to accrue to her grandchildren, if any. We had six years and two children, and then Jack announced very casually that he would not indulge further, that it was too likely to bring on a heart attack. He has a great fear of dying. First he brought in a stud, and he wanted to watch. But I don't think sex is a spectator sport, and I wouldn't have any part of it. Then he hired a stable boy with form-fitting dungarees, and I refused to take the bait. So Jack and I made a bargain, and it's in writing somewhere: I was to have perfect freedom, any liaison I desire, with one reservation. I was not, under any circumstances, to become emotionally involved with any lover. So I have Jack's blessing with you. But only up to a point. No emotional strings."

"Meg, that's all right with me, and I think you know that. I wasn't looking for a mistress."

"I know, and that's why I came. But you make it very difficult for me."

"In what way?"

"It's just that you're so damned *decent.* How does one go to bed with you and not become involved? There is the quick lay, which is easily forgotten, and then there is the relationship that is caring."

"Just remember the old masculine rule of thumb, which has been the excuse for rape, incest, I don't know what all—a stiff prick has no conscience."

"And a feminine rule which is not so generally acknowledged, probably because it is feminine—a wet cunt does not discriminate."

"A stand-off for sure, and maybe we can keep it on that basis."

"We can. But you have to know something. It might make a difference."

"Yes?"

"If I were not forbidden to fall in love, I would love you."

"I believe you, Meg. And I want you to know that you are one of the nicest people I have ever been with."

"Screwed, you mean."

"How the hell else do you know anyone?" I asked.

She laughed. "You can't. Not really. The mat. It tells everything."

"How much one is willing to give, and withhold. The protective instinct. The all-too-niceness. A woman who is not whorish in bed is not worth the trouble."

"Am I whorish?"

"Beyond any quality of redemption."

"Would you pay me?"

"Thirty pieces of silver."

"You are a lewd alluder."

"What did you major in? Bible?"

"Literature. With a lot of Bible. The convent."

"I'll give you a doctoral examination in literature."

"Are we going to play doctoral and nurse?"

"A shabby joke. Off with the lace. This is going to be a complete examination."

She slipped easily out of the negligée and I placed my hand lightly on the pubic hair. " 'The mount was of a classical femininity, round and smooth and plump.' "

"I know that."

"No, you don't."

"Edmund G. Wilson. *Memoirs of Hecate County.* "

"That is damn good."

"But I am not the Princess with the Golden Hair."

"You are the Madonna with the Silken Hair. And I prefer

the Madonna. The Princess, you may recall, was pretty cold mutton. Try another." I rolled over on her and pressed very firmly with my pelvis and said in a strident voice, "Repent, for the Kingdom of Heaven is at hand."

She pushed me away sharply. "Now, that is sacrilege!"

"And you're against sacrilege? Not against fornication or adultery, but sacrilege? I live by the adulterous Bible. What was it?"

"Do I have to say?"

"The rules of the game."

"All right, then. The Sermon on the Mount."

"I give you A plus."

"Just in lit?"

"No. In the other, too."

"Am I really good? Every woman wonders."

"You're exceptional. A moving map. You have a way of bringing the points of interest to the seeker, a prescience about it."

"Do you care to study the map a bit more?"

"Every back road and byway."

"Is that a mountain I see rising?"

"A mirage."

"It seems real. Shall I sample it?"

"Any test you wish to make. If you'll promise me an oasis."

She busied herself, momentarily, in a most delicious way, and it was not a mirage, nor fleeting. "Don't make me come now," I said. "I'm old-fashioned."

"I wouldn't deprive myself."

"Do I need a password?"

"Not when you have the key."

It took longer, but she didn't weary of the game or lie wooden. The torso rose and fell expertly, meeting the summons, and when it overcame her she flexed the tiny muscles that are most intimate. After a while we slept, my left hand on her left breast, the fingers encasing the nipple. In the night she awakened, roused me, and got over me to direct the action. I wasn't sure I hadn't dreamed it.

I got up early, pulled on my pajamas, gathered the light robe about me, brushed my teeth, and foraged in the kitchen. She hadn't forgotten anything, and I had the orange juice, the coffee, the bacon and eggs going when she stumbled in. "You are one of God's good souls," she said. "I love breakfast, but I hate to make it."

"Would coffee help?" I asked, pouring her a mug.

She held the cup in both hands. "I had a dream," she said.

"It was no dream."

"Was it as good as my dream?"

"Better, even if rather exhausting. And tenderizing."

"Are you tender?"

"In a few spots. I'm not used to really concentrated fucking. I suppose one learns how to deal with it."

She laughed in her cup. "What do you want to do today?"

"Besides the obvious? Take a long walk. Go to a seafood restaurant. I need oysters. About six dozen."

"Do you think there's anything to that?"

"No, but Molly Bloom did. And would I argue with Joyce?"

"You're a good cook."

"In a good cause."

"When we've finished here, let's take a nice, long, slow, warm shower."

"If you're game." And we did, with the natural consequences, standing up, our bodies snake-like, without a holding point except where we joined, and we pawed and sloshed our way through it.

That is the way the weekend went, without care for a single other person, selfishly indulging ourselves in each other and our whims, giving all, taking all, and on Sunday afternoon she said to me, "I've been thinking."

"I had noticed some cerebral activity."

"You should go to her," Meg said with finality.

"But she said . . ."

"It doesn't matter what she said. She needs you most urgently. Not for this, what we have had, the sex. She needs your emotional and spiritual support."

"And you think it wouldn't frustrate her?"

"No. I think of what I'd want. Above all, I'd want you."

"I guess I have to trust your instincts, Meg."

"And I've been thinking some more."

"About what?"

"That this weekend that brought us together, it will never happen again. Will it?"

"I don't know."

"I think you do. You'll go back to Trish, with a little bit of guilt, and you will devote yourself to her. And Meg will be . . ."

"Stop it, Meg. You're putting on the hair shirt. So let me tell you something. You are the most beautiful creature I have ever held in my arms. You are a lot of fun. In the future, I'll probably see you many times. And whenever I do, regardless of the circumstances, I'll relive part of these moments at the Roost. I'll never forget you."

"I won't forget you, either. I didn't really know what it was like to be loved by a sensitive, generous, sharing man. I have not much liked myself these last two years, the careless, hasty liaisons. But this has been more, so much more, and if it were allowed, I could love you. So very deeply."

"Don't say it, Meg."

"I didn't say it. But I have a request. Before you go, one more time. For me. Just for me, and my little idiosyncracies and aberrations. For me. Just for me. No other consideration."

I nodded. "All right. I'm your slave. But before we get into that, while we are speaking truly and from the heart, there's one other thing I have to say."

"Yes?"

"Thank you, Meg, you Madonna with the lovely, silken hair, for being here, when I needed you most."

"There's a better way to thank me."

I laughed.

And thanked her most generously.

On Monday afternoon I drove the Studebaker up to the entrance of Mason's Bluff, and Peyton came out and his dark features lifted and he said, "Ah'm glad youah heah, Mistuh Harry."

"Where's Trish?" I asked.

He nodded toward the river. "Down there. I been worried about her. She's not herself."

"Take my bag in, Peyton. I'll go down to her."

I walked down the hill toward the landing, jutting out into the river, and far to the south I could make out a small, forlorn figure. I whistled and she turned and saw me, and she began to run toward me, and as if impelled by some invisible force I threw myself toward her, my legs churning in the soft winter earth of the riverbank. We met almost in full stride, clasped each other and fell, and she held me very close and released the demon that had been holding her, crying, crying, crying. There was nothing I could say, nothing that she seemed to want me to say. I just held her until the wracking waves subsided into hiccups, soothed by the stroking, the embrace, the closeness. Finally, I helped her to her feet and headed her toward the house, but she took my hand and turned again toward the water.

"There's something I have to tell you," she said. "That's why I left. I was trying to put the words together. I couldn't face you. And I haven't been able to face myself."

"Trish, I know."

"From Selma?"

"Yes."

She took this as something wondrous, and she beheld me with love. "But you don't know why."

"In some muddy way, I think I do."

"I have to tell you. I think I have to say it. For myself as well as for you. But it will never be the same. Between us. I ruined it."

"Trish . . ."

"No. Let me tell it. I thought my father was going to jail, and I was resigned to it, and I could have lived with it. And the loss of this place, which I also could have lived with. And then Sam showed up at the trial, and he kept my father out of jail, and he saved Mason's Bluff, and I knew that this man, this creature whom I totally despised, had done these good things. So when he called that Thursday, and told me that I owed him, I had to pay. In the only coin a woman has." She was crying again, and I put my arm around her waist protectively. "I thought I could go, and pay, but not really give anything, that I could separate myself from my body, somehow, and he would have a shell that would be meaningless."

I sensed that she had reached a very difficult point, and I wanted her to stop, but she had to go on. This was the moment she had been dreading. She had to go through with it now, as catharsis.

"You don't know what it's like to be ravished, Harry.

"Sam is impotent. He can't get it up.

"So he goes down.

"And he was like an animal. He actually *bit* me, *gnawed* on me. There are teeth marks on my breasts, and on my legs. It was a nightmare. I had never been with any man except you, and I didn't know that there were *beasts* running around loose. And he kept me there and kept me there and kept humiliating me.

"I wish my life were a strip of film, and that I could cut out those ugly frames.

"But they'll always be with me, and they'll always be between us."

"Then I won't go back, Trish. The agency . . ."

"But don't you see? You have to. If you allow this to make a difference, he has defeated us. The Sam Bradfords are the winners. Can't you see that?"

"No I can't. He has done me . . ."

"Done *you?* Done you what? A cruel injustice? He didn't do you. He did *me.*"

"Isn't it the same?"

"No, no. There is some figuring you have to do. But, more importantly, how do you feel about me?"

"Trish, little girl, my little blond love, if you had been raped, I wouldn't turn my back on you. Essentially, you have been raped. We both have. And what you think about at a time like this is retribution. I love you, Trish. That's how I feel about you."

And I did go back to the Senate Office Building and Sam Bradford, and I wasn't quite sure why, except that there was a half-formed resolve, too nebulous to articulate, blending itself within me, not yet fully realized, but a black presence without form in the dark when I reached out to her and felt her cringe, draw away from the lover's touch, deny me her sore and swollen breasts, coil up in rejection when I searched the lover's mount, brushed the pudenda, sought to explore flesh now forbidden. For I had lost her. I had had her snatched away. And that became part of the dark resolve. But I didn't know it, and only later would I be able to fit the parts together. All the merriment, all the innocence, all the carefree abandon was gone. Gone the sweatshirt. She no more made homecoming the big event of the day. She sat in silence, in darkness, transformed by bestiality into a dark arena which I could not penetrate. And in the night I cried. Where, oh where, is my love gone, where the innocence, where the child that I knew? Oh, where is the angel with gossamer wings? Speak to me, man of letters, where the leaf, the stone, the unfound door? There are those of us who cry, and we cry in our loneliness.

Where, princess, oh where?

☆ II ☆

MY RETURN TO THE OFFICE was not without awkwardness. My desk was piled high with congressional trivia, and Sam, when he walked through, did not know exactly what to say.

"Glad to have you back aboard," was the best he could manage, and there were undertones and overtones which I could not cope with. I did not go gladly into his office for the ritual spirits, and on the whole I performed rather perfunctorily. I think above all, Selma was glad to have me back in my accustomed place.

In that spring two events of some importance had their origin in the office of Sam Bradford, United States Senator from the Free State of Maryland. One was the notice, which Sam mentioned casually in the morning hour and spread liberally on the pages of the *Congressional Record,* that the Sanford, Ohio, paper which had written bad things about him for the Appendix had changed ownership, or direction. Emmons was out. A young editor named Foust, gung-ho for rooting Communists out of places of influence, was editor, a transformation to which editors hither and yon should pay heed. There were even laudatory editorials about Sam Bradford which he duly entered into the Appendix. What did not appear in the *Record* was the fact that the transition from Emmons to Foust had cost the Bradford war chest in the neighborhood of $30,000, and that Sam was not disposed to buy many editors. The word, nevertheless, got through to the National Conference of Editorial Writers, and the drain on the treasury was a small price to pay, considering the mileage Sam got out of Emmons's humbling. He and I had, in effect, made Emmons eat shit, and if there were any other shit-eaters out there, they would have to contend with the Bradford Syndrome, or the Bradford Brigade, if Sam chose to turn them loose on some unwary printing plant.

The second development came to my notice without warning, and I was a little piqued. At about 2 P.M. on a Thursday my telephone rang and there was a State Department type on the line who said his name was Hermitage. I didn't know Hermitage and I didn't know what the hell he was babbling about.

"Look," I said, "let me call you back on a clear line. We don't know what may be bugged."

"Okay. Hermitage. State 2770."

"I'll get right back to you." I walked down the hall and took the elevator to the lobby and enclosed myself in a wood-phone booth and dialed State and asked for extension 2770 and Hermitage himself came on the line. I didn't have to go through any intermediaries. "This is Dodge," I said. "What the hell are you talking about?"

"You must not be very close to your boss," he said. "Some time ago Senator Bradford sent over the name of Jack Symington as a nominee for the ambassadorship to the Court of Saint James's."

"I'd say that you were joking," I said, "but you sound like a humorless man."

"I'm not very funny. What do you think of Symington as Ambassador to England?"

"Eminently qualified," I said. "My recollection is that he

gave the appropriate sums to the general's election as President, he has a good old Maryland name, quality background, good stock, and he can personally afford to defray the expenses of the Fourth of July party. He has a young, vivacious wife, small children, family man. The British like the family standard. He'd suit you to a 'T.' "

"That is not why I called you."

"Then why?"

"Symington's wife. We hear she's a nympho."

"Oh, hell no. That implies utter lack of discrimination. Bellhops. Greengrocers. That sort of rabble. Meg is not that way."

"What way is she?"

"Very careful."

"But she sleeps around?"

"I wouldn't deny that."

"Would she screw everything up to and including the Prince of Wales?"

"I don't even know the Prince of Wales."

"I don't think there is one, at the moment. Maybe two years old. She's into quality people, nevertheless? No notoriety, low-key. But hot pants?"

"I guess so. The Symingtons don't cohabit. And she looks for the discreet opportunities."

"Do you know what this would do to us if the *Sunday Express* got hold of it?"

"It would sure jazz up foreign relations. But in the cause of Anglo-American relations, what harm?"

"You don't get it. Caesar's wife. All that horse shit."

"Do you go through this with everybody?"

"Oh, hell, no."

"Then why Meg? The Symingtons?"

"Look, if he had been nominated for Jakarta or Tel Aviv or Oslo, it'd be automatic. His wife could screw the twelve tribes of Israel and it wouldn't matter. But every bastard who gives

$50,000 thinks he has bought himself Grosvenor Square. And that ain't the way it works. This is one of the show places, demanding absolute rectitude. And the fact that Symington is a Bradford candidate doesn't help. The British do not like to be reminded."

"So your present inclination is to put Symington at the bottom of the heap? I suppose there's a heap?"

"Oh, there's a heap, and you said it. Symington goes to the bottom of the pile."

"Are you prepared to take some heat on this?"

"From whom?"

"Sam is going to be very distressed. Symington has been with him all the way."

"Fuck Sam."

"Easy to say. But when he starts boring in? He'll make an issue of it. Heavy pressure on Foreign Relations, and maybe even a personal crusade against State. And I should warn you. Sam doesn't follow the rules. None of that Marquis of Queensberry crap. Bare knuckles."

"You know, Dodge, I don't give a damn. I'm about ready for retirement. I'll be gone by the time a nomination goes up to Foreign Relations. So somebody else gets the flak. Not me. I'm going to shaft old Jack. Flag him with red. With a dozen better risks on top. And if Sam wants to bust some heads, I'll be fishing off Tampa. How does that grab you?"

"Sam is very close to the Navy, and he will personally order out a warship. He'll sink your fuckin' fishin' boat."

"But first he has to find out which one."

"That's not the way Sam does it. He'll sink the whole damn fleet."

"Well, I won't be out there that day, anyway. I got tipsters in the Navy Department."

"Hermitage," I said, "you are a scrofulous old son of a bitch, but it was a pleasure doing business with you. One thought, though, is over-riding. How the hell did you happen to call me?"

"Dodge, we have got about two miles of film on you."

"Film, for God's sake? What have I done to deserve such attention?"

"You cavorted with Meg Symington. And I must say, you're quite an athlete. I admired your acrobatic invention."

"Hell, you don't have to invent with Meg. But why me?"

"Aw, you were just incidental. When we first got wind of Mrs. Symington's proclivities, we put a film crew on her."

"The bastards with the fishing poles. They didn't look genuine to me."

"They've got all kinds of gear. In particular some infrared film developed by the CIA and made available to us. They can take pictures in the dark. Heat seeking. They shot her with about half a dozen guys. A lot of heat. One of them was a jockey, for God's sake. Little scrawny son of a bitch. A respected Baltimore lawyer. Episcopal priest. Actually, we've got enough without bringing you into it. Tell you what I'll do. We'll crop your footage, so the face never shows. Just a man, obviously not her husband. But if you'd like a couple beautiful blowups, I'll be glad to send them over."

"I'd like to have them. Really, I would."

"Give me twenty-four hours."

"And you won't spread them around?"

"No. Unless the President asks why Symington didn't make it. Then we'd give him a fill."

"But I could still be only a headless body?"

"Oh, sure."

I thanked him and went back to the office and felt a little strange about being a film star, but I'd almost forgotten it when, about two weeks later, Meg called and asked if we could have lunch.

"I've got to be in Washington next Tuesday," she said,

"and I'll be tied up most of the morning. Could we meet at about two at the King's Arms?"

"Sure," I said, and entered it on my appointment pad and didn't think anything more about it until the morning of that day. I got to the lounge at about 1:45 and told the headwaiter I was expecting a lady, and he gave me a corner table and brought me a martini and I sipped at it until she swept in, turning every head in the place, customers and management. She spoke to the maitre d', who was obsequiously attentive, and he brought her over to my table and made a great show of seating her and I told him to bring her some Chivas Regal on the rocks, one ice cube.

I reached over and took her left hand. She was wearing the Symington rocks, which were earth shaking, and I supposed that her business in Washington had been legitimate. She smiled at me, lighting up the dim room and making me wonder if I had only dreamed that I had once made desperate love to her.

When her drink came she ordered a Western omelet and I asked for the chicken à la king, and she was bursting with something she had to tell. "Okay, Meg," I said, "what the hell is it?"

"Do you know where I've been all morning?"

"I don't think you have been gladdening the heart of some wayfarer, which is your calling in life."

"Something Sam set up," she said, "if you can believe that. I've been over to State Department protocol learning how to be an ambassador's wife."

"Protocol invited you over?"

"Very proper lady there. Wanted to be sure I knew all the social graces."

"No problem for you?"

"No problem."

"You passed the test?"

"Nothing to it. I have been schooled."

Our plates came, and I didn't know how to tell her, how to tell her the worst part or how to explain that at State every department does not coordinate with every other.

I sampled the chicken on its flaky biscuit and said, "Meg, where is Jack going to be ambassador to?"

"I bet you couldn't guess."

"I don't play that game with my clothes on. Where?"

"London. Do you believe it? London!"

I was silent, fumbling with my fork and a load of peas, and Meg said impatiently, "Well, aren't you going to say anything?"

"Yes, but you're not going to like it."

She looked at me in puzzlement. "You're serious, aren't you? You really do know something."

I nodded. "Enough," I said.

"What, then?"

"That Jack isn't going to get that appointment."

"Why?"

How do you tell? How do you tell a silken Madonna that it has been fun, but the games were more than we had anticipated. I decided to rely on truth. "A camera crew has been following you around."

Meg's face fell. "That truck at the beach," she said slowly. "I thought I'd seen it before. It just didn't register. Will it all come out?"

"No. Jack's name just won't go up to the Foreign Relations Committee."

"Is there anybody I can talk to?"

"I could call a man."

"Would you?"

I got up and went to a pay phone near the entrance and got Hermitage. "I'm having lunch at the King's Arms with a lady who'd like to talk to you," I said.

"Who's the lady?"

"Your favorite movie star."

"Maureen O'Hara?"

"Not quite. But close."

There was a slight pause. "All right, I'll come, Harry," he said. "But don't use my name. I've still got those few months to go."

"Agreed," I said. I went back to the table and ordered a fresh round of drinks and we sat rather uncomfortably trying to make small talk, some of it painful for us both.

"How's Patricia?" she asked at one point.

"Fine," I said flatly.

She picked up the emptiness in my voice and said, "All that bad?"

"Worse. She's destroyed."

"She'll come around. And Sam?"

"Out of his mind."

"Par for the course. Is that the man?"

Hermitage was large, in a sports coat and matching trousers, and he came to our table and I pushed out a chair for him. "This is the man from State," I told Meg. "Mrs. Symington. Could I order you something?"

"Just a beer," he said, and I called the waiter and ordered him a Carlsen, which was Jack's brewery, and it came quickly with a frosted mug and Hermitage looked questioningly at Meg.

"A simple question," Meg said. "Is there anything, anything on God's green earth, that I can do?"

"I'm afraid not, Mrs. Symington," Hermitage said. "Things have proceeded—pretty far."

"Suppose I gave an affidavit? Absolutely no playing around. Would that help?"

"Would you give such an affidavit?"

"Sure."

"And abide by it?"

"Well, that is another question."

"There is one possibility," Hermitage said. "A different appointment."

Meg seized on it. "Like where?"

"The Ivory Coast. San Salvador. Something obscure."

"Jack would be insulted. He has been so looking forward to that ride to Buckingham Palace."

Hermitage shook his head and drank his beer. "London is going to a Midwest publisher," he said.

"With a faithful wife," Meg said wryly.

"Fat, fiftyish and formidable," State said. He drained his glass and stood up to go.

"Let me tell you one thing," Meg said. "If that had been the price, my purity, if I had been told—I wouldn't have paid it."

Hermitage nodded compassionately and we watched him go.

Meg took my hand, lacing my fingers through hers. "I am of a mind to get a room in the Willard Hotel," she said. "Do you want to come up?"

"Yes," I said fervently.

"But if I get a room in the Willard Hotel, and wait for you, you are not going to come up?"

"No."

"Then don't leave with me. The goddamn photographers might be outside." She smiled and left and she did not turn around to wave.

☆ 12 ☆

By THE SPRING OF 1952, Sam Bradford was one of the most powerful men in America. In terms of political prestige, he probably had no equal, not even at the White House. His periodic investigations into every conceivable crevice of American life in which Communists might be chipping away had made him the beloved of the faceless millions, who were all too eager to believe that the hand of Moscow was at work in mysterious ways wherever Americans congregated, and those who were not believers were fearfully silent.

Bradford Brigades were formed in almost every community in the country, and, following the tune of the senate piper, they were ready to retaliate against anyone who dared question the methods or the motives of the Man from Maryland. Autographed pictures of the Senator, copies, of course, were sent out of his office by the thousands. His portrait was hung along with the American flag in schools, lodges and patriotic fraternities. To the active Bradford clubs a newsletter was circulated by his self-appointed courtiers; the letters went much further than the newspapers could. They named Communist suspects in local government, business, literature, education, religion and show business, and to be mentioned in the column of unreliables could cost one his job or his patronage.

Bradfordism was a national disease, fed by a public mentality which had been seeking an outlet for frustrated energy. The non-believers, whether in the press or the pulpit, found it the better part of wisdom to remain silent, and one of the strangest developments ever to emerge in American history was recorded: led not by law, not by its constituted leadership, the nation was on the brink of a fanaticism utterly alien to American principles. Those who did not love Bradford and despised what he stood for lived in fear, not only for themselves but for the future of the country.

I took one of the many newsletters which flooded the office into Sam's Sanctum and thrust it in front of him. "They want to draft you to run for the presidency," I said.

Sam picked up the paper, scanned it, and laughed. "Why would I want to be President?" he asked. "I have more power in this office, right here in this room, than I'd have in the White House."

"You can't declare war," I said.

"Hell," Sam said, "I've declared war. And I've got the biggest damn army in history."

"Little old ladies in tennis shoes," I joked.

"Yeah," Sam said, unperturbed, "and they can claw and they can scratch. But you know damn well there are a lot of others. It's not all little old ladies. The arthritis set."

"I know," I admitted, "I've seen the checks."

"Harry," Sam said, "I've got to get away. I've got a heavy committee schedule coming up, and it looks like I'm going to be booked for about a speech a week. What would you say to going up to Camp Abigail for a few days? Bring the missus."

"I can see Patricia going up to Camp Abigail," I said.

"She hates my guts, doesn't she?" Sam said.

"In a kind of general way. Yes, that would express it."

"Well, what about you and me and Numeriano going up there? Just the three of us. Take a case of good hooch. Shoot some clay pigeons."

"I wouldn't mind. I can send Trish to Richmond."

I called Patricia and dispatched her for the weekend. She answered woodenly, and I knew that she would woodenly put the M.G. on U.S. 1, woodenly tool through the long line of motels, come to life only as an effort to cheer up Colonel Mason. I didn't tell myself, consciously, but I know that in my heart I was glad to be relieved of the ordeal of Georgetown for a few days. We pulled away from the Senate Office Building right after lunch, with Numeriano at the wheel of the Cad, and before we left the District we stopped at a liquor store and Sam gave his driver a hundred-dollar bill and told him to load up on White Horse, Gordon's and Jack Daniels. Numeriano came back shortly and started to stow the heavy box in the trunk, but Sam called to him, "Give us one for the road."

The Filipino climbed back under the wheel, started the limousine and turned to us with two bottles, one of the Tennessee whiskey and one of scotch, and with them two plastic glasses. He had prepared a cooler of ice, and he passed it back wordlessly, put the Cad in gear and headed out through Rockville toward Hagerstown. The miles and the drinks flew by swiftly.

Camp Abigail was on a hillside off a dirt road half way between Thurmont and Emmittsburg. As the crow flies it was less than twenty miles from Camp David, the name the General had given to the Presidential retreat, with its guest compound and tight security. I suppose Sam had bought the property for its proximity to greatness, but he had not attempted splendor. From his investment income he had built a rather Spartan lodge, with a great room that served as the living and dining space, a modest kitchen and, toward the rear, four bedrooms that shared two baths. The great attraction of the common room was a tremendous stone fireplace, and Numeriano had it roaring within twenty minutes of our arrival. We lugged the booze in and sent Numeriano back to Thurmont to buy groceries, again with the hundred-dollar bill which was the only kind Sam ever seemed to carry.

Sam and I sat on benches at a slab table. He was taking his scotch neat, to hell with the ice, and when he was appropriately lubricated he again asked the question that had been hanging between us for months. "Trish," he said. "She hates me, doesn't she?"

"Yeah," I said candidly. "I think you could say that."

"It was just one of those things," Sam said.

"No, it wasn't. You made her feel obligated. It's not an easy cross to bear."

"Do you hate me, too?"

"No. I should, but I don't."

"You were pretty mad."

"Yeah. Damn mad."

"Why'd you come back?"

"Trish wanted it."

"I don't understand intelligent people. Why haven't you whipped my ass?"

"It's not my way of doing things."

"I'll tell you something, Harry."

"What?"

"I know you. I know how you think. In some way, you're gonna beat the hell out of me."

"I'm not a violent man."

"Yes, you are," he said. He studied his drink. "You are a violent person, even if you aren't aware of it. I've known you in war and in peace. You could pull a trigger on a machine gun. Without mercy. And you could shut up that asshole editor. Without qualm. You are one mean son of a bitch."

I laughed, although I knew he spoke the truth. The tension of the moment was broken by Numeriano, who brought in a load of meat and stowed it in the refrigerator.

"We're gonna shoot some," Sam called, and Numeriano wordlessly brought the shotgun out of the closet and a box of shells and took up a position in the yard with a bag of targets.

"Pull," Sam would yell, and Numeriano would toss one of the birds in the air and Sam would fire and miss it cleanly. He didn't care about the shots; he loved to hear the blast of the shotgun, to feel its kick against his shoulder.

We had been handing the weapon back and forth for about a half hour when a sheriff's car drove up into the clearing. A slim, gaunt man in khaki uniform with a shoulder patch got out and touched his short-billed cap respectfully. Sam went over and took his hand. "Harry, this is Sheriff Thompson. Manley, we call him. Harry Dodge, my administrative assistant. And you know Numeriano."

Manley traded handshakes politely and said, "I heard gunfire. Thought I'd just look in. We've had some vandalism in some of these places."

" 'Preciate it," Sam said. "How about a drink?"

"Don't mind," the Sheriff said, and we all went inside and had a stiff one.

As Thompson and Sam sat talking, Numeriano sidled up to me and said, "Lieutenant?" I looked at him and he said, "Could we line up some bottles?" He had his automatic out, and we collected some beer and whiskey empties and went out front and put them on a rail fence and Numeriano unloaded a clip at them.

"You're getting better," I said. "You got one."

"It wasn't the one I was aiming for," Numeriano said.

"Let me put up a target," I said. I found a piece of cardboard and drew some rough circles on it in pencil and got a rusty nail and fixed it to a tree down near the fence. I went back to Numeriano and said, "Now aim very carefully. Take your time. Bring the gun up and think of it as an extension of your hand and squeeze the trigger, very deliberately."

Numeriano drew a bead from about fifty feet and closed in on the target and fired six times and I didn't see the cardboard ripple. Disgustedly he refilled the clip, started to move closer to the target, tripped over a root in the path and reflexively shot a pane of glass out of the front window of the lodge. Sheriff Thompson came roaring out, pistol in hand, and I pointed to Numeriano on the ground and said, "He misfired."

"Damn near took my ear off," the Sheriff said, holstering his revolver. "Numeriano, put that damn thing away before you hurt somebody. You could blow your balls off."

We were standing there yakking, with a quite crestfallen Numeriano examining himself for broken limbs, when another black Cad, its parking lights on as the shadows lengthened, purred up in front of the lodge.

"Your Excellency," Sam said as Jack Symington got out of the car.

"Bullshit," Jack said and waved at the Sheriff's departing car.

We went inside and Numeriano busied himself at the stove while Jack and Sam and I sat at the slab table with some fresh firewater.

"Have you heard anything?" Jack asked Sam.

"Nah," Sam said, making a sweeping motion of dismissal with his glass. "Doesn't mean anything. I put you up, didn't I? You think that doesn't carry any weight?"

"I've been daydreaming about it," Jack said. "You know, I've been in London a couple times. Did the tourist bit with Meg. Westminster Abbey. The Tower of London. Saw the square where Eisenhower directed the invasion. Changing of the Guard. All that folderol. But we were just tourists. It'll mean something to be on the inside, to be the power at Grosvenor Square. I only saw it from a distance."

Sam raised his glass a bit unsteadily. "Excellency, I've never been to London. But when you get set up, I'll be over. That's a promise."

"We'll fire cannon for you," Jack said. "Turn out the Marine guard, all spit and polish. Very Important Personage. You can't know how much I want this."

Numeriano came over with sirloin tips and home fries and asparagus in butter sauce, and he tapped a bottle of some very good red that Jack had brought, and we sat around stuffing ourselves and making toasts to their majesties across the water, and I kept my whiskey glass full and sipped at it hard along with the wine, mixing the grain with the grape. By the time Numeriano came to clear away the debris, I was crocked enough that it no longer mattered to me how much they enjoyed their fool's paradise. I took the wine bottle and squeezed it very hard and not a drop came out, and I put it on the table and spun it and poured myself another very liberal helping of straight sour mash and stood up unsteadily and said, "Gen'mun, I have'n 'nouncement to make."

"The dead walk," Sam said, quaffing deeply of his scotch. "What you gonna 'nounce?"

"Jack," I said, and burped loudly for emphasis, "ain't gonna go ta Lunnon."

Sam looked at me in amazement and disbelief. "Just what the hell are you sayin'?" he asked with exaggerated politeness. "I don't get you at all."

I wavered but stood my ground. "Jack ain't goin' ta Lunnon."

Sam was sober enough to get my drift, although Jack himself was floating back and forth. "What the fuck you talkin' 'bout?" Sam exploded.

"Wa' the fuck?" Jack echoed.

"All you bassards sober up," I ordered. "I been listenin' around in the Congressional Club, an' the Lunnon Embassy is goin' ta Rutledge, an Indian—Indian-ap-o-lis publisher."

The shock did indeed sober Sam and Jack up. "The Congressional Club," Sam sneered. "What do they know?"

" 'Nuff," I said, although I was no longer as drunk as I appeared to be. "An' I have had my ear to the groun'." I pulled at my right lobe. "This ear. I checked. Sta' Department. Lunnon is goin' ta Rutledge."

"I doan unnerstand," Jack said. "Why?"

"Campaign contrib—contributions. Rutledge gave over a hunnerd thousand. 'Djou give that much?"

"No, I di'n't," Jack said. "Something like twenty-five or thirty. But I would've."

"Nah, nah," Sam said. "It ain't money. This is gettin' at me. Who'd you talk to at State?"

"I own know. European desk."

"Jezus," Jack said. "Meg had so counted on bein' presented at court. Wha'm I gonna tell 'er? They even had 'er over to portucol. Proto—what the hell ever."

Sam threw his glass at the fireplace, missing broadly. "They tell you'f they got anything in mine fer Jack?"

"San fuckin' Salvador," I said. "Afferica. Eurasia. The Panama Canal. I own know. I cou'n't make sense out of it."

"I am going to get those sons of bitches," Sam swore. "I have never asked for anything—not anything—an' they pull this shit on me. I'm gunna investigate the fuckin' State Department." He slapped the table with his fist. "I'm gunna git'm."

Jack was quite himself and in command of the situation. "Sam," he said instructively, "I don't want you to do that. I mean, I want you to give the State Department the hots, but not on account of me. Wait until it cools off. Nothing to do with the nomination. And then go get 'em. Understood?"

"Yeah," Sam said. "Unnerstood. Harry, make a note of that. Get the State Department, but don't tie it to Jack."

"Duly noted," I said. "But wassamatter, Jack? Don't you wanna be ambassador plenipotentiary to the Celebes?"

"I don't think so," Jack said. "And if Numeriano will show me where I'm bunking, I'll turn in. This has been quite a shock."

Jack left and Sam spilled some scotch toward his glass and said, "Harry, you shouldn't ought to've done that."

"Why not?" I said.

"He could've dreamed a little. He's an old man, 'n he needs dreams."

"It wouldn't have changed it. He had to know."

"I guess he did. We all have to know. You know what I wish we had?"

"No."

"Coupla broads."

"Ah-h."

"I could go to that telephone right now an' call a guy in Hagerstown an' inna hour he'd have two cunts up here. You think I should?"

"Not for me."

"All right. But Jack's leavin' in the morning. Tomorrow night I'm bringin' in a babe, 'n don' you fuck up."

"Look, I'll ride back to Baltimore with Jack and take the train to Washington. You can have the place running over with the female of the gender. Would that suit you?"

"Fuckin' right."

"Okay. Would it suit you if I turned in now?"

"Fuckin' right."

In April, the name of Seymour Rutledge was sent up from the White House to the Senate Foreign Relations Committee as nominee for the ambassadorship to the Court of St. James's. England. "Go over and take a look at this bastard," Sam instructed me, and I attended the hearings and gained a healthy respect for the man from Indianapolis. He was intelligent, he was articulate, he had been a Rhodes Scholar and studied at Cambridge, he understood Anglo-American relations, and his nomination was approved without a dissenting vote. He would make an excellent envoy.

I reported to Sam that the nominee was duly installed, and he nodded as if it were of little moment. "There is some kind of May Day rally on the Mall," he said. "In front of the Washington Monument. Mostly veterans, I think. I've got to appear on the podium. Put something together."

"Any particular slant?"

"The usual stuff. Rehash. Communists in government. But don't mention State. It's too soon to start on that."

So I took a couple days and put together a speech, and I wasn't very careful, because I knew he wouldn't follow the text, anyway. Mostly I scavenged old texts, inserting a few new phrases, and I typed it out for him and he made a few notations and I gave it to Selma to do the final draft on the machine with the big, easy-to-read letters. I went with him on May Day, and there was a big platform in front of the obelisk and the TV cameras were there because nothing else was going on, and Sam looked over the multitude and saw that there was hay to be made, and I knew that his mind was whirring, thrown into overdrive. When he was called upon as the featured speaker he read a few of my fairly conventional lines into the mikes, and then he started ad-libbing. His ad-libs I had heard many times, and he delivered them passionately and deliberately and caused a lot of uproar among the beer-swillers out front. I didn't pay much attention until he began to perorate.

"There is something I want to tell you," he shouted, "to show you just how diligently the Communist conspiracy is at work to undermine our common cause. It has just been brought to my notice that a member of my own staff belongs to a Communist-front organization."

I sat bolt upright in my folding chair, because I knew that I might have to battle my way off that speakers' stand.

"A member of my own staff," Sam said, "one in whom I reposed utmost confidence, has been placed there at the direction of the Communist apparatus. She is a member of the Polish-American Friendship Society, an organization which has been identified by the Attorney General's office as a Communist-front organization. Her name is Selma Gadowski, and I don't know who her contact is, but I promise you this: I'm going to find out. The Communists will not have access to my files!"

Sam sat down to a roar of applause, and I walked over to him and hissed in his ear, "Until this very moment, you shit ass, I think I never really gauged the depth of your cruelty or your recklessness. Have you no sense of decency left?"

But he was not listening to me. He was hearing the roar of the crowd, and I dashed off the platform and made my way through the jungle of bodies. I knew that Selma would have been watching the TV set in the office and I wanted to get to her so that I could explain that the Sam Bradford on whom she doted was just bull-shitting, that he was playing to the galleries, that he probably hadn't even thought about what he was saying. Finally, I did get a cab, but it made its way along Constitution more slowly than I could walk, and I gave the driver five dollars and hopped out and ran until I was exhausted and then walked and then ran some more, a pain wracking my side. I finally did reach the Senate Office Building and bounded up the stairs, but except for a tempo from the typing pool there was no one in our suite. Selma had taken her coat and hat and bag, and she was not there. Frantically, I called her Capitol Heights number, but she had hardly had time to get home, and I called Patricia and she was sobbing, "Yes, I heard him," but, "No, Selma hasn't been in touch." I hung up and ran out and walked the streets looking for her in bars and lounges, making sporadic calls to the few friends I knew she cherished, and long after dark, when the crowds had found places in the drinking stalls, I took a taxi to her apartment, and when she didn't answer my knocking and calling I got the super to let me in, and she was there, sprawled out on the bed, with the empty tube of sleeping pills on the night table, that lovely, sensitive clod, her laughter now forever silent, and I knelt at the side of her bed, taking the cold hand and praying for forgiveness.

There was a note. It was addressed to me.

"Mr. Dodge: I know you will find this, because you are the only one here who cares. Please try to understand. See that my people get my things. I have $1,800 in a savings account. It should go to my parents. Tell Senator Sam that he was wrong."

I jammed the note in my pocket and made the few official calls that I knew were necessary. After the formalities were over I went down the stairs and out into the dark streets of that cold, friendless capital city. Blindly, staggering from pure hatred, I walked the miles from that one-time slum near the Capitol toward the place where I lived, which had once been a black ghetto. I was passing the flood-lit house that had been built for Presidents when it suddenly came to me, the resolve that had been given birth, all unrecognized, when my wife had been demoralized, turned to chalk, given focus and impetus in this senseless death of an innocent young woman. I was passing Old State, the Executive Office Building, when my step halted and I threw my clenched fist into the air and said aloud: "Sam Bradford, I am going to destroy you! This time I am going to collect my debts!"

And all the rest of the way home, I felt a lot better.

☆ 13 ☆

O N THE MONDAY FOLLOWING, I called Sam, and I said, "I don't think I'm going to be in for a while. I've got to think."

He was very understanding. "Sure," he said. "I know you do. Take all the time you need. But I want you to know one thing."

"What?"

"I didn't mean it to turn out that way. With the Polack. It just jumped into my mind. Something to say. How the hell did I know she'd take it that way?"

"Sam, she adored you."

"But I . . ."

"The ground you walked on. She was funny that way."

"Harry, we could have shipped her back to the Baltimore office. I tell you truly. I really didn't know."

"Sure, Sam," I said. "We coulda shipped her out. Look, I'll be in touch."

I hung up, and Patricia had been listening and her expression didn't change. "You're taking some time off?"

"I have to make a few telephone calls, and after that I have to go to Florida."

"You want me to hibernate?"

"If you like, you can go with me."

"I never thought it was a woman."

"No. I have a woman."

"Who do you have to see?"

"A man. A State Department type."

"Why Florida?"

"He's retired. In one of those places where people go to die."

"How can he help you?"

"I'm not sure. I just have to try."

"Do what you have to do."

So Patricia went off to the James River, and I went out to Washington National, and in a few hours I was at Tampa and I rented a car and went out to a little peninsula and there was a man at a slip chipping at the deck of a cabin cruiser and I parked the Ford and went over there and said, "Hermitage?"

He put down the scraper and came over to me, tan in his T-shirt and grey shorts, and he said, "Dodge, isn't it?"

I nodded. "I need some advice."

He looked out over the bay and he didn't see anything and his mind was going back, over a lot of years, and he said, "I'm not in that business anymore."

"I know you're not. Not official. But you guys never retire."

"Sit over there," he said, and gestured toward a redwood table with matching benches, and I sat there until he came back with a pitcher of gin and Wink. "I'm drained," he said. "Out to pasture."

"I know," I said, "but there's a lot floating around in your head that isn't retired. You can't turn off the grey cells. I don't think the pasture does that."

"Symington didn't make it," he asked, but it was more a statement of fact.

"No, Rutledge went to London, as you had surmised. He's a good man. He'll make a fine ambassador."

"I thought so," Hermitage said. "But you didn't come about that."

"No."

"Are you going to tell me?"

"I'm looking for a straw man."

"For what reason?"

"I want to destroy a United States Senator."

"Heaven bless us," Hermitage said. "I'm not into that line of work. Did you bring anything casual? To wear?"

"Sure."

"Go in the house and change. My wife Ann will show you where. Meantime I'll get that old scow into the water and we'll go out and wet a line."

"I don't fish."

"You do now. Go change."

I went to the Ford and got the bag and went into the house, and a very nice lady met me and directed me to a bedroom and I pulled on some khakis and some tennis shoes. I went out to the dock, and Hermitage had the old wreck in the water and was swearing at the Chrysler marine engine, and in a little while it was putting and we cruised out past the breakwater. "What the hell are we going to catch?" I asked.

"I'm damned if I know," Hermitage said, "I've never caught anything."

We baited the hooks with shrimp and I cast a few times and jigged a little and pretty soon I landed a fairly decent pompano. "Jesus Christ," Hermitage said, "that's the first time anybody ever caught anything off this scow. We ought to put up a flag or a broom or something."

"You're pullin' my damn leg."

"Nah, honest. This rig scares the damn fish away."

We fished real hard for about an hour, and Hermitage had a big piece of trash that he played for about half an hour before it broke his line and I had some little stuff and we reeled the lines in.

"Have to eat," Hermitage said. "There's some sardines and pork and beans and plastic spoons and you are supposed to be ravenous. Like saltines?"

"I don't like any of that damn stuff," I said. "Do you have some beer?"

He ate the sardines and pork and beans and I drank beer, and I sensed that we were approaching a resolution. "What you want to do," Hermitage said, "it isn't going to be easy."

"That's why I came to you. I need help."

"Are you fully aware of what's involved? You're talking about Bradford, of course? He's a god."

"I know. I helped make him one."

"And now you want to unmake him?"

"In a word."

"It's a lot harder."

"I haven't got a handle."

Hermitage bowed his head and rubbed his eyes with his thumbs. "In six months, I'll be blind," he said. "Glaucoma."

"I'm sorry."

"Of no consequence. You know, I've been thinking about it, while you been casting that damn spinner, even when the ray was on my line. It can be done."

"How?"

"Your man is power-crazed. He believes everything he says. For him to put it into words, that makes it truth."

"And I make words for him."

"So you make truth. Manufacture it. And he turns the lead into gold. I assume it's State. Otherwise you wouldn't be here."

"Yeah. Really growing out of the Symington turndown. He can't say that, but it should be understood. You grieved him."

"I couldn't help it if Symington's wife had hot pants."

"Cuts no ice."

"You know your man is a megalomaniac?"

"Sam?"

"Yeah. Delusions of grandeur. All-powerful. The king can do no wrong."

"If that's megalomania, that's Sam. He destroyed a perfectly innocent girl. Two, really, one of them very close to me. And he feels no remorse whatsoever."

"No, he wouldn't. But how to attack it?"

"That's why I'm here."

"I think in stages. Beginning with little people, a lot of them. I can suggest the manufacture of some dossiers. All very vulnerable. My recollection is that Sam never checks out raw files. We can provide the basic data. And then work right up to the top."

"Meaning the Secretary?"

"Yeah."

"It would take a great deal of finesse."

"But if you brought him along, a step at a time."

"Okay, I can manage that. But I'm not sure that would do it."

"What I propose is a non-war. No response at the lower level. So each time he aims a little higher, and he attacks the Secretary, and there's dead silence."

"So what do we accomplish?"

"The General."

"That's fantastic. Who would dare?"

"Bradford. You see, your Senator thinks he's above the law, and he will be until the wrath of God descends upon him."

"You're a devil, Hermitage."

"I think so. I'll send some papers up to the Hollow. Clue them in. You're right, old man. I'm still a consultant."

"Well, hell, why not shoot the works?"

"Exactly my thought. My wife is in there stewing up some

kind of gumbo. I told her you'd be devouring it with us. It'll damn near kill you. She is the worst damn cook in the world. But pretend you are overcome with its deliciousness. And get sick as quietly as possible." He stood up and put a hand on my shoulder. "I didn't like you a whole hell of a lot in the films. Too goddamn athletic. Reminded me of lost youth, lost opportunities. But, Dodge, today we have served the cause, and I have to admire you for your willingness to do that. You really care, don't you?"

"Maybe not for the right reasons," I said, embarrassed.

"But you care."

I laughed, and was sick for most of the night. I have known people who have become deathly ill in supping on bouillabaisse, for no reason that makes sense. I got sick to the gut on Ann Hermitage's chowder, and I don't really know why.

Sam was off on some fishing expedition when I returned to Washington. He had a pair of his gumshoes crepe-soling their way through Europe, and they had been very careful, visiting the military bases, checking in with the embassies, giving them full scrutiny. And they scared the hell out of a lot of career officers.

A girl had been brought in from the steno pool when I returned to the office, and I was always too aware of her. She sat in the chair that had been Selma's, clicked the typewriter that had been Selma's, used the well-worn eraser that had been Selma's, and on the first day I felt like walking over to her and shouting, "Just what the hell are you doing here?" But I didn't. I bled a little inside and held my tongue; she could not have known that she filled in for a ghost, a beloved ghost. And in a few days Sam came back and called me in and waved all sorts of incriminating reports.

"Do you know," he shouted, "that they are keeping a German national on the payroll in Bonn because she gives good blow jobs?"

"I can't believe that," I said. "She could make more money setting up in business for herself. What do we pay embassy help there? A hundred dollars a month? At ten dollars a job, which is a quite reasonable rate, she could double her take."

Sam laughed. "Actually, they can't fire her. They're in a real box. She has bedded ninety percent of the career people— it's all documented—and she's threatened to spill the beans if they sack her."

"Probably types two hundred words a minute," I said. "That kind of help, along with personal service, is damned hard to find. But a question. How soon do you want to start devouring State?"

"I gotta work it in," he said. "I've given my word on that. But we got all these fuckin' hearings."

"Schools?"

"Yeah. The NEA. Every damn disgruntled principal between here and Tacoma. Why don't we take the opening plunge July 4? I have to make an Independence Day speech in Richmond. The American Legion or VFW or some horse-shit sponsor."

"Okay. I'm working on a kind of strategy. First the little stuff. A hundred minor counselors in outposts all over the world. Feeding the pink stuff to the USIA. Censoring Voice of America broadcasts. Just chip away at first. And then bring in the heavy artillery. There has been one curious development."

"Nothing is curious to me anymore. What is it?"

"We got an anonymous mailing from State. Performance records on about a half dozen people. I think somebody over there knows what you want."

"Save that stuff for later," he said. "Could be dynamite. But just use crap for Richmond. They don't know from nothing down there, anyway. I could recite the goddamn alphabet backwards and they'd think it was the State of the Union."

"Okay. Will do. But, Sam. If you're really going after State, sooner or later there have to be some big names. Maybe all the way to the top."

"No sweat. If it comes down to the truth on who's soft on Communism, who do you think the people of this country are going to believe?"

"No question."

"Then work up some cream of wheat for Richmond. You know. Fourth of July. Independence Day. God, mother and apple pie. All the fuckin' virtues."

So I loaded a slingshot for Richmond, and we drove down there in the Cad and met all the half-drunk Legion types, and at about one o'clock we were conveyed over to a wooden platform that had been thrown up in front of a statue of Robert E. Lee on horseback. Sam was duly acknowledged, and he made proper obeisance to the flower of the Confederacy and kind of dragged one leg behind him over to the lectern.

"You will have to forgive the infirmities of the flesh," he said. "In this right leg I am carrying about a pound of shrapnel—you Legion folk will understand that—and it gives me a little stiffness now and then. But I would give my life for this country. I have offered to, as many of you have, and what is a gimpy leg?"

Everybody on the plaza had been drinking beer and celebrating the Declaration of Independence, and Sam very insidiously launched into the prelude to the State Department assault, and if he said the State Department was full of mumbo-jumbos, here was the crowd that would believe him. It was all going very well. It was until I looked into the crowd and saw one very intense flat Polish face, and it was Justin Gadowski, with whom I had drunk very strong vodka, and he was edging closer and elbowing with a hand in his pocket, and I watched him and when he was about twenty feet from the grandstand he pulled out a rusty horse pistol and aimed it at Sam. There was just one thought in my mind: "No, no. It can't end this way." I launched myself toward the lectern just as the old cannon roared and simultaneously I felt the hot, jolting, sharp tearing of the flesh. Off behind me, dully, to my right, there was the roar of Numeriano's automatic, and I didn't see it but they told me that he very neatly drilled three holes within a four-inch space in Justin's chest.

I remember the wail of the ambulances and the quick, sterile efficiency of the emergency room at the Medical College of Virginia, and beside me there was a long, gasping lump. I held Justin's rough old hand as the life escaped from him and blamed myself. His daughter I had thrust into the jaws of a particular kind of hell, and he had followed, in blind revenge, and I remember as in a dream that Patricia was there, caring, and that I was reassembled in a sterile room with my blond wife at my bedside and Sam raging in the corridor. My leg ached and my head hurt. The leg had been shot; the head had been lacerated and diminished by a small concussion as I sought to shield the body of the Senator from Maryland, target of an assassin's bullet.

Sam blustered in, pregnant with concern, saying that he would take care of all the expenses and not to worry about a thing. Patricia turned her face from him and walked over to a window, looking out over Richmond, not seeing this man or hearing what he said. I knew what she was reliving in her tormented mind, the terror and humiliation revivified, the shame reborn, but this was not the time to speak of it.

In a moment of what passed for him as tenderness, Sam leaned over me and said, "Harry, I didn't really know that you were that devoted to me. When that old fart blasted away, everybody on that platform was scrambling for cover. Do you know that you actually shielded my body with yours?"

"Mostly reflexive, Sam," I said. "When I spotted Gadowski in that crowd I guess I knew what he was going to try. I have an old-fashioned view of politics. I don't think Senators of the United States should have their asses shot off."

"I want to thank you. He could have killed me. Thank you."

"So you've thanked me. Enough is enough."

"I'm going back to Washington, now that I'm sure you're all right. You made all the afternoon papers. Hero. You up-staged hell out of me."

"Sorry. Have a good trip."

When he left Patricia came back to the bed and sat beside me. "Why did you do it, Harry?" she asked. "Risk your life for his? It's not a fair trade."

"I didn't want Justin to be responsible. I didn't want Sam to go like that. A martyr."

She sat briefly without speaking, and then she said, "But there's more to it?"

I nodded, and she didn't pursue it. Once she would have. She would have had to have known every detail, and she would have conspired with me, coming up with outlandish embroidery on the central theme. But that old spark which I had so treasured, if it were any longer alive at all, was buried very deeply. I dozed off, and when I awakened she was still there, but hardly a presence.

Colonel Mason visited, a shell of the man I had first met regarding a minor traffic incident, haggard, thin, his tweeds unaltered and bagging, his tie slightly askew. He shook my hand with a limp grip, and Patricia got another chair and drew it up beside the hospital bed.

"Are you in much pain, son?" he asked.

The "son" was a fairly recent addition. Adversity in some ways had drawn us all closer.

"Why did you do it?" he asked. I looked at Patricia, who

had heard all the variations of my reasons given to friends, reporters, doctors, senate investigators. She got up and trailed off into the corridor, in search of some small nameless comfort.

"Colonel," I said, "there isn't any answer. I don't love Sam enough to make Patricia a widow."

"And I want grandchildren," Mason said. "When are you and Patricia going to get around to that? Or did you have to get shot up first?"

"Oh, I think the grandchildren will get here."

"I worry about Patricia," the Colonel said. "She doesn't seem herself."

I couldn't tell him—that she had been touched by the Sam Bradford blight, as the whole nation had—and I said imprecisely, "These have been difficult times for her. She worried a great deal about you. Still does. And she's had a lot on her mind."

Mason leaned close to my ear. "Can I tell you something? In confidence? I wouldn't want Patricia to know."

"Sure."

"I don't like Bradford."

"You're not by yourself."

The colonel pulled away and said thoughtfully, "I know he did me a tremendous personal favor. But somehow I get the feeling that it was all an act. Playing to the galleries. Grandstanding. That his concern wasn't for me at all. Almost as if he had an ulterior motive." He stopped and cleared his throat. "This all may sound ungracious. Except for him I might be doing time. But you know something?"

"What?"

"Sometimes, I'd almost rather have gone to jail."

I laughed, and it wasn't easy, considering all the ramifications. "I don't think you'd have pulled time, anyway," I said. "It would have been like sending Thomas Jefferson to jail."

Patricia came back in with something soft in a paper cup and handed the remnants to me, and the colonel got up to leave. "When they let you out of here," he said, "come out and recuperate at the Bluff. You know, we're farming the place? Peyton's boys have a lot of old ground under cultivation. It makes my day, to watch the green things growing. Come out, Harry."

And I did. We took over Trish's room and rearranged a large landing for sitting with the TV, and sometimes we caught glimpses of Sam, exorcising the Communist demons from the American body corporate. As the leg healed we went for long walks, and I watched her for signs of revival, as the plantation lived once more. But the heaviness was still upon her, and there were times in the night, as we lay there woodenly aware of another time and another spirit, that I thought of Meg and the hot desire which seemed barely satiable. And as I drifted in that limbo just before sleep came I reproached myself, that the Princess with the Silken Hair was so readily available, so instantly available, and that I did not avail myself. Meg! Oh, Meg! Once I caught myself, in my sleep, pulling frantically at the long blond mane, taming the wild mare, a mount that had ridden off into some deep impenetrable wood, riderless even if saddled.

In August we returned to Georgetown, in the worst month for Washington, when the humidity is intolerable and the hot nights endless. The air conditioners rattled in the windows and did little good. The office, I found, was a disaster. Sam had not bothered to get dedicated help but had relied on temps, calling on committee secretaries to do his correspondence, and I had to set up everything afresh. I brought over a grey lady from the Baltimore office and gave her a $5,000 raise to make it worth her while, and with her help and that of the building porters I moved everything around and rearranged it so that it would no longer be the office that Selma had run so efficiently. With dividers I built a cubicle for my-self and one for Numeriano, who could shoot straight when he had to, and when Mrs. Maisel, the new girl of fifty, asked if there were anything we could do for Sam's precincts, I told her that we would leave any rearrangement there to his imag-ination. The success of our efforts was supported by Sam him-self, who started into the office and then backed out, thinking he had invaded the wrong premises. But he saw me and took the chance.

"Sam," I said, "you remember Mrs. Maisel?"

"Sure'n I know a good Baltimore Catholic," he said. "You were the second in command over there, weren't you?"

"After Mrs. Garmische."

"Will you like it here?"

"I don't know. I think so. Mr. Dodge came over and told me I was being transferred, and here I am. One thing I do like. The pay. I just hope I can satisfy."

"You'll do fine," Sam said, "and welcome aboard. If you have any questions, any questions at all, Mr. Dodge has all the answers. Just do what he says, and you won't go wrong. Come in, Harry."

We went into the Star Chamber, and as he was making the drinks he asked, "How's the leg?"

I slapped it. "No problem. Amazing how the flesh regener-ates itself."

"Much scarring?"

"A little mark."

"You have my personal Purple Heart."

"I already got one around somewhere. I don't even know where those things are."

"If you were running for office, you'd know. But essentially, you're all whole?"

"Sound as ever. Maybe a little gun-shy."

Sam laughed. "That's natural. Look, I've got this tour com-ing up. A whirlwind in the Midwest. They love me out there.

I can harp on pretty much the same theme, but we need to substitute some names and places. New victims. Can you turn out a standard text and then have that old bat out there do about six versions, changing the situations and the culprits?"

"No problem, and it's kind of ironic that this opportunity should arise now. I told you about the fat envelope under the State Department frank. Had photostats of the service records and confidential memoranda on a dozen Foreign Service officers. I don't have any reason to doubt the authenticity of the stuff. I can check if you'd like. But it seems there are questionables in just about every embassy and consulate on the face of the earth."

"If it looks genuine, use it," Sam said. "I think we have friends at State, people on our side. So pour it on. Milk it for all it's worth. But remember the ground rules. There should never be any hint that we're retaliating for Jack."

"Oh, hell, yeah, I know that. They'll never know what hit 'em." Nor would Sam know, until it was too late, what had hit him, because that little State Department packet was the careful devising of Hermitage and his gang of ruffians. A lot of very precise thought had gone into composing those phonied transcripts.

So it was with a great deal of mirth that I batted out about half a dozen orations, with the interchangeable names of a dozen little fish alleged to have been allied at one time or another with left-wing causes and strategems. I told Mrs. Maisel how to do the busy work, and Sam went off on his tour, with some of his committee staff and with Numeriano and his automatic pistol. Sam made the inevitable headlines with frontal assaults on the State Department, which apparently was undoing with one hand everything it had done with the other. No continent was safely supervised. The traitors had infiltrated Europe, South America, Asia, the Balkans, the Middle East, the Orient—everywhere except Antarctica—and Sam had the names and associations to go with his charges.

It made awfully good copy and was the inspiration for any number of editorials from Chicago to Milwaukee, but the State Department provided no help whatsoever. In the daily press briefings the spokesman at Foggy Bottom fell back on "No comment" whenever the name of any Bradford target was mentioned. It was an infuriating ploy, one that Sam had never before encountered. Always before, when there had been accusations there had been denials, with long and detailed defenses. But when the State press officer said merely, "No comment," there was nothing to do except charge "cover-up," and there was very little mileage in that.

Sam returned to Washington in a state of annoyance and perplexity. "We're eatin' their asses out," he said, "and they want to be coy about it. What kind of game are they playing?"

"Damned if I know," I said. "You'd think they'd make some pretense at rebuttal."

And while he was there in Washington, the hearings went on and on, endlessly. At one point he was into UNICEF, The United Nations International Children's Emergency Fund, and to "Trick or Treat" for UNICEF or to buy UNICEF Christmas cards was to entangle oneself with the international Communist conspiracy. On another occasion he was pounding away at the Methodists and Communist influence in their Federation of Social Action. According to the evidence supplied by very unsavory characters with strange glints in their eyes, 2,109 Methodist ministers were suspected of Communist inclination. As the inquiry broadened it included 614 Presbyterian ministers, 1,411 Protestant Episcopal rectors, 660 Baptist preachers, half of the Unitarian clergymen in the United States and its possessions, 450 rabbis, 30 of the 95 men who had worked on the Revised Standard Version of the Bible and 658 clergymen and laymen connected with the National Council of Churches. I, for one, did not see how any right-thinking person could take religion seriously any more.

Surprisingly enough, the mail did not condemn Bradford but commended him. I spent several days classifying the response to the committee's hearings on the church, and ninety percent of the respondents were glad to learn that the ministers in whom they had reposed their hope of heaven were really pawns of Moscow. In the so-called fundamentalist areas the suspicion was highest.

Naturally the committeee charade got a good press. The church is an easy target. There is no central clearing house, no person authorized to speak for the Protestant faith. But I noted that Sam had clearly exempted one area—he had called no witness who might speak to Communist perversion of Catholicism. I, of course, would not believe that the Vatican had been infiltrated. But there were some nuts out there—we got letters from them—who not only believed it but who could document it: Catholic pandering to the Polish Communist regime, here a compromise, there an arrangement, certainly circumstantial accommodations. But the "war chest" had been fattened by the Catholic Church. Sam was not about to turn on his backers. And so Catholicism came through unblemished.

The church inquiry was piddling stuff, though, and Sam knew it. He needed a frontal assault, badly. His press was sagging into inside shorts. By Thanksgiving the editorial writers, who are not a faithful bunch, were paying him lip service, minor heed. He needed another big one, and we went into council.

"What can I do?" he asked. "We keep pecking away, in the committee, and we do expose things. But I admit this to you, it's peanuts. We've had witnesses in droves. I think we have demonstrated to the American public that Communism is hammering away at the foundations of American life. Oh, very insidiously, I'll grant you that. But we don't have the big name. There have to be pyrotechnics."

"How high are you willing to go?" I asked coachingly.

"I don't think anybody is above reproach."

"The Secretary of State?"

Sam looked at me in surprise. "That old fuddy-duddy?"

"If you analyze his record, he is soft on Communism."

"I hadn't even thought of it."

"But just think. Has there ever been a direct confrontation? Do you know what we should have done, while we had the superiority? We should have bombed the shit out of the Russians. But the Secretary held back. Now I ask you, why the fuck why? They got the bomb, stolen from us, but they had no reliable delivery system. We did. We could have blasted the Communist menace off the face of the earth. Did you ever think of that?"

"It never occurred to me."

"It should have. First they get the bomb. Right? And next they turn to delivery systems. The time to get them was when they had the fuckin' explosive without the capacity to spread it around."

"All right. I see what you're talking about. The Secretary has stood for appeasement."

"Right. And who appeases? The fuckin' sympathizers."

"Okay. Crank it out. I have something to do in Muskogee. Thanksgiving. I don't even know if there's a phone line into Muskogee. But maybe the AP has a pony express rider there. Aim it for an Oklahoma audience."

Boy, did I aim it. I happened to think that the Secretary, despite his engummed choppers, was an honorable man. But I had never written what I thought. I had written what Sam was supposed to think. And Sam was now supposed to think that the Secretary, knowingly, unknowingly, by design or stupidity, had sacrificed the future of this country because of a soft feeling toward its principal antagonist. I pulled out all the stops, portraying him on the one hand as a weakling, on the other as a calculated cynic. In Sam's speeches, such discrepancies didn't matter.

Naturally in Muskogee Sam embroidered on the framework I had provided for him, and naturally the Secretary came out as black as sin. The wire services did jump on it, the newspapers did display it in railroad Gothic, and the State Department said, "No comment."

Sam came back to Washington more annoyed than ever. "Just what do I do to get those bastards over there riled up?" he asked. "I put their fuckin' archangel through the mill, and all I get is 'No comment.' When'n the hell are they going to comment?"

"You know what I think we ought to do?" I said.

"What?"

"Put the Oklahoma speech in the *Record*. With all the elaborations we can produce."

"That's easy enough."

"Maybe we'll get some reaction from the Senate symps."

"Lot of 'em over there."

"I think you have to goad them into some kind of reprisal."

"Well, I'll make the proper motions. But sometimes I think the Senate is composed of a bunch of yellow bellies. They don't react unless their own personal, private interests are touched. We haven't hit a nerve."

"You want to hit a nerve?"

"Of course."

"Let me think about it."

Sam went off to the senate, and in the morning hour he made the proper noises about the Secretary of State and entered in the *Record* not only his own Muskogee speech but the editorials which had commented on it. Thus they became part of the permanent record of the United States. The Appendix is temporal, not actually permanent, but any historian researching the history of the period would sort through the

Appendix, which is mostly full of crap, but which cannot be ignored. In the morning hour, when Sam made his entry and his elaborations, no senator of the United States rose to challenge what he had said. Oh, the wires picked up a few fragments, because there wasn't much else to report, but it was not front page stuff without a confrontation. And there was no confrontation; no one would square off with Bradford. Sam came back to the office in a low mood.

We went in for a drink, and as he was tossing the first one down he said, "What in God's name have I got to do?"

"What do you want to do, Sam?" I asked.

He looked at me squarely and said with a kind of passionate conviction that he could not have mustered two years earlier, "I want the American people to understand how widespread the Communist conspiracy is."

I was a little shaken. From the first, Sam had not been a believer. He had latched onto a cause which he knew was phony. But he had performed the impossible. This cynic, this political animal, *had actually convinced himself.* And there was more to it than that: *it had become a psychosis.* Even a year earlier we would have joked with the press about the hearings, the speeches, the conjured-up bugaboo. But as I looked at Sam that day I realized, frighteningly, that he had begun to believe his own lies. That was quite telling, quite revealing, because Sam was not by nature a believer in anything. He was a pragmatist, a disciple of expediency, or so I had always thought. But he had succeeded in brainwashing himself, and that made him all the more dangerous. Now he would pursue his quarry with evangelical vengeance, in the manner of a John Brown or a William Lloyd Garrison, both mad. Now he would believe, in all sincerity, that the words that fell from his lips were truth because he had uttered them. And he couldn't utter a lie.

It came to me that he was far more dangerous than I had

ever suspected. Formerly I had known, or thought, that we were devising a charade, that it was all part of the great game of politics, that we could call time out, that we could, if need be, quit the field altogether. But that was no longer true. This man saw shadows where there were none. For him the ghosts walked; there was, indeed, a grand Soviet strategy to take over the United States. *Sam believed.*

And so that made it incredibly simple.

They had not responded, I told the senator, because he was getting very close to the heart of the matter. They had no wish to see the piercing spotlight, to be placed under the great magnifying glass, to have to account for their every action. Sam had made the terrain dangerous; there was even the possibility of a popular uprising to weed out the Comsymps, so great was his popular following. So he must take the initiative, in a way that only a dedicated, respected Senator, one of his undeniable stature, could.

"I don't think I know what you mean," Sam said when I explained all this to him. He never was very bright.

"You have to think about it," I said. "Analyze it. You have attacked the Secretary, and there has been no denial."

"No."

"You expected denials, didn't you?"

"Of course."

"And that there were none was practically an admission that what you said was true."

"That's the way I interpret it."

"And the way most Americans interpret it. Now think about this, very carefully. Who appointed the Secretary?"

He looked at me, eyes widening, suddenly aware of the awful implications. "The General," he whispered.

"Exactly," I said. "You have to expose the General."

"My God," he said. *"Lese majesty."*

I didn't even know the bastard knew the term. "No," I

countered. "Truth. I think it can be shown. Maybe not direct involvement, but such gross inattention to the day-to-day workings that it *amounts* to conspiracy."

Sam pounded his desk with his fist. "That is it," he said maniacally. "That is the key. I don't know why I didn't see it before. That is why all the silence. We were getting too close!"

"I think so," I said, and in my mind there appeared the vision of the little devil, goading the innocent onward. Except that Sam wasn't innocent.

"Have you got anything?" Sam asked feverishly.

"Little bits and pieces."

"Can you put them all together?"

"In a kind of roundabout way. It involves his brother."

"The smart one?"

"Much the smarter, and more devious."

"And the brother, as a university president, with access to secret contracts, has been whispering in the General's ear?"

"That's the way I see it," I said. "Hopkins has some very fat projects, in very hush-hush fields."

"Je-zus," Sam said, and exhaled elaborately. "I never thought it would come to this."

"Does it scare you? You can back off."

"Sam Bradford never backed off from a fight in his life. You know that."

"So I should put it together?"

"Very carefully."

"When is your next major speaking engagement?"

"I don't know. Early next year, I'd imagine."

"Well, the hearings can keep you going until then."

"Oh, we've got enough material for the next ten years. Education coming up. And then labor unions. The Communists have bored in everywhere. Good inside stuff. But this piece. It's banner headlines. All over."

"Maybe a lot of flak, too. He got a pile of votes."

"Because he was a war hero. Hell, I'm a war hero."

"Yeah, with all that shrapnel." He didn't detect the irony. "I bet the General never even got shot at."

"Oh, hell, no. But he's got all those ribbons."

"And that smile."

"The smile. Yeah. But what does it hide? The sell-out. I always wondered why we didn't light into the Russians after Berlin fell. Do you know we gave them East Germany? Most of it. We sold out a lot of good people. And now it all comes into focus. The General wanted it that way. A Russian advantage. And all those poor Germans in—where the hell was it?"

"Leipzig. Brandenburg. We withdrew. Handed all that real estate over to the Red Army."

"And the American people were so blind. Nobody realized. Nobody protested. And it was clear even then."

"Sam, I'll work on it. Real hard. All the background. All the compromises. The negligence. We'll point the finger."

"Just head me in the right direction. I'll take it from there. You don't have to spell it out for me."

I nodded and left his office, and Mrs. Maisel, who had no clue, remarked that for the first time in our association I was actually smiling.

I had made the appointment for 11 A.M., when I knew Sam would be holding forth in committee against the demons. A few minutes before the hour, I picked up my briefcase and walked down the corridor and down one flight of steps and down another corridor and around a turn to the East Wing. The receptionist was wearing a grey tailored suit and her hair was cut short and she favored me with an eyebrow and I said, "Dodge."

"He's expecting you. Go on in."

I nodded to the few other Hill types and tapped lightly on his door and opened it, and he was leaning back in his chair with his feet on his desk reading the *Record*. The shoes were high-topped, scuffed, a design I hadn't seen in twenty years. He put the pamphlet down and nodded toward a chair. "I don't know why I agreed to see you," he said. "To my mind the senator you represent is beneath contempt."

"Which is why I asked to see you," I said.

"You aren't trying to sell me on one of his pet schemes? I throw people like that out every day."

"I have something to sell you," I said, "but not as Senator Bradford's man." I flipped open my briefcase and took out the sheaf of State Department photostats. "I would like you to examine these," I said. "Every name in this file has been a Bradford target in the last few months. Look at the originals, and then scan through the explanatory statement attached to each."

I handed him the packet, and he began to leaf through the pages, and when he came to the notes a smile played across the gross old features. We sat without speaking for twenty minutes, while he got an impression of what I had given him. Then he leaned back and adjusted his spectacles and said, "How did you manage this?"

"A team at the State Department worked for about two weeks manufacturing the data. It took a lot of ingenuity. There are some sharp guys over there."

"I know them from Foreign Relations. A dedicated bunch. Why did you get mixed up in it?"

"Senator, forgive me if I seem to sound disloyal. But I love this country. I love its people. I believe the Constitution means what it says. I want to see our way of life preserved. And I think Sam Bradford is a menace to it."

"Why didn't you take this to the newspapers? Pearson, somebody like that?"

"Because I think it's a senate matter."

"How soon would you suggest that I use this?"

"Not yet. He is going to make a speech in which he brands

the President of the United States as a traitor. I would think some time after that."

"Most appropriate. I am an old hand at choosing the moment."

"I know you are." I stood up to leave, and he came around from behind the desk, smaller than he had seemed behind it.

"I would like to shake your hand, Mr. Dodge," he said. "On this day you may have saved the Republic."

"I wouldn't want credit for it, sir."

"I know. But it occurs to me that in a few months you may be needing a job. There would always be a place for you here."

"I appreciate that. But I don't expect to make politics a career."

"Why?"

"Begging your pardon, sir, but it is a very dirty business."

☆ 14 ☆

THE ASSAULT ON THE presidency was delayed. There was the long Christmas recess, and then there were matters pending before the Select Committee, and then Jack Symington died.

Died.

Somehow it was a breach of trust.

Here was a man who had renounced conjugal relations with his beautiful and willing young wife, leaving her to search out adulterous pastures. But he bred racehorses, without notable success, and then one day at Bowie a nag by the name of Gracias, its jockey no doubt inflamed by Meg's spectacular ministrations, came from very far behind, a mudder, and broke across the finish line ahead of the pack in the Fairfield Stakes, which were respectable. Jack had not anticipated the victory as a gift of Gracias, nothing out of nobody, but he nevertheless went to the laureate circle, and as the floral wreath was being placed around the neck of the winner, Jack succumbed to the excitement, fell prostrate and gave up the ghost. He would have enjoyed life—and death—more had he fallen before Meg's bountiful favors, but he died on the track in full view of the wagering public, without a shred of dignity. The speculators on the longshot loved him, but there were not enough to give a damn.

So Sam and I had to be among the mourners, and we went into the little chapel at My Lady's Manor and paid our respects. Not very willingly. "I detest funerals," Sam said. "They remind me of my own mortality."

"I kind of like them," I said perversely. "Every time I go to a funeral, I know that someone else is being entombed, not me. Goodbye, Jack."

"Oh, hell, yes," Sam said. "Goodbye, Jack, you old son of a bitch."

"Now, why would you say that to this so shortly departed?"

"Because he always hedged his support."

"Well, the hell with him. We have never needed the lukewarm."

Meg went into mourning for about two weeks, and then she called me at the office and her voice was honey in the horn and she could be most persuasive, most inviting. "Harry," she began, "don't mention names."

"Okay."

"But you know?"

"Yes."

"I'm a very rich widow."

"I'd imagine so."

"Oh, it's not all settled. The will, I mean. But we had a contract, and I'm good for about ten million."

"It's a nice, round figure."

"Well, I won't be left at the poverty level."

"So what can I do for you, Meg?"

"I am rich, and I am panting. I think you know. An arrangement. It was never the same with anyone else."

"Are you talking about another weekend?"

"No. Something more permanent. Vows and all that. After

a respectable interval, of course. But the enjoyments don't have to wait."

"I couldn't do it, Meg. Not for ten. Not for fifty."

"Harry, why the hell not? You are living in some kind of never never land. That pistol doesn't go off anymore."

"You're dead right, Meg. But I have to sweat it out. There is something there, something reclaimable, something that I have to breathe life into again, to revivify."

"And you won't pull out?"

I weighed the consequences and was silent, but eventually, laboriously, I said, "No."

She was furious. "Harry, I come to you on bended knee. It's not a posture I enjoy."

"I don't think your knee is bent."

"Why?"

"Meg, you're used to having things your own way. I think ultimately you would tire of me. I'm a pretty square son of a bitch."

"That's not the real reason."

"No."

"You are being faithful to that jaded flower. Jeezuz, Harry!"

"I can't help it. It's my nature."

"Until you said that, Harry, I was going to say, 'Never call my number again.' But I'm here, Harry. If you get the urge."

"Meg?"

"Yes?"

"In some perverse way, in some secret little part of my heart, I love you. Thank you. You've made it tolerable."

"Don't thank me, Harry. It wasn't a gift. You made it tolerable for me, too. But I have to get on."

"Goodbye, pretty lady."

After she hung up, I went in to talk to Sam. He was grieving, in the rather unconvincing way that came naturally to him. "Jack's death," Sam said. "That took a lot out of me."

"And Jack was the occasion for the State Department vendetta. Are you going to give it up now?"

"Oh, hell, no. I can't help Jack, but I can get a little satisfaction."

"I've been working on the drafts."

"Keep at it."

And so I kept polishing the attacks on the general, knowing full well that Sam would take the criticisms as departure points and add his own personal touches. It developed that the blow was to fall at a Lincoln's Day dinner in Chicago. Because his favorites among the investigative staff were tied up, I went with Sam, and it turned out just as I had imagined. Not just the influence of the older brother, who was smarter. Not just the questionable appointments, but the general was, in Sam's vocabulary, and these were his words, not mine, "a willing advocate of the Communist conspiracy in the United States." Sam never knew what caution meant. He had to steam in with the whistles blowing to make his landing.

Obviously he got a good press. No one of any stature accuses a President of the United States of Soviet complicity and comes away without a line in the newspapers. I enjoyed Lincoln's Day hugely, because I felt that Sam finally had ventured upon forbidden ground. And indeed he had, because for the first time, after years of treading softly around the deadly inquisitor, the big newspapers opened up on him editorially.

If was almost as if it had been orchestrated, because *The Times* and the *Post* fired immediate salvos, not only accusing Sam of recklessness but also questioning the state of his mentality. The lesser journals took up the refrain, and the senator who up until that time could do no wrong found himself the target of every Podunk sharpshooter who had too long muzzled the barking dogs of the editorial pages.

Sam tried to laugh the whole thing off. "Who reads the

editorial pages?" he said uneasily. "As long as the people are with me."

But if the people were with him, the United States Senate was not. Old Royster, who had never been a Bradford advocate, rose on the Senate floor after the Lincoln's Day recess, this hunchback of a man, bald with years, wearing the rimless spectacles and occasionally stroking his paunch, and said, "I have a matter of serious gravity to bring before this body today. To make myself clear beyond any doubt, I refer to the curious antics of the junior Senator from Maryland, who has grossly maligned one of the most heroic figures this country has ever produced."

On a hunch I had gone with Sam to the floor that day, and I stood in the back of the chamber, near the center door. I looked at Sam as Royster bore in on him, and Bradford wore that cynical little smile, barely tolerating the rantings of this senile old man from Vermont. The smile did not intimidate Royster, however. He was of tough stock, fighting stock, and from the humblest of beginnings he had clawed his way to power and influence in the New England states. He asserted in that early afternoon meeting that Bradford was a divisive influence in American life, throwing even his own Catholic Church into disarray and frightening and confusing minorities of whatever persuasion.

"The Senator from Maryland," Royster said, "and you will note that I do not refer to him as 'distinguished,' is addicted to tactics so close to those of Adolf Hitler that they have struck fear into the hearts of many good people in this country. Neighbor has been turned against neighbor, parents against teachers, parishioners against their pastors. He asserts that he is the primary investigator of alien influences in our culture, but in fact he has never documented a single charge that he so carelessly flung about on the evil winds he has created. In the last few months he has been intent upon dismantling the State Department, slandering a body of men who are among this nation's most patriotic and useful citizens.

"In doing so, he has resorted to pure fabrication.

"At one point he described a 'Mary K. Evans' as a known sympathizer with Communist causes who 'holds a sensitive position on the Far Eastern desk' at the State Department. The truth is that the only 'Mary K. Evans' in the employ of the State Department is a washroom attendant.

"At another point he cited the questionable associations of one Russell X. Whittaker. The only person of that name ever on the State Department payroll was an assistant secretary in the administration of James K. Polk. He has been dead for eighty years.

"Other persons he accused were figments of his imagination. They never were associated with the State Department at all.

"This one accusation, though, I must share with you. It concerns a female named 'Myra' whom Bradford referred to as 'a Red bitch who is privy to the innermost secrets of the Secretary of State.' Gentlemen, 'Myra' does exist. She is the Secretary's Irish setter and does often go with him on long walks. I don't think she is a security risk.

"Even the Secretary, known to every one of us, his integrity beyond question, he has attempted to defame. I compliment the Secretary for his restraint, and in the name of the United States Senate, I apologize to all of Bradford's victims.

"I send to the Chair Senate Resolution 261, which I should like to have spread upon the record and read to this honorable body."

The Vice President, who was presiding, said, "The resolution will be received." A page darted toward Royster, took the paper and ran with it to the Senate clerk. "The clerk will read the resolution," the Vice President said.

"Senate Resolution Number 261: 'Resolved, that the conduct of the junior Senator from Maryland is unbecoming a member of the United States Senate, is contrary to senatorial traditions, and tends to bring the Senate into disrepute, and such conduct is hereby condemned.' "

In the hubbub that followed, Bradford was recognized, and as he rose the chamber quieted. "Mr. President," he said, "I have listened to this attack. I have listened, and I have held my tongue. But I must propound an inquiry. Must the precious time of this body be wasted out of courtesy to the wild ramblings of a senile old man?"

Senator McIntyre jumped in and shouted, "I call the senator to order. His characterization of the Senator from Vermont is an insult to the dignity of this chamber."

"The clerk will strike from the record the unacceptable characterization of the Senator from Vermont, and the Chair warns the Senator from Maryland to be more circumspect in his language."

Sam laughed hollowly. "I can't believe what I'm hearing here," he said. "The Senator from Vermont has branded me a liar and a Fascist . . ."

"And will continue to do so," Royster piped up.

"And yet I am not allowed to respond in kind. What kind of bending of the rules is this?"

The Vice President responded from his lofty perch. "The rules are not being bent. It is simply that the Senator from Maryland does not quite understand the nuances."

"Nuances, hell!" Sam exploded. "The Senator from Maryland has the feeling that he is playing against a stacked deck."

Old Senator Ennis, of Mississippi, spoke up. "Mr. President," he said, "the resolution which we have just been handed requires rather extreme action. I would suggest that a special bipartisan ad hoc committee be appointed to consider it."

"That was my purpose," the Vice President responded, "and so the Chair appoints to the Committee to consider Senate Resolution Number 261 the following members: Royster, of Vermont, who introduced it; Albright of Arkansas, and Ennis of Mississippi; Jenson of Colorado, Cash of South Dakota, and Wilding of Wisconsin. The members will note that the committee is completely bipartisan, three Republicans and three Democrats. Mr. Jenson will serve as chairman, and in addition to the counsel authorized for the committee the Senator from Maryland is at liberty to engage his own counsel. The Chair would expect that the committee would make its report within three weeks, although such time as required will be allowed."

Those were the three wildest weeks on record in Washington, a town which in its time has seen very many zany periods. The committee drew up a series of charges against Bradford, none of which really went to the heart of the matter, and Jenson, as chairman, was barely able to keep the hearings civilized. Sam had employed the best legal talent available in Washington, and he attempted to prove that Jenson, who was his judge, was in actuality a fellow traveler.

But when Sam argued that Jenson was a pinko, Jenson simply ruled that Sam was out of order, gaveling him into silence. An excerpt from the transcript shows how this crippled Bradford:

To a charge that Jenson was getting his direction from "leftist" newspapers, Jenson ruled, "The Senator is out of order."

Bradford: "Can't I get the Senator to tell me . . . ?"

Jenson: "The Senator is out of order."

Bradford: ". . . whether it is true or false?"

Jenson: "The Senator is out of order. We are not going to be diverted by these sideline excursions."

Naturally, Sam was frustrated. Sideline, unrehearsed diversions were his stock in trade. He could occasionally get in his licks, by calling the Democratic Senator Albright "Halfbright," and he attempted other obstructionist and delaying tactics. But as for defense, he had none. Royster could prove, with the help of State Department personnel officers, that Bradford, with no attempt at checking, had spread wide the contents of manufactured dossiers.

The net result was that the ad hoc committee presented a report to the senate which contained the following charges: that Bradford had collected funds to fight communism which were in fact diverted to other purposes inuring to his own personal advantage; that certain of Bradford's official acts (as in the vendetta against the State Department) were motivated by self-interest; that certain of his activities in senatorial campaigns, as in the war against Miller, involved violations of the làw and that his conduct was contumacious toward the Senate and injurious to its effectiveness, dignity, responsibilities, processes and prestige.

There were other matters which the committee considered, as Sam's encouragement of federal employees to feed him classified information, it following that he received secret papers which should not have been in his hands. There was also some consideration of chastising him for his abuse of other members of the senate. But the committee staked out its ground and the issue was sent to the world's greatest deliberative body.

The world's greatest deliberative body, however, was considerably harassed. Sam's supporters, mobilized by retired admirals and generals, marched almost a million people on Washington, objecting to the proposed censure. Half a dozen vice chairmen of the pro-Bradford forces operated out of three of Washington's most prestigious hotels, and Bradford zealots poured into Washington by bus, train and plane, to take temporary housing in the private homes of Bradford adherents.

These were sober Americans, seduced in their thinking to believe that if the symbol of anti-Communism in America, Sam Bradford, were put down, the Soviets would have won a victory so colossal that the entire apparatus of government could be taken over by Moscow.

On the Senate floor Bradford zealots, unwilling to accept the verified details, denounced the committee report as a Communist plot and argued with froth-lipped passion that if Bradford were censured the next move would be against the FBI, last bulwark of American freedom. The senate, quite raggedly, debated the case of Sam Bradford for seven days and in the end it voted not to "censure" him but to "condemn" him. The vote for "condemnation" was sixty-seven to twenty-two—a good working majority, but certainly not unanimous.

The vote was not so much a slap at Sam as it was a defense of the senate. The "club" tradition had been tarnished and this was a means of setting things in order, of doing a little housecleaning. I expected to see Sam come out fighting, but I was wrong, and I really can't explain Bradford's sudden deflation. In fact, the most incredible aspect of Sam Bradford's career is that a vote of condemnation could so thoroughly demolish him. But it did. He had not been deprived of his senate seat. He had not lost his committee assignments. But he had been publicly repudiated by the one body that in his heart of hearts he had sought most to impress.

In the days that followed the decision Sam Bradford was not himself. Deprived of the imprimatur of the United States Senate, he was doomed. Daily I watched him wither, shrink, retreat into the no-man's-land of drink and mindless depression from which there is little hope of recovery. He was desolate.

I was not desolate. I wish to be forgiven by those who still care, but I exulted. I had engaged him on treacherous ground; I had pitted him against the day's most beloved American hero, the President of the United States.

Sam had lost.

I had won.

And the crazy bastard didn't even know it.

☆ 15 ☆

WE MEANDERED AROUND Washington for a few weeks, paying no attention to senate deliberations, committee work or the office routine. Mostly, we drank. Or Sam drank. I watered mine heavily, but Sam had an edge on by mid-morning, and he kept honing it. Then he took it in his head to get away, to spend a few days at Camp Abigail.

I said, "Sure," and made the necessary arrangements with Patricia. I would be gone a week at most. It would perhaps be best if she would go down to Mason's Bluff, there to commune with her father. She was compliant; she didn't naysay me. And on a Friday afternoon we went out to Camp Abigail, amply stocked with booze, and Sam was quiet, somnolent on the back seat.

What happened after we got to Abigail I have told so many times that I can recite it by rote. It's in the history books, a matter of permanent record.

It was the third day, and Numeriano and I had fired several clips from the automatic, the Filipino shooting so erratically that I wondered again how he had drilled Gadowski's breast. We were resting at a wrought-iron table when Sam bolted out of the house with the shotgun at a low angle. "I'm gonna get those Commie bastards," he shouted, and as he ran toward the fence he exploded one round of the double-barrel. He reached the root, and because he was drunkenly dragging his feet he tripped, fell and the shotgun bounced away and discharged, the blast catching him in his chest. He was dead when we reached him.

To the last, he had been blasting away at the Soviet menace, and it is said that he gave his life to warn his country of the dangers posed internally and externally by the Red tide.

It is said, but I don't say it.

There are only two of us who know the truth, and Numeriano, wherever he is, isn't talking.

We had, indeed, been shooting, just as I said, and we were resting for a moment when we heard the shotgun blast away inside the cottage. Numeriano and I both sprinted. We knew the extent of his depression, and we could have guessed the scene we would find. Sam was there in the living room, the shotgun beside him and his chest in fragments, and I said, "Sam, what the hell?"

Sam was dying, and he looked at me with the first truly understanding gaze I had seen on his face in months, and he said, "Harry, you set me up, didn't you?"

At the time his way of resolving it seemed perfectly natural to me. I couldn't deny him, because in the presence of death there is no reason to dissimulate, and I said, "Yes, Sam, I jobbed you."

"But why, Harry?"

The pathetic thing was that he really didn't know and I had to tell him. "For Patricia, Sam, the sweet innocent, and you won't understand that. And for Selma, too, whom you utterly destroyed without a shred of reason. For Justin, that lump of flesh who was her father."

"And that's .it?" He was overcome by the triviality of it, and I had to tell him the rest.

"No, that's not all. For the country, for all the little people who were scared. I did it for them."

"Christ!" Sam wheezed. "A fuckin' idealist."

And then he died.

By this time Numeriano had Sam's head in his lap, and the gushing from the wound, the great venting beat of the heart, was more than I could endure and I turned away.

"Lieutenant," Numeriano called, and his voice was imperative, "I don't want it to be this way. I don't want all those people—the jerks he hated—to know how it was. You have to help me."

"Okay," I said, "we'll take him down to the tree root, where you fell, and make it look like an accident."

"All right."

We wrapped Sam in a blanket and took him down to the wall, near the outgrowth, and we set him down very gently. We went back and got the shotgun and fired the second round harmlessly into the air and placed it beside him, off a little bit, where it might have fallen, engineering it to look like what it was not.

And then we called Sheriff Thompson, explaining that there had been a terrible accident.

He was, to his credit, very discreet, although I don't think for a moment that we fooled him—Numeriano, still cradling the head in his lap and covered with blood, flecks of blood and mucous spattering me. He did make very precise diagrams, he did have a photographer take the death shots, he did very pointedly neglect to go into the cabin to see if there were signs we had not volunteered. I think he admired Sam, but he nevertheless caused to be released the news that Sam Bradford, lately junior Senator from Maryland, had been killed by the accidental discharge of a .12 gauge shotgun. Numeriano and the Sheriff and I coordinated our stories, and we clung to the fabricated accounts before a coroner's jury, before the minuscule senate inquiry, even to the FBI. Sam was killed by accident, and to the church and to his many admirers across this broad land that made all the difference.

What I have set down here is the truth as I know it, despite the differing accounts carried in the history books. But books often lie, and in any case they don't tell everything.

They don't tell, for example, that with the death of Sam Bradford I got my wife back. Patricia had been crippled, mentally subdued, but with her total release from the Senator of the Free State of Maryland she recovered her old vivaciousness, the joy of life, the exuberant, seeking partner in bedding. Had I known that would have been the result I would have been tempted to shoot the bastard much earlier, but I didn't understand the exact trauma which had disabled Trish. Somehow, the finality of the roar of that shotgun blew the cobwebs away. The capital life we enjoyed, so I took a public relations job with BBD & O and was very good at it because I knew so many people and was privy to congressional byways.

When we began to present Stanwick B. the grandchildren he longed for, we sold the small carriage house in Georgetown at a nice profit, buying into Chevy Chase before Washington real estate prices began to be ridiculous. Upon the death of the colonel, Patricia sold Mason's Bluff to a developer. It was no doing of mine, but I think Patricia did not want to be reminded, ever again, that it had been bought with very strange coin, and that she had put up part of it herself. The Bluff no longer exists as we knew it. It has been turned into a very posh housing retreat, with gates and passes, and we have never been back. Some memories are not meant to be preserved.

I don't mean to harp on the theme, but I can't tell you how good it is to claim one's kin. It would be nice enough if it were one's cousin or brother-in-law, a maiden aunt. But to rediscover one's wife is something very special. She didn't intrude it upon me, or burst forth into overnight blossom, but in a very short time the old desire was there once more, not carnality but an urgency to share in physical communion the cares of the day. My touch no longer caused her to wither, nor did any part of love making. She bore a small scar on her right breast, but essentially she was whole once more.

At times she was curious about the interim. "What did you do, Harry, while I was gone?"

"I was celibate," I said, and I wondered, still wonder, how she would have reacted had I told her, "Trish, I had a ball with Meg."

But I never told her, and they actually became very good friends. If I said today, "Trish, what woman are you closest to?" she would respond unhesitatingly, "Meg Clements."

"Clements," because Meg did remarry. She joined her fortune with another old Maryland name, almost as moneyed, choosing as husband an older man, one who had put in some time as a tea planter in Ceylon. He was of English custom and bearing, but Meg confided to me in a rare moment of candor that she had checked him out and that he could be "entertaining." Not that Meg ever gave up her wanderlust. She has always required new diversions, young blood, and Trish knows this and excuses it.

And if I would say to Patricia, "Doesn't it bother you that Meg requires extramarital attention?" Trish would say to me, "Harry, you really don't understand women like Meg. She is a mature, healthy woman. With a very healthy appetite."

I will never tell her it is an appetite I have shared. Nor will Meg. I admire Meg deeply, but I don't tell her so. There are sometimes important sacrifices which one must make, and Meg is one of mine.

So things returned to a kind of normalcy, to the moment of our conjunction here, and the letter to which I must respond out of courtesy is before me. I have written hundreds of replies to such queries, and I muse over what a jolt it might create in the American Historical Association pamphlets if I really told the truth.

But this, of course, is not the time for it. I think of my place in history, the footnote, and I am properly chastened. To the professor at Auburn I dispatch historical truth, that which has been gospel for all these years:

"Dear Sir:

"I was indeed very close to Sam Bradford, and you honor me with your inquiry.

"To my mind Senator Bradford was the epitome of the loyal American, as subsequent events have proven. He was cruelly used by the United States Senate, which I believe contributed to his premature death. He had much to offer, much more to offer than he was ever given credit for. I don't think that even now he would apologize for his thinking: America first, America for Americans. In the context of our times, I don't think that was such a bad philosophy.

"If I can be of further service to you, do not hesitate to call on me.

> "Very truly yours,
> "Harry Dodge,
> "Administrative Assistant to
> Senator Sam Bradford."